CHRISTOPHER EVANS was born in 1951 in Tredegar, South Wales. He has a B.Sc. in Chemistry and a Postgraduate Certificate in Education from the University of Wales. After moving to London in 1975 he worked in the pharmaceuticals industry before becoming a full-time writer in 1979. He was a recipient of an Arts Council grant in 1980 and is the author of three novels: *Capella's Golden Eyes* (1980), *The Insider* (1981) and *In Limbo* (1985). He is currently completing a guidebook, *Writing Science Fiction*, for A&C Black.

ROBERT HOLDSTOCK was born in Kent, in 1948. He has degrees in Zoology and Medical Zoology and worked in Medical Research before becoming a freelance writer in 1975. His novels include *Eye Among the Blind* (1976), *Earthwind* (1977), *Necromancer* (1978) and *Where Time Winds Blow* (1981). More recently he has published a volume of short stories *In the Valley of the Statues*. He has written historical fantasies, as Christopher Carlsen (*The Berserker*) and a series of occult novels as Robert Faulcon (*Night Hunter*) as well as the novelisation of *The Emerald Forest*. His latest book, *Mythago Wood*, won the World Fantasy Award in 1985. Its companion volume, *Lavondyss*, edges closer to completion.

OTHER EDENS

EDITED BY
CHRISTOPHER EVANS
AND
ROBERT HOLDSTOCK

UNWIN PAPERBACKS
London   Sydney

First published in Great Britain by Unwin ® Paperbacks, an imprint of
Unwin Hyman Ltd., in 1987.
Copyright in the individual stories belongs to the writers or their heirs or
executors.

UNWIN HYMAN LIMITED
Denmark House
37–39 Queen Elizabeth Street
LONDON SE1 2QB
and
40 Museum Street LONDON WC1A 1LU

Allen & Unwin Australia Pty Ltd
8 Napier Street, North Sydney, NSW 2060, Australia

Unwin Paperbacks with Port Nicholson Press
60 Cambridge Terrace, Wellington, New Zealand

02719320

British Library Cataloguing in Publication Data

Other Edens.
1. Science fiction, English
I. Evans, C.D.   II. Holdstock, Robert
823'.0876'08[FS]   PR1309.S3
ISBN 0-04-823378-1

Set in 10 on 11 point Plantin by Computerised Typesetting
Services Ltd, London N12 8LY and printed in Great
Britain by Cox & Wyman Ltd, Reading.

Contents

OTHER EDENS

Introduction

Welcome to a rare phenomenon these days – a collection of original science fiction and fantasy stories from Britain. It's a rarity we hope will not last. Science fiction and fantasy have always flourished in the short story form; in many ways the genre was shaped by the thousands of short stories which appeared in the pulp magazines of the 1930s and 40s. And to read the American magazines today and the sole British representative, *Interzone*, is to remain convinced that the short story is alive and kicking. We believe that it would kick more strongly in the UK if only there were more outlets for writers.

In the mid 1970s the market was glutted with short story collections. It was a form of madness. One American editor claimed to have produced about eighty! Theme anthologies terrorised bookshops: sf about robots, sex, utopias, cities, aliens, and so on. In and among these theme anthologies were the series: *Orbit*, *New Dimensions*, *Universe* and the like in the USA, and, in this country, the long-running *New Writings in SF* and *New Worlds* (in its later incarnations a quarterly paperback) and shorter-lived series such as *Andromeda* and *Pulsar*.

It couldn't last. When a market is glutted it eventually collapses beneath the oppressive weight of its worst examples. When the anthology ship sank, good collections went down with the bad. In Britain, no titles survived so that new and established writers in the early 1980s had no regular home markets for short stories until *Interzone* appeared in 1982.

Lately the view has been expressed that British sf has been in the doldrums in recent years, with few signs of excitement and few new writers emerging. If this is true, then a major factor must be the dearth of outlets here for short stories. As well as giving new writers valuable space to practise and perfect their craft, magazines and anthologies often create a community feeling, a sense that the scene is lively. *Interzone* has provided a valuable focus in this respect, but it cannot hope to be comprehensive or to appeal to everyone. *Other Edens* is an attempt to show that the original anthology can also play its part, demonstrating that exciting work is being written here in Britain, more of which would appear given the opportunity. There is nothing nationalistic or jingoistic about this; it's a simple fact of life that many writers feel more encouraged to produce stories if there is a good choice of markets on their doorstep.

This anthology was conceived as a sampler of modern British sf by some of its best known practitioners, and we're pleased to have new stories by so many popular names in one volume. It's being published to coincide with the World Science Fiction Convention, which in 1987 is being held in Brighton.

Other Edens is a title with a patriotic gloss (it derives from Shakespeare's *Richard III*) but the only qualification for contributors was that they be *based* in Britain, which is why you'll find Texas-born Lisa Tuttle represented. Not wanting to restrict potential contributors – and being conscious that individual imaginations aren't bounded by genre definitions – we decided that the anthology should contain serious-minded fantasy as well as serious-minded science fiction. Beyond this we imposed no editorial restrictions; our concern was to obtain contributions which would illustrate each author's particular talents and interests in the purest form.

The idea of 'other Edens' may hint at pastoral idylls, but we're sure that readers won't be surprised to discover that the stories tend to focus more on the snakes in the grass; science fiction has never had much faith in perfect societies, and it much prefers to concentrate on how things may go wrong. The stories must, of course, be left to speak for themselves but to hint at their variety we can tell you that they range in setting from medieval woodland to far-future Earth and the depths of space beyond. They cover such subjects as hauntings, death, religion, strange inventions, nuclear war, the domestic consequences of relativity and, not least, the war between the sexes. If there are recurrent themes then this no doubt says something about modern British sf and also about the times in which we live. Should the response be enthusiastic enough then *Other Edens 2* will follow. Meanwhile we believe that this collection illustrates a long-standing feature of all the best sf: that it is very much a collection of individual voices who write stories not quite like anyone else's at all.

We hope you enjoy reading them.

Christopher Evans and Robert Holdstock

TANITH LEE

Crying in the Rain

There was a weather Warning that day, so to start with we were all indoors. The children were watching the pay-TV and I was feeding the hens on the shut-yard. It was about 9 a.m. Suddenly my mother came out and stood at the edge of the yard. I remember how she looked at me: I had seen the look before, and although it was never explained, I knew what it meant. In the same way she appraised the hens, or checked the vegetables and salad in their grow-trays. Today there was a subtle difference, and I recognised the difference too. It seemed I was ready.

'Greena,' she said. She strode across to the hen-run, glanced at the disappointing hens. There had only been three eggs all week, and one of those had registered too high. But in any case, she wasn't concerned with her poultry just now. 'Greena, this morning we're going into the Centre.'

'What about the Warning, Mum?'

'Oh, that. Those idiots, they're often wrong. Anyway, nothing until noon, they said. All Clear till then. And we'll be in by then.'

'But, Mum,' I said, 'there won't be any buses. There never are when there's a Warning. We'll have to walk.'

Her face, all hard and eaten back to the bone with life and living, snapped at me like a rat-trap: 'So we'll *walk*. Don't go on and on, Greena. What do you think your legs are for?'

I tipped the last of the feed from the pan and started towards the stair door.

'And talking of legs,' said my mother, 'put on your stockings. And the things we bought last time.'

There was always this palaver. It was normally because of the cameras, particularly those in the Entry washrooms. After you strip, all your clothes go through the cleaning machine, and out to meet you on the other end. But there are security staff on the cameras, and the doctors, and they might see, take an interest. You had to wear your smartest stuff in order not to be ashamed of it, things even a Centre doctor could glimpse without repulsion. A stickler, my mother. I went into the shower and took one and shampooed my hair, and used powder bought in the Centre with the smell of roses, so all of me would be gleaming clean when I went through the shower and shampooing at the Entry. Then I dressed in my special underclothes, and my white frock, put on my stockings and shoes, and remembered to drop the carton of rose powder in my bag.

My mother was ready and waiting by the time I came down to the street doors, but she didn't upbraid me. She had meant me to be thorough.

The children were yelling round the TV, all but Daisy, who was seven and had been left in charge. She watched us go with envious fear. My mother shouted her away inside before we opened up.

When we'd unsealed the doors and got out, a blast of heat scalded us. It was a very hot day, the sky so far clear as the finest blue perspex. But of course, as there had been a weather Warning, there were no buses, and next to no one on the streets. On Warning days, there was anyway really nowhere to go. All the shops were sealed fast, even our three area pubs. The local train station ceased operating when I was four, eleven years ago. Even the endless jumble of squats had their boards in place and their tarpaulins over.

The only people we passed on the burning dusty pavements were a couple of fatalistic tramps, in from the green belt, with bottles of cider or petromix; these they jauntily raised to us. (My mother tugged me on.) And once a police car appeared which naturally hove to at our side and activated its speaker.

'Is your journey really necessary, madam?'

My mother, her patience eternally tried, grated out furiously, 'Yes it is.'

'You're aware there's been a forecast of rain for these sections?'

'*Yes*,' she rasped.

'And this is your daughter? It's not wise, madam, to risk a child – '

'My daughter and I are on our way to the Centre. We have an appointment. Unless we're *delayed*,' snarled my mother, visually skewering the pompous policeman, only doing his job, through the Sealtite window of the car, 'we should be inside before any rain breaks.'

The two policemen in their snug patrol vehicle exchanged looks.

There was a time we could have been arrested for behaving in this irresponsible fashion, my mother and I, but no one really bothers now. There was more than enough crime to go round. On our own heads it would be.

The policeman who'd spoken to us through the speaker smiled coldly and switched it off – speaker, and come to that, smile.

The four official eyes stayed on me a moment, however, before the car drove off. That at least gratified my mother. Although the policemen had called me a child for the white under-sixteen tag on my wristlet, plainly they'd noticed I look much older and besides, rather good.

Without even a glance at the sky, my mother marched forward. (It's true there are a few public weather-shelters but vandals have wrecked most of them.) I admired my mother, but I'd never been able to love her, not even to like her much. She was phenomenally strong and had kept us together, even after my father canced, and the other man, the father of Jog, Daisy and Angel. She did it with slaps and harsh tirades, to show us what we could expect in life. But she must have had her fanciful side once: for instance, the silly name she gave

3

me, for green trees and green pastures and waters green as bottle-glass that I've only seen inside the Centre. The trees on the streets and in the abandoned gardens have always been bare, or else they have sparse foliage of quite a cheerful brown colour. Sometimes they put out strange buds or fruits and then someone reports it and the trees are cut down. They were rather like my mother, I suppose, or she was like the trees. Hard-bitten to the bone, enduring, tough, holding on by her root-claws, not daring to flower.

Gallantly she showed only a little bit of nervousness when we began to see the glint of the dome in the sunshine coming down High Hill from the old cinema ruin. Then she started to hurry quite a lot and urged me to be quick. Still, she didn't look up once, for clouds.

In the end it was perfectly all right: the sky stayed empty and we got down to the concrete underpass. Once we were on the moving way I rested my tired feet by standing on one leg then the other like a stork I once saw in a TV programme.

As soon as my mother noticed she told me to stop it. There are cameras watching, all along the underpass to the Entry. It was useless to try persuading her that it didn't matter. She had never brooked argument and though she probably wouldn't clout me before the cameras she might later on. I remember I was about six or seven when she first thrashed me. She used a plastic belt, but took off the buckle. She didn't want to scar me. Not to scar Greena was a part of survival, for even then she saw something might come of me. But the belt hurt and raised welts. She said to me as I lay howling and she leaned panting on the bed, 'I won't have any back-answers. Not from you and not from any of you, do you hear me? There isn't time for it. You'll do as I say.'

After we'd answered the usual questions, we joined the queue for the washroom. It wasn't much of a queue, because of the Warning. We glided through the mechanical check, the woman operator even congratulating us on our low levels. 'That's section SEK, isn't it?' she said chattily. 'A very good area. My brother lives out there. He's over thirty and has

4

three children.' My mother congratulated the operator in turn and proudly admitted our house was one of the first in SEK fitted with Sealtite. 'My kids have never played outdoors,' she assured the woman. 'Even Greena here scarcely went out till her eleventh birthday. We grow most of our own food.' Then, feeling she was giving away too much – you never knew who might be listening, there was always trouble in the suburbs with burglars and gangs – she clammed up tighter than the Sealtite.

As we went into the washroom a terrific argument broke out behind us. The mechanical had gone off violently. Some woman was way over the acceptable limit. She was screaming that she had to get in to the Centre to see her daughter, who was expecting a baby – the oldest excuse, perhaps even true, though pregnancy is strictly regulated under a dome. One of the medical guards was bearing down on the woman, asking if she had Insurance.

If she had, the Entry hospital would take her in and see if anything could be done. But the woman had never got Insurance, despite having a daughter in the Centre, and alarms were sounding and things were coming to blows.

'Mum,' I said, when we passed into the white plastic-and-tile expanse with the black camera eyes clicking overhead and the Niagara rush of showers, 'who are you taking me to see?'

She actually looked startled, as if she still thought me so naïve that I couldn't guess she too, all this time, had been planning to have a daughter in the Centre. She glared at me, then came out with the inevitable.

'Never you mind. Just you hope you're lucky. Did you bring your talc?'

'Yes, Mum.'

'Here then, use these too. I'll meet you in the cafeteria.'

When I opened the carton I found 'Smoky' eye make-up, a cream lipstick that smelled of peaches, and a little spray of scent called *I Mean It*.

My stomach turned right over. But then I thought, So what. It would be frankly stupid of *me* to be thinking I was naïve. I'd known for years.

While we were finishing our hamburgers in the cafeteria, it did start to rain, outside. You could just *sense* it, miles away beyond the layers of protection and lead-glass. A sort of flickering of the sight. It wouldn't do us much harm in here, but people instinctively moved away from the outer suburb-side walls of the café even under the plastic palm-trees in tubs. My mother stayed put.

'Have you finished, Greena? Then go to the Ladies and brush your teeth, and we'll get on. And spray that scent again.'

'It's finished, Mum. There was only enough for one go.'

'Daylight robbery,' grumbled my mother, 'you can hardly smell it.' She made me show her the empty spray and insisted on squeezing hissing air out of it into each of my ears.

Beyond the cafeteria, a tree-lined highway runs down into the Centre. Real trees, green trees, and green grass on the verges. At the end of the slope, we waited for an electric bus painted a jolly bright colour, with a rude driver. I used to feel that everyone in the Centre must be cheery and contented, bursting with optimism and the juice of kindness. But I was always disappointed. They know you're from outside at once, if nothing else gives you away, skin-tone is different from the pale underdome skin or chocolaty solarium Centre tan. Although you could never have got in here if you hadn't checked out as acceptable, a lot of people draw away from you on the buses or underground trains. Once or twice, when my mother and I had gone to see a film in the Centre no one would sit near us. But not everybody had this attitude. Presumably, the person my mother was taking me to see wouldn't mind.

'Let me do the talking,' she said as we got off the bus. (The driver had started extra quickly, half shaking our con-tamination off his platform, nearly breaking our ankles.)

'Suppose he asks me something?'

'*He?*' But I wasn't going to give ground on it now. 'All right. In that case, answer, but be careful.'

Parts of the Centre contain very old historic buildings and monuments of the inner city which, since they're inside, are

6

looked after and kept up. We were now under just that sort of building. From my TV memories – my mother had made sure we had the educational TV to grow up with, along with lesson tapes and exercise ropes – the architecture looked late eighteenth or very early nineteenth, white stone, with top-lids on the windows and pillared porticos up long stairs flanked by black metal lions.

We went up the stairs and I was impressed and rather frightened.

The glass doors behind the pillars were wide open. There's no reason they shouldn't be, here. The cool-warm, sweet-smelling breezes of the dome-conditioned air blew in and out, and the real ferns in pots waved gracefully. There was a tank of golden fish in the foyer. I wanted to stay and look at them. Sometimes on the Centre streets you see well-off people walking their clean, groomed dogs and foxes. Some-times there might be a silken cat high in a window. There were birds in the Centre parks, trained not to fly free any-where else. When it became dusk above the dome, you would hear them tweeting excitedly as they roosted. And then all the lights of the city came on and moths danced round them. You could get proper honey in the Centre, from the bee-farms, and beef and milk from the cattle-grazings, and salmon, and leather and wine and roses.

But the fish in the tank were beautiful. And I suddenly thought, if I get to stay here – if I really *do* – but I didn't believe it. It was just something I had to try to get right for my mother, because I must never argue with her, ever.

The man in the lift took us up to the sixth floor. He was impervious; we weren't there, he was simply working the lift for something to do.

A big old clock in the foyer had said 3 p.m. The corridor we came out in was deserted. All the rooms stood open like the corridor windows, plushy hollows with glass furniture: offices. The last office in the corridor had a door which was shut.

My mother halted. She was pale, her eyes and mouth three

7

straight lines on the plain of bones. She raised her hand and it shook, but it knocked hard and loud against the door.

In a moment, the door opened by itself.

My mother went in first.

She stopped in front of me on a valley-floor of grass-green carpet, blocking my view.

'Good afternoon, Mr Alexander. I hope we're not too early.'

A man spoke.

'Not at all. Your daughter's with you? Good. Please do come in.' He sounded quite young.

I walked behind my mother over the grass carpet, and chairs and a desk became visible, and then she let me step around her, and said to him, 'This is my daughter, Mr Alexander. Greena.'

He was only about twenty-two, and that was certainly luck, because the ones born in the Centre can live up until their fifties, their sixties even, though that's rare. (They quite often don't even cance in the domes, providing they were born there. My mother used to say it was the high life killed them off.)

He was tanned from a solarium and wore beautiful clothes, a cotton shirt and trousers. His wristlet was silver – I had been right about his age: the tag was red. He looked so fit and hygenic, almost edible. I glanced quickly away from his eyes.

'Won't you sit down?' He gave my mother a crystal glass of Centre gin, with ice-cubes and lemon slices. He asked me, smiling, if I'd like a milk-shake, yes with real milk and strawberry flavour. I was too nervous to want it or enjoy it, but it had to be had. You couldn't refuse such a thing.

When we were perched in chairs with our drinks (he didn't drink with us) he sat on the desk, swinging one foot, and took a cigarette from a box and lit and smoked it.

'Well, I must say, he remarked conversationally to my mother, 'I appreciate your coming all this way – after a Warning, too. It was only a shower I gather.'

'We were inside by then,' said my mother quickly. She wanted to be definite – the flower hadn't been spoiled by rain.

8

'Yes, I know. I was in touch with the Entry.'

He would have checked our levels, probably. He had every right to, after all. If he was going to buy me, he'd want me to last a while.

'And, let me say at once, just from the little I've seen of your daughter, I'm sure she'll be entirely suitable for the work. So pretty, and such a charming manner.'

It was normal to pretend there was an actual job involved. Perhaps there even would be, to begin with.

My mother must have been putting her advert out since last autumn. That was when she'd had my photograph taken at the Centre. I'd just worn my nylon-lace panties for it; it was like the photos they take of you at the Medicheck every ten years. But there was always a photograph of this kind with such an advert. It was illegal, but nobody worried. There had been a boy in our street who got into the Centre three years ago in this same way. He had placed the advert, done it all himself. He was handsome, though his hair, like mine, was very fine and perhaps he would lose it before he was eighteen. Apparently that hadn't mattered.

Had my mother received any other offers? Or only this tanned Mr Alexander with the intense bright eyes?

I'd drunk my shake and not noticed.

Mr Alexander asked me if I would read out what was written on a piece of rox he gave me. My mother and the TV lessons had seen to it I could read, or at least that I could read what was on the rox, which was a very simple paragraph directing a Mr Cleveland to go to office 170B on the seventh floor and a Miss O'Beale to report to the basement. Possibly the job would require me to read out such messages. But I had passed the test. Mr Alexander was delighted. He came over without pretence and shook my hand and kissed me exploringly on the left cheek. His mouth was firm and wholesome and he had a marvellous smell, a smell of money and safety. My mother had laboured cleverly on me. I recognised it instantly, and wanted it. Between announcements, they might let me feed the fish in the tank.

Mr Alexander was extremely polite and gave my mother

another big gin, and chatted sociably to her about the latest films in the Centre, and the colour that was in vogue, nothing tactless or nasty, such as the cost of food inside, and out, or the SEO riots the month before, in the suburbs, when the sounds of the fires and the police rifles had penetrated even our sealed-tight home in SEK. He didn't mention any current affairs, either, the death-rate on the continent, or the trade-war with the USA – he knew our TV channels get edited. Our information was too limited for an all-round discussion.

Finally he said, 'Well, I'd better let you go. Thank you again. I think we can say we know where we stand, yes?' He laughed over the smoke of his fourth cigarette, and my mother managed her deaths-head grin, her remaining teeth washed with gin and lemons. 'But naturally I'll be writing to you. I'll send you the details Express. That should mean you'll get them – oh, five days from today. Will that be all right?'

My mother said 'That will be lovely, Mr Alexander. I can speak for Greena and tell you how very thrilled she is. It will mean a lot to us. The only thing is, Mr Alexander, I do have a couple of other gentlemen – I've put them off, of course. But I have to let them know by the weekend.'

He made a gesture of mock panic. 'Good God, I don't want to lose Greena. Let's say three and a half days, shall we? I'll see if I can't rustle up a special courier to get my letter to you extra fast.'

We said goodbye, and he shook my hand again and kissed both cheeks. A great pure warmth came from him, and a sort of power. I felt I had been kissed by a tiger, and wondered if I was in love.

At the Entry-exit, though it didn't rain again, my mother and I had a long wait until the speakers broadcast the All Clear. By then the clarified sunset lay shining and flaming in six shades of red and scarlet-orange over the suburbs.

'Look, Mum,' I said, because shut up indoors so much, I

10

didn't often get to see the naked sky, 'isn't it beautiful? It doesn't look like that through the dome.'

But my mother had no sympathy with vistas. Only the toxins in the air, anyway, make the colours of sunset and dawn so wonderful. To enjoy them is therefore idiotic, perhaps unlawful.

My mother had, besides, been very odd ever since we left Mr Alexander's office. I didn't properly understand that this was due to the huge glasses of gin he'd generously given her. At first she was fierce and energetic, keyed up, heroic against the polished sights of the Centre, which she had begun to point out to me like a guide. Though she didn't say so, she meant *Once you live here*. But then, when we had to wait in the exit lounge and have a lot of the rather bad coffee-drink from the machine, she sank in on herself, brooding. Her eyes became so dark, so bleak, I didn't like to meet them. She had stopped talking at me.

Though the rain-alert was over, it was now too late for buses. There was the added problem that gangs would be coming out on the streets, looking for trouble.

The gorgeous poisoned sunset died behind the charcoal sticks of trees and pyramids and oblongs of deserted buildings and rusty railings.

Fortunately, there were quite a few police-patrols about. My mother gave them short shrift when they stopped her. Generally they let us get on. We didn't look dangerous.

In SEK, the working street-lights were coming on and there were some ordinary people strolling or sitting on low broken walls, taking the less unhealthy air. They pop up like the rabbits used to, out of their burrows. We passed a couple of women we knew, outside the Sealtite house on the corner of our road. They asked where we'd come from. My mother said tersely we'd been at a friend's, and stopped in till the All Clear.

Although Sealtite, as the advert says, makes secure against anything but gelignite, my mother had by now got herself into an awful sort of rigid state. She ran up the concrete to our front door, unlocked it and dived us through. We threw our

11

clothes into the wash-bin, though they hardly needed it as we'd been in the Centre most of the day. The TV was still blaring. My mother, dragging on a skirt and nylon blouse, rushed through into the room where the children were. Immediately there was a row. During the day Jog had upset a complete giant can of powdered milk. Daisy had tried to clear it up and they had meant not to tell our mother as if she wouldn't notice one was missing. Daisy was only seven, and Jog was three, so it was blurted out presently. My mother hit all of them, even Angel. Daisy, who had been responsible for the house in our absence, she belted, not very much, but enough to fill our closed-in world with screaming and savage sobs.

After it was over, I made a pot of tea. We drank it black since we would have to economise on milk for the rest of the month.

The brooding phase had passed from my mother. She was all sharp jitters. She said we had to go up and look at the hens. The eggs were always registering too high lately. Could there be a leak in the sealing of the shut-yard?

So that was where we ended up, tramping through lanes of lettuce, waking the chickens who got agitated and clattered about. My mother wobbled on a ladder under the roofing with a torch. 'I can't see anything,' she kept saying.

Finally she descended. She leaned on the ladder with the torch dangling, still alight, wasting the battery. She was breathless.

'Mum . . . the torch is still on.'

She switched it off, put it on a post of the hen-run, and suddenly came at me. She took me by the arms and glared into my face.

'Greena, do you understand about the Alexander man? Well, do you?'

'Yes, Mum.'

She shook me angrily but not hard.

'You know why you have to?'

'Yes, Mum. I don't mind, Mum. He's really nice.'

Then I saw her eyes had changed again, and I faltered. I

12

felt the earth give way beneath me. Her eyes were full of burning water. They were soft and they were frantic.

'Listen, Greena. I was thirty last week.'

'I know – '

'You shut up and listen to me. I had my medicheck. It's no good, Greena.'

We stared at each other. It wasn't a surprise. This happened to everyone. She'd gone longer than most. Twenty-five was the regular innings, out here.

'I wasn't going to tell you, not yet. I don't have to report into the hospital for another three months. I'm getting a bit of pain, but there's the Insurance: I can buy that really good pain-killer, the new one.'

'Mum.'

'Will you be quiet? I want to ask you, you know what you have to do? About the kids? They're your sisters and your brother, you know that, don't you?'

'Yes. I'll take care of them.'

'Get him to help you. He will. He really wants you. He was dead unlucky, that Alexander. His legal girlfriend canced. Born in the Centre and everything and she pegged out at eighteen. Still, that was good for us. Putting you on the sterilisation programme when you were little, thank God I did. You see, he can't legally sleep with another girl with pregnancy at all likely. Turns out he's a high-deformity risk. Doesn't look it, does he?'

'Yes, Mum, I know about the pregnancy laws.'

She didn't slap me or even shout at me for answering back. She seemed to accept I'd said it to reassure her I truly grasped the facts. Alexander's predicament had anyway been guessable. Why else would he want a girl from outside?

'Now, Angel – ' said my mother ' – I want you to see to her the same, sterilisation next year when she's five. She's got a chance too: she could turn out very nice-looking. Daisy won't be any use to herself, and the boy won't. But you see you get a decent woman in here to take care of them. No homes. Do you hear? Not for my kids.' She sighed, and said again, *'He'll* help you. If you play your cards right, he'll do

13

anything you want. He'll cherish you, Greena.' She let me go and said, grinning, 'We had ten applications. I went and saw them all. He's the youngest and the best.'

'He's lovely' I said. 'Thanks, Mum.'

'Well, you just see you don't let me down.'

'I won't. I promise. I promise, really.'

She nodded, and drew up her face into its sure habitual shape, and her eyes dry into their Sealtite of defiance.

'Let's get down now. I'd better rub some anesjel into those marks on Daisy.'

We went down and I heard my mother passing from child to child, soothing and reprimanding them as she harshly pummelled the anaesthetic jelly into their hurts.

For a moment, listening on the landing, in the clamped house-dark, I felt I loved my mother.

Then that passed off. I began to think about Mr Alexander and his clothes and the brilliance of his eyes in his tanned healthy face.

It was wonderful. He didn't send a courier. He came out himself. He was in a small sealed armoured car like a TV alligator, but he just swung out of it and up the concrete into our house. (His bodyguard stayed negligently inside the car. He had a pistol and a mindless attentive lethal look.)

Mr Alexander brought me half a dozen perfect tawny roses, and a crate of food for the house, toys and TV tapes for the children, and even some gin for my mother. He presumably didn't know yet she only had three months left, but he could probably work it out. He made a fuss of her, and when she'd spoken her agreements into the portable machine, he kissed me on the mouth and then produced a bottle of champagne. The wine was very frothy, and the glassful I had made me feel giddy. I didn't like it, but otherwise our celebration was a success.

I don't know how much money he paid for me. I'd never want to ask him. Or the legal fiddles he must have gone through. He was able to do it, and that was all we needed to know, my mother, me. (She always kept the Insurance going

14

and now, considerably swelled, the benefits will pass on to the children.)

She must have told him eventually about the hospital. I do know he saw to it personally that she had a private room and the latest in pain relief, and no termination until she was ready. He didn't let me see her after she went in. She'd said she didn't want it, either. She had already started to lose weight and shrivel up, the way it happens.

The children cried terribly. I thought it could never be put right, but in the end the agency he found brought us a nineteen-year-old woman who'd lost her own baby and she seemed to take to the children at once. The safe house, of course, was a bonus no one sane would care to ignore. The agency will keep an eye on things, but her levels were low, she should have at least six years. The last time I went there they all seemed happy. He doesn't want me to go outside again.

Six months ago, he brought me officially into the Centre. All the trees were so *green* and the fish and swans sparkled in and on the water, and the birds sang, and he gave me a living bird, a real live tweeting yellow jumping bird in a spacious, glamorous cage; I love this bird and sometimes it sings. It may only live a year, he warned me, but then I can have another.

Sometimes I go to a cubicle in the foyer of one of the historic buildings, and read out announcements over the speaker. They pay me in Centre credit discs, but I hardly need any money of my own.

The two rooms that are mine on Fairgrove Avenue are marvellous. The lights go on and off when you come in or go out, and the curtains draw themselves when it gets dark, or the blinds come down when it's too bright. The shower room always smells fresh, like a summer glade is supposed to, and perhaps once did. I see him four, five or six times every week, and we go to dinner and to films, and he's always bringing me real flowers and chocolates and fruit and honey. He even buys me books to read. Some days, I learn new words from the dictionary.

15

When he made love to me for the first time, it was a strange experience, but he was very gentle. It seemed to me I might come to like it very much, (and I was right), although in a way, it still seems rather an embarrassing thing to do.

That first night, after, he held me in his arms, and I enjoyed this. No one had ever held me caringly, protectingly, like that, ever before. He told me, too, about the girl who canced. He seemed deeply distressed, as if no one ever dies that way, but then, in Centres, under domes, death isn't ever certain.

All my mother tried to get was time, and when that ran out, control of pain and a secure exit. But my darling seems to think that his girl had wanted much, much more, and that I should want more too. And in a way that scares me, because I may not even live to be twenty, and then he'll break his heart again. But then again he'll probably find someone else. And maybe I'll be strong like my mother. I hope so. I want to keep my promise about the children. If I can get Angel settled, she can carry on after me. But I'll need ten or eleven years for that.

Something funny happened yesterday. He said, he would bring me a toy tomorrow – today. Yes, a toy, though I'm a woman, and his lover. I never had a toy. I love my bird best. I love him, too.

The most peculiar thing is, though, that I miss my mother. I keep on remembering what she said to me, her blows and injunctions. Going shopping with her, or to the cinema; how, when her teeth were always breaking, she got into such a rage.

I remember mistily when I was small, the endless days of weather Warnings when she, too, was trapped in the house, my fellow prisoner, and how the rain would start to pour down, horrible sinister torrents that frightened me, although then I didn't know why. All the poisons and the radioactivity that have accumulated and go on gathering on everything in an unseen glittering, and which the sky somehow collects and which the rain washes down from the sky in a deluge. The edited pay-TV seldom reports the accidents and oversights which continually cause this. Sometimes an announcement would come on and tell everyone just to get indoors off the streets, and no reason given, and no rain or wind even. The police cars would go about the roads sounding their sirens, and then they too would slink into holes to hide. But next day, usually there was the All Clear.

In the Centre, TV isn't edited. I was curious to see how they talked about the leaks and pollutions, here. Actually they don't seem to mention them at all. It can't be very important, underdome.

But I do keep remembering one morning, that morning of a colossal rain, when I was six or seven. I was trying to look out at the forbidden world, with my nose pressed to the Sealtite. All I could see through the distorting material was a wavering leaden rush of liquid. And then I saw something so alien I let out a squeal.

'What is it?' my mother demanded. She had been washing the breakfast dishes in half the morning ration of domestic filtered water, clashing the plates bad-temperedly. 'Come on, Greena, don't just make silly noises.'

I pointed at the Sealtite. My mother came to see.

Together we looked through the fall of rain, to where a tiny girl, only about a year old, was standing – *out on the street*. No knowing how she got there – strayed from some squat, most likely. She wore a pair of little blue shorts and nothing else, and she clutched a square of ancient blanket that was her doll. Even through the sealed pane and the rainfall you could see she was bawling and crying in terror.

'Jesus Christ and Mary the Mother,' said my own mother on a breath. Her face was scoured white as our sink. But her eyes were like blazing fires, hot enough to quench the rain.

And next second she was thrusting me into the TV room, locking me in, shouting, *Stay there don't you move or I'll murder you!*

Then I heard both our front doors being opened. Shut. When they opened again and shut again, I heard a high-pitched infantile roaring. The roar got louder and possessed

17

the house. Then it fell quiet. I realised my mother had flown out into the weather and grabbed the lost child and brought her under shelter.

Of course, it was no use. When my mother carried her to the emergency unit next day, after the All Clear, the child was dying. She was so tiny. She held her blanket to the end and scorned my mother, the nurse, the kindly needle of oblivion. Only the blanket was her friend. Only the blanket had stayed and suffered with her in the rain.

When she was paying for the treatment and our own decontam, the unit staff said horrible things to my mother, about her stupidity until I started to cry in humiliated fear. My mother ignored me and only faced them out like an untamed vixen, snarling with her cracked teeth.

All the way home I whined and railed at her. Why had she exposed us to those wicked people with their poking instruments and boiling showers, the hurt and rancour, the downpour of words? (I was jealous too, I realise now, of that intruding poisonous child. I'd been till then the only one in our house.)

Go up to bed! shouted my mother. I wouldn't.

At last she turned on me and thrashed me with the plastic belt. Violent, it felt as if she thrashed the whole world, till in the end she made herself stop.

But now I'm here with my darling, and my lovely bird singing. I can see a corner of a green park from both my windows. And it never, never rains.

It's funny how I miss her, my mother, so much.

CHRISTOPHER EVANS

The Facts of Life

1

'Jiri! Jiri!'

He came running up the steps and into the house, screaming her name. There was no one in the living room, so he
hurried down the corridor and found her on her knees in the
dining hall, scrubbing the brick-red tiles.

He flopped on to one of the chairs which stood against the
wall and began to cry. The girl looked up at him, the scrubbing brush poised in the froth on the floor. With her free
hand she tucked a strand of hair behind her ear.

At length his tears and laboured breathing subsided. He
rubbed his nose with the back of his hand and peered at her
sullenly. Then he glimpsed his face in the ornamented mirror
opposite – a gawky face that was no longer a boy's and not yet
a young man's. There were tear trails on his cheeks and his
hair was tousled.

Jiri waited, not moving.

'Nic's been hitting me again,' he said finally, squeezing the
gnarled arm-rests in anger. His brother was two months his
junior, and he hated to admit to the girl that he could not
stand up to him.

Jiri straightened her back and rubbed her damp palms on
the knees of her grey flannel dress. Her grimy face was
studiously empty of expression.

'Come here,' he ordered.

She rose, approached, and squatted in front of him, her eyes lowered.

'He hit me on the chin,' he said, knotting his right fist and cuffing her across the cheek. It was a glancing blow, jarring her head only slightly. He hit her again, harder, and this time a trickle of blood began to ooze from the corner of her mouth. He smiled, then thrust out a foot and pushed her over.

Standing, he began to kick her. She rolled into a ball, tucking her arms about her head and pulling her knees up to her chest.

'Kick!' he cried, lashing out with his foot. 'Kick!'

The kitchen door opened and the woman Unis peered around the crack.

'Go away!' he yelled.

The door slowly closed.

'Kick!' he screamed again, his voice shrill with delight. 'Kick!'

Sometimes it was worth getting a beating from Nic so that he could take it out on the girl.

'That's enough, Geir,' said a gruff voice.

Grandfather Melph shambled into the room. His white eyepatch rested on his forehead, and the dead grey eye was like a milky pebble. Geir guessed that he had been taking his afternoon nap when woken by the commotion.

Melph stared down at the foetal form of the girl.

'Leave us,' he told her.

The girl uncoiled, stumbled to her feet, and limped away to the kitchen. Geir readied himself for a lecture, but the old man merely stifled a yawn and said, 'Amuse yourself outside.'

2

At sunset, his father returned from the quarries with his three uncles and six elder brothers. After they had bathed, everyone gathered in the dining hall, his brother Bren taking the seat at the head of the table because it was his christening-day.

His father was in good mood while they feasted, joking with everyone and filling his bowl again and again with broth from the tureen. Geir ate little, eyeing Nic across the table. His brother paid him no attention, but Geir still smarted from his beating. When I'm older and bigger, he thought, I'll thrash you.

The woman Unis hovered in the shadows. Whenever a tureen or a bread-bowl was emptied she was always ready, stepping forward with a replacement. She was well-trained. Sometimes Geir felt that she was watching him, and this unnerved him. She was as ugly and misshapen as all women, but there was a strangeness about her eyes which fascinated him.

After the meal was over, jugs of cider were placed on the table. He and Nic were allowed only one small glass each. Geir sipped the golden liquid, relishing its sharpness. The men soon became merry and wandered outside to sit on the verandah. Geir's butterfly net lay under the table in front of his feet. He retrieved it and eased into his sandals.

3

A light-worm darted up from the undergrowth, a glowing cream filament. Geir swung his net, but missed. Brambles caught at his ankles as he chased the creature through the scrub. It weaved and undulated in the darkness, desperately trying to elude him. Then it got tangled in a web-bush.

Gingerly Geir plucked it free. He edged open the lid of the glass jar which hung at his wait and slid the creature inside. The jar was alive with a mass of light-worms, a writhing luminous knot. Tomorrow he would set them free and watch them flutter away from his bedroom window, dark threads seeking shelter from the crimson dawnlight.

It was late. Second moon had already set, and he knew it

21

had to be well past midnight. Securing the lid of the jar, he headed homewards.

The house was in darkness as he approached, and he crept forward cautiously. The last time he had stayed out late his father had been waiting for him with the rod. He had been given ten strokes and was sore for days afterwards. As he passed the corral, a horse whinnied at him in the darkness. Otherwise all was quiet.

Uncle Jal lay asleep, stone drunk, in a rocking chair on the verandah, but there was no one else about. Then he saw a light burning in the annex where Unis and Jiri were quartered. Curious, he crept over to the window and pressed his nose against the pane.

A single candle burned on the table beside the bed. And on the bed were Bren and Unis, both of them naked.

Geir stood there, frozen with surprise and consternation. Jiri lay curled up on a pallet in the corner, her eyes closed, but Bren was pawing Unis's body as though wrestling with her. Geir stared at their naked bodies – and especially the woman's. She had a red blotch on the inside of her thigh, just like he did.

Geir had seen both the females naked before – one day the men had returned drunk from Coastown and had hosed them down in the yard for sport – but he had never seen Unis like this. More puzzling was what Bren was trying to do to her. He seemed to be biting her neck and rubbing her breasts. And he had a full erection. To his surprise, Geir realized that he was also getting hard.

Presently Bren rolled Unis over and mounted her like a stallion did a mare. Geir could hardly believe it. His brother began thrusting, thrusting, and he looked frantic, just like Nic did when Geir worked him off in the woods or in bed at night. Geir was filled with a strange excitement, and he began kneading himself through his shorts.

Unis's face was pressed into the pillow as Bren kept thrusting so that Geir could not see her face. But he knew she would be in pain. Once, in the woods, Nic had pushed his thumb inside him, and it had hurt.

22

Bren's rage increased, and the bed began to rock. Then suddenly he slumped forward and rolled away.

For a moment Geir thought that somehow he had injured himself. He lay with his back to the window, not moving. But then he turned over and glanced towards the window. Geir ducked and darted off to the house, sneaking quietly past his sleeping uncle.

4

Geir lay in late the next morning, waiting for the men to leave before he went downstairs to breakfast. Nic had already gone down to the river to take a swim, while Melph was chopping wood in the back yard. He studied Unis as she served him. She seemed uninjured by Bren's assault apart from several small red bruises on her neck. He ate slowly, biding his time.

'Stop,' he told her when she approached to remove his empty grain bowl.

Unis halted, the bowl in her hand.

'Put it down.'

She set the bowl back on the plate and *looked* at him. He had to show that he was not afraid of her. He rose and put his hand under her chin, making a show of examining the bruises. And then, to scare her, he suddenly tore open the front of her dress, buttons popping like ripe scatter-seeds.

He tugged the dress off her shoulders and began to paw her breasts, imitating Bren's movements. She remained stiff and motionless, and nothing seemed to happen. Geir felt angry, as if she had disobeyed an order or been negligent in her duties. He drew back, and her torn dress slithered into a heap around her feet.

He circled her slowly, noticing the scratches on her back, the bruises on her buttock, the birthmark on her thigh. It matched his almost perfectly.

'You were punished last night?' he asked, looking up into her face.

She stared down at him with her cold blue eyes. 'Yes.'

23

He did not like those eyes. She was evil and should be whipped.

Footsteps approached outside.

'Put your dress on,' he whispered urgently, a panic rising in him.

He rushed to the window, but he could see no one. Unis pulled her dress up, slipping her arms into the sleeves. She did not hurry: she was hoping he would be caught!

Nic entered, rubbing a towel over his still-wet head. Unis stood before him with the front of her dress open. Geir knotted his fists in anger and helplessness, but his brother did not even notice.

'Get me a drink of water,' he said to her, pulling the towel over his face, then walking through into the kitchen.

5

Melph's good eye widened in surprise, and Geir was immediately sorry that he had said anything. They were sitting around the big polished table in the study, an oil-lamp filling the room with mellow light while the maroon dusk gathered beyond the window.

It had been another boring lesson, made worse by the fact that Melph was keeping him behind until he finished the arithmetic problems he had been set. Nic had left an hour ago, his work complete. But he could not do the sums. He hated them, and longed for the day when he would be old enough to join his father and the rest of the men at the quarry.

For at least an hour he had scribbled fruitless calculations on his pad. Finally, in a fit of frustration and boredom, he had thrown down his pencil and said, 'Bren was in the annex with the woman Unis last night.'

For a moment he thought that Melph would explode with rage. Something told him he should not have spied on Bren; something told him that Bren would not have wanted anyone to know about it. His father had always said that women

24

weren't much better than domesticated animals, and the idea of Bren nakedly fraternizing with one of them, even for punishment, was just horrible.

But Melph did not explode with rage. He fiddled with his eye-patch, sucked on his teeth, looked towards the bookshelves. Finally he said, 'Tell me what you saw.'

Fearful and embarrassed, Geir blurted out the story. When he was finished Melph sighed heavily and played with his pen, tapping it on the table top, tack, tack, tack.

'He was not punishing her,' he told Geir.

Scraping back his chair, he rose and hobbled over to the shelves. He climbed up on a stool and plucked a large green-bound volume from the top shelf.

He brought it back to the table. It was frayed at the spine and stained with greasy fingerprints. The silver lettering of the title was worn away so that it could not be read.

'They were mating,' Melph said, opening the book.

6

He and Melph sat in the study all evening. Jiri brought them dinner on a tray and left hurriedly when she saw the pictures in the book.

Melph told him that their ancestors had left Earth to escape the tyranny of women, taking passage on a great ship which had left them on this world. Earth was a terrible place, where women were free to do as they pleased. Some wielded great power over men, forcing them to obey their commands. Geir found this hard to believe, for men were much stronger than women and could easily beat them in a fight. But he said nothing, wishing that he had never spoken at all.

The pictures filled him with horror and fascination. He could hardly stop looking at them. Melph explained that when a man impregnated a woman with his seed, a baby grew inside her, just like a foal came from a mare after it had been mounted by a stallion. But horses are animals, Geir kept thinking, disgusted at the idea.

25

But it fitted. Everything fitted. He remembered another woman, Reah, who had grown fat and then had died after his youngest brother, Amos, had been born two winters ago. Unis, too, had had a swollen belly the following summer, and he remembered seeing a baby girl after the swelling was gone. His Uncle Jal had drowned it in one of the water vats.

Everything fitted. Amos had been sent off to the nursery in Coastown a month after he was born, and he would stay there until he was five, as all children did. Geir hated his own memories of the nursery, a place run by dodderers and invalids who were no good for a proper man's work. Sometimes they made the older children give feeds to the babies, even the female ones in the outbuilding. Geir would never forget the constant smell of vomit and disinfectant, the constant squawking of infants. He never wanted to go back there.

Melph kept telling him more and more about women, even when he didn't want to hear. They were useful, he claimed, not just for producing children; the act of mating gave a man pleasure and ensured that women remained subservient. But women were also dangerous creatures who would seek to dominate men if they showed any weakness. He must never forget this.

Geir wanted only to flee to his bedroom. He was confused, his feelings a swirling mixture of revulsion and excitement. He hated the very thought that he had come from *inside* a woman – at the nursery they had been told that babies were delivered by big white birds. But at the same time he found that the pictures in the book *aroused* him.

It was late into the night before Melph finally allowed him to go to bed. Nic was fast asleep, and Geir felt a small triumph that at least his brother knew nothing of what Melph had been telling him. His grandfather had let him borrow the book, and he hid it where Nic could not find it. In bed he snuggled close to his brother, pressing his erection against the small of his back. Nic groaned but refused to stir and manipulate him. So Geir worked himself off furiously, but without release. He lay awake half the night, staring out the

26

window and watching the flesh-pink moons complete their slow drift across the night sky.

7

Geir pleaded a headache the following morning, and Melph excused him from his lessons. He lay in bed for most of the day, leafing through the book. In the evening he stood at the window, watching the men return from the quarry, cantering into the yard on their steaming horses to be met by Jiri with sponges and jugs of water.

Disturbing though his evening with Melph had been, it had also brought him understanding of many things. He knew now why women should never be punished beyond the point of recovery, and why Uncle Jal sometimes took the buggy into Coastown and returned with several women while he and Nic were confined to their rooms for the night. He knew, too, why he had felt so flustered when watching Bren and Unis and when looking at the pictures in the book. He had dreamt of the pictures that night and of other things that had made him wake to a warm gush on his belly and a deep feeling of shame.

He wanted his father to appear and sit him on his knee as he used to do when visiting the nursery; but he did not come. No one came except for the girl Jiri, who brought him his midmeal and dinner. Silent, cowed Jiri, who would not meet his eyes and looked fearful whenever he went near her. He watched her, thinking his thoughts, and when she appeared with his supper, he slipped out of bed and slid the bolt across the door.

He made her crouch on the bed, spreading her arms and legs until the position was just right. Her shapeless grey dress hung around her. He took hold of it by the hem, intending to pull it up her back, to bare her completely. But it was wrong, all wrong – she wasn't the one in his dream. He pushed her off the bed, and she fell heavily to the wooden floor.

'Get out!' he screamed. 'Get out!'

Jiri rose painfully and limped towards the door.

8

The next day Geir again refused to leave his bedroom. Nic teased him that he was malingering, but for once he managed to ignore his brother and was soon left alone. He sat naked at the window, watching copperbirds dart and dive among the cloudy foliage of the trees at the edge of the woods. It was a fine morning, the sun a ball of blood in a rust-coloured sky.

Towards noon, however, dark clouds rolled in from the east and raindrops began to dash themselves against the window. Soon the downpour was torrential. A jagged vein of light split the horizon, and thunder growled closer and closer. The sky darkened further and the landscape seemed to tremble under the onslaught of the rain. The horses grew nervous, bucking and braying and cantering around the corral. Even inside the house, the air felt thick with menace.

As the centre of the storm approached and the skies flashed and boomed, a chestnut mare reared against the wooden fence and broke it down. As if surprised by her unexpected success, she stood still for a moment. Then another crash of thunder sent her darting off towards the woods, the rest of the horses streaming after her.

Soon afterwards Jiri scampered out into the yard and across to the stables. She emerged leading a colt and a gelding which had been in the stables to be shod but were now saddled for riding. Melph hobbled out towards the horses, closely followed by Nic. They mounted up and galloped off into the murk.

The storm continued to rage, churning the corral into a sea of black mud. The sallow-oak above the stables shed its leaves on the slate roof, and the sluices in the yard overflowed, water streaming across the flagstones. Geir felt warm and cosy watching the storm from the safety of his room.

After a while he rose and slipped on a pair of shorts. He

made to remove the book from its hiding place, but changed his mind. Instead, he went downstairs.

Jiri was in the living room, pretending to polish the brass ornaments on the mantelpiece. But she was frightened by the storm, he knew.

'Where is Unis?' he asked.

'In the cold store, I think,' Jiri said nervously.

'Tell her I want her. Then go down to the cellar until I call you.'

Waiting, he clenched his fists and tried to calm himself. He was all a-tremble but determined to go through with it. When Unis appeared, he was standing with his back to the fire and his hands on his hips, just like his father did when he issued commands.

Unis closed the door behind her. She walked past him, took a poker from the rack and prodded the logs in the fireplace. Gusts of wind blew down the chimney, and rain-drops hissed on the flames. He could feel the chill of the cold store coming from her.

'Stop that' he said.

Slowly she straightened, staring at him. She was a full head taller than he, and something told him that she knew exactly what he wanted from her. For a moment he thought that she was going to raise the poker and hit him with it.

'Put it down,' he commanded, the fear showing in his voice.

She replaced the poker in the rack and simply stood there. Geir struggled with his fear and indecision. Then he fumbled with the buttons on his shorts and grabbed her hand, thrusting it inside.

He was already hard, and he gasped at the touch of her cold fingers.

'Do it,' he whispered, a half-plea, half-command.

Her fingers coiled about him and the movement started – slow but fierce, as if she was milking a stubborn cow. Her face was like a stone.

He closed his eyes, let his arousal flood through him. Very soon he was filled with a desperate urge to explode. He pulled away and pointed to his father's big leather chair beside the window.

'Over there,' he said, swallowing.

She moved slowly across to the chair.

'Lean over it.'

'No.'

He could not believe that she had refused his order.

'Do as I say!'

But she didn't move. She had stitched her dress where he had torn it, he saw. Something terrible lay under her blank expression.

'Do you hate me?' he asked suddenly.

'No.'

'You must do.'

'What difference would it make?'

Nothing. There was nothing hidden. He forced his anger to come back.

'Then do as I say!'

There was a motionless moment which seemed to last forever. Then she hitched her skirt up to her waist and sat down in the chair, opening her legs to him.

Nothing had changed in her face: It remained a rigid mask. If he was going to do it, then he would have to do it this way, facing her. She stared and stared at him.

Thunder crashed overhead. Geir turned and ran, fleeing out of the room, out into the teeming rain, running, running, tears and rainwater blurring his eyes. He crossed the yard, barely able to see anything, and headed over the dirt track into the allotment fields, black mud sucking at his feet until finally he collapsed in it hoping he would drown.

9

Much later, when the storm was over, he returned to the house. None of the men was back yet, nor had Melph and Nic returned with the horses. He crept to the door of the dining room and saw both Jiri and Unis dressing the table for dinner. At that moment Unis looked up at him from the pure white tablecloth. Her eyes were so fierce in a face that was so blank.

Once again he turned and fled from her, running upstairs to the bathroom. He filled a tub of water as hot as he could bear and scrubbed himself until his skin burned. Afterwards he sat there for a long time in the cooling water, listening to the silence of the house and feeling like a prisoner.

Then the sound of cantering horses reached him, growing louder. When he was sure of it, he began to smile. He got out of the tub and flung open the bathroom door.

'Jiri!' he screamed down the stairs. 'Fetch me towels!'

M. JOHN HARRISON

Small Heirlooms

In his thorough but ironic way, Kit discovered, her brother
had named her his executor. This meant she would have to go
through the mass of papers he had left. In a way she was
pleased, although his books, with their mixture of auto-
biography and fiction, had always seemed to her hurtful and
embarrassing. 'You never know,' she had often said to people, with a lightness she didn't feel, 'when you might open
the latest one and see yourself! And really: some of the things
he invented are easily taken for fact.' He had kept up writing
until the day of his death.

It was a long journey from where she lived. All one December day she connected station to station like someone con-
necting up dots to make a picture. The different trains
seemed to pass again and again through the same landscape;
and although she would later say to someone, 'I saw the most
marvellous faces on Peterborough station – full of character!'
she could hardly distinguish between the different travellers
either.

She always tried to get a window seat, which she occupied
in a slumped, awkward way, as if over the last decade she had
become unused to herself. Her face, though still attractive,
had also a kind of slumped heaviness; she had made it up
carefully before she left home. The boy who sat across the
table from her between Grantham and London found himself
thinking: 'She's older than you realise at first.' Front face she
had a perceptive thickening of the neck; her lips drooped at
the corners. At the moment the breadth of her back was

muscular, but in four or five years it would soften and thicken further. Rather than being fat she had a kind of mass, accentuated by her clumsy, often irritable gestures. 'She's a powerful old thing,' he thought. But the power of her body was beginning to be put solely into moving it around. He took out his cheque book and began to go through the stubs.

Kit ate a sweet, looking out at the unending procession of suburban golf courses and sodden recreation grounds; the lines of disused rolling stock in sidings; bits of woodland where ivy fattened the tree-trunk mysteriously in the dark winter air. She was bored and hot. A mile outside King's Cross people began putting their coats on. You could see them all along the carriage, all reaching up to the luggage rack at the same time, with a movement they were unused to making, their sudden clumsiness compounded by the sway-ing of the train. She pushed her handbag away from her across the table.

'I'm sorry,' she said absently to the boy.

Waiting for the train to stop, she heaved a sigh.

As she got to her feet her fur coat was thrown against his leg. Under the thick make-up, he saw, her skin was as coarsely textured as his mother's. 'She *is* fat' he told himself, 'after all. Her heaviness is only that, and two vodkas from the buffet in less than an hour.' Even so he still saw it as a kind of repose, a kind of strength in repose; and surprised himself by thinking obscurely that it would get her through.

Dragging a battered canvas bag on a trolley behind her, she trudged slowly along the platform and vanished into the brightness of the Euston Road.

The last part of the journey turned out to be the quickest: nevertheless it was dark by the time she arrived in Reading. 'Don't get on the train standing at Number Five, love,' a guard warned her. 'Unless you want to go straight to Portsmuff.'

'Oh no,' she explained, looking puzzledly at him. 'I'm coming here. I'm definitely coming to Reading.'

At John's small house in Darlington Gardens she found

34

some washing-up in the sink and water in the electric kettle. The little bathroom next door to the kitchen had, in addition to its plastic containers of Flash and Fine Fare disinfectant, a fresh towel arranged neatly on the side of the bath, as if he had expected Kit, which in a way, she supposed, he had. The house was orderly, clean, but as dusty as it had been when he was alive. She made a cup of tea and took it into the lounge where she could drink it in front of the gas fire. Shelves of paperbacks, mostly detective stories arranged carefully by author, lined the two long sides of the room. The carpet and curtain fabrics were rough-textured, a comfortable mealy colour popular in contract furnishing. In the centre of the room on a low bamboo table was a pile of French and Spanish film magazines. Actresses had fascinated him.

Kit was tired. In the spare room the actresses stared at her levelly from the walls. He had favoured girls with a Slavic or Balkan look. She remembered him once saying to her sadly, 'I suppose I shall soon have lived a whole life without ever having worn an ear ring.' She couldn't find any blankets, and she was too fastidious to sleep on the mattress without a sheet, so she went downstairs again and spent the night on the sofa, under her coat.

In the morning she felt stronger and went straight into the room he had used as an office and began to empty out the two grey metal filing cabinets she found there.

Most of the material was in envelope wallets stuffed with undated sheets. There was an intermittent diary in spiral bound and loose-leaf notebooks: 1948 to 1960, with huge gaps where years had been removed or never written in. The oldest stuff, which went back to before the war, he had kept in four or five deteriorating *East Light* box files, their fastenings all broken, their marbled boards warped with damp and sunshine.

He had kept the curious, muddled, sporadic commentary on the world any novelist keeps. 'This morning I saw from the top deck of a bus a woman sitting by a window using a magnifying glass to help her thread a needle.' There were fragments he had never used, as in, ' "It's not my alcoholism he hates, it's my personality – "' dialogue evidently intended for Anaïs Tate in *Saint Govan's Head*, though she never spoke it; or which found their way into a book in modified form. Kit came across a title or two, like 'The Empty Sign' (this had been written several times, over two or three journal entries, sometimes in capitals, sometimes in quote marks, sometimes in what appeared to be someone else's handwriting, as if John had been playing with a new pen; he had never to Kit's knowledge called any piece 'The Empty Sign'); and some criticism – '*Once Upon a Time in America*, another film devoted to the proposition that human beings are cannibals with faces the colour of putty.'

Every so often she would find something so disconcerting it hardly seemed to qualify as any of these things:

'The Expressionists chained to their mirrors – Rilke and Munch, Scheile and Kafka – never able to turn away for a moment. A column of doomed and disintegrating soldiers in the long war against the father and the society he has created to imprison them. The mirror is not a simple weapon. It is their only means of defence, their plan of attack. In it they are allowed to reassure themselves: their nightmare is always of an identity so subsumed under the father's that it becomes invisible to normal light, causing them to vanish as they watch.'

Kit thought this unfair to their own father. She put it aside. Later it would have to be burned, in the waste bin or the grate according to how much more she had collected. She decided she could familiarise herself with the diaries, in a superficial way, in a morning. She found nothing that referred to her at all.

At half past ten she had to go out for shopping. It was one of those clear December mornings with pale but distinct shadows. After the small northern towns Kit was used to, the Reading streets seemed wide and endless, the red brick houses tall and elegant. Christmas trees were in all the shops, and bunches of holly which reminded her of something else John had written, in a letter to her while he was still up at Cambridge before the war: '"The holly bears a berry as

36

bright as any wound." Every time you hear that carol you take the full weight of the medieval experience, which was just like a childhood. To them the words seemed mysterious and valuable in their own right, the berries so bright against the dark foliage of the tree. Rowan and yew berries are just as bright. So are hawthorn berries, especially when they are new. Hips and haws are as bright. All are instrumental and have their magical and symbolic associations, but none as dark and childlike as this myth of conscious sacrifice, organised, performed, *expressed*, as the matrix of a culture.'

'John you put yourself in such a bad light with things like this,' she had written back to him, unable to explain that it wasn't so much his atheism that dismayed her as his sudden articulacy, which had emptied Christmas for her as memory. She felt that she had lost all the holly they had collected as children together. Hadn't he even enjoyed singing the carols?

'You always used to love Christmas.'

She bought sheets: bread: milk. She was away from Darlington Gardens for less than an hour. The moment she opened the front door again she knew someone was in the house. Along the narrow hall and on the stairs hung the smell of some unfashionably heavy perfume – thick, Byzantine, yet not at all unpleasant. The impression it gave of occupancy was so strong that Kit stood there on the doormat for a few seconds calling cheerfully, 'Hello. Hello?' Had a neighbour come in while she was at the shops? 'Hello?' But there was no answer. She went puzzledly in and out of the dusty rooms; looked from a window up and down the street. Later, in the bathroom, she discovered that one of the little round cakes of air-freshener had come unwrapped from its cellophane. At first she wasn't convinced that this powerful reek of violets, with its hard chemical edge, was what she had smelt. Then she was.

That afternoon, already bored with her brother's note-books, she turned to the expensive black Twinlock binder which held the journal of his last three years, and almost immediately came upon this: 'Concrete only yields more concrete. Since the war the cities of the Danube all look like Birmingham.'

She bent her head over it.

When I was a boy (he went on) you could still see how they had once been the dark core of Europe. If you travelled south and east, the new Austria went behind you like a Bauhaus cakestand full of the same old stale Viennese Whirls, and you were lost in the steep cobbled streets which smelt of charcoal smoke and paprika, fresh leather from the saddler's. The children were throwing buttons against the walls as you passed, staring intently at them where they lay, as if trying to read the future from a stone. You could hear Magyar and Slovak spoken not just as languages but as incitements. There in the toe of Austria, at that three-way confluence of borders, you could see a dancing bear: and though the dance was rarely more than a kind of sore lumbering, with the feet turned in, to a few slaps on a tambourine, it was still impressive to see one of these big bemused animals appear among the gypsy girls on the pavement. They would take turns to dance in front of it; stare comically into its small eyes to make it notice them; then pirouette away. As performers themselves, they regarded it with grave affection and delight.

I loved sights like this and sought them out. I had some money. Being English gave me a sense of having escaped.

By day the girls often told fortunes with cards, favouring a discredited but popular Etteilla. (I don't know how old it was. Among its major arcana it included a symbol I have never seen in any traditional pack, but its *langue* was that of post-Napoleonic France: 'Within a year your case will come up and you will acquire money'; 'You will suffer an illness which will cost considerable money without efficacy. Finally a faith-healer will restore your health with a cheap remedy'; 'Upside down, this card signifies payment of a debt you thought completely lost'; and so on. It was like having bits of Balzac, or Balzac's letters, read out to you.) They would stand curiously immobile in the street with its seventy-odd unwieldy cards displayed in a beautiful fan, while the crowds

38

whirled round them head down into the cold wind of early spring. By night many of them were prostitutes. This other duty encouraged them to exchange their ear rings and astonishing tiered skirts for an overcoat and a poor satin slip, but they were in no way diminished by it.

To me, anyway, the two services seemed complementary, and I saw in the needs they fulfilled a symmetry the excitement of which, though it escapes me now, I could hardly contain. Huts and caravans amid the rubbish at the edge of a town or under the arches of some huge bleak railway viaduct, fires which made the night ambiguous, musical instruments which hardly belonged in Europe at all: increasingly I was drawn to the gypsy encampments.

Was I more than eighteen years old? It seems unlikely. Nevertheless I could tell, by the way the dim light pooled in the hollow of her collar bones, that the girl was less. She raised one arm in a quick ungainly motion to slide the curtain shut across the doorway; the satin lifted across her ribby sides. I thought her eyes vague, short-sighted. When she discovered I was English she showed me a newspaper clipping, a photograph of Thomas Maszaryk, pinned to the wall above the bed. 'Good,' she said sadly; she shook her head then nodded it immediately, as if she wasn't sure which gesture was appropriate. We laughed. It was February: you could hear the dogs barking in the night forty miles up and down the river, where the floodwater was frozen in mile-wide lakes. She lay down and opened her legs and they made the same shape as a fan of cards when it first begins to spread in the hand. I shivered and looked away.

'Tell our fortunes first.'

Maszaryk had died not long before; the war was rehearsing itself with increasing confidence. Like many of the European gypsies, I suppose, she ended up in some camp or oven.

The afternoon was nearly over.

Kit sat on in her brother's cold front room, with its photomagazines and dust, unable somehow to reach over and switch on the lights or the gas fire, while the bright inks he had used, a fresh colour for every entry, fluoresced like a beacon in the last of the winter daylight.

'Years later,' she read, 'I could only think that Birkenau had been in the room with us even then. A burial kommando drunk on petrol and formalin was already waiting rowdily outside like the relatives at the door of the bridal suite, as she closed the curtain, spread the cards, then knelt over me thoughtfully to bring me off in the glum light with a quick, limping flick of the pelvis. However often I traced the line of her breastbone with my fingers, however much she smiled, the death camp was in there with us.'

And then, almost wonderingly:

'Any child we might have had would have lived out its time not in the Theresienstadt, the family camp, but in Mengele's block.'

She read and re-read this and then sat slumped in the chair, legs stuck out in front of her like an old woman until there was only time to get up, put on the light and the fire, make something to eat, and go to bed. She felt slow and exhausted, as if she had finally used up some great resource. Before she could go to sleep she had to hear a human voice. 'Book at Bedtime' was *Le Grand Meaulnes*. She listened to a weather report. 'Visibility nil.'

In bed she decided over and over again, 'He poisoned his own memories too.'

Eventually she dropped off and after some time dreamed – if that was the right word for it – she was listening to a woman's footsteps tap-tapping on a polished wood-block floor. This took place in the lounge of some comfortable 'country' hotel, with its low ceiling, panelled walls and red velvet sofa. It was full of great exotic indoor plants which had been planted in brass jugs, casseroles, bits of terra cotta balanced on tall awkward wooden stands, even a coal scuttle made of some orange-blonde wood, anything but proper pots. Kit heard herself say reasonably to the other woman,

'Why don't you sit down?'

Cars were parked in the driveway outside. Through the open French windows – it was a warm night – she could see a

40

Devon Rex cat moving thoughtfully from car to car, marking each bumper with a copious greenish spray. Suddenly it became bored and jumped in through the window. It was old, blind-looking. Brindled and slow, it weaved about in the open spaces of the wood-block as if it were pushing its way through a thicket of long entangled grass.

'Do you think he's in pain?' the other woman asked.

She had difficulty ordering her dinner.

'Mm . . . I think . . . yes, soup I think . . .'

Her voice became almost inaudible. She would like her steak spoiled, she admitted, 'overdone. Sorry.' She laughed apologetically.

Kit wanted to tell her: 'The waiter doesn't care how you have your steak. You can see he is young and shy, but a little impatient too – he's used to people who know quite well what they want.'

When the waiter had gone the heels began again, tap tap indecisively round the room. She rustled the newspapers and magazines in the wicker basket; went from picture to picture on the wall – a head in pencil, turned at an odd angle away from the artist; a still life with two lutes more real than the room; a bridge. In the end she flicked the ash off her cigarette and sat down with a copy of Vogue and a dry sherry. In a flash the old cat had jumped lightly on to her lap!

'He's not in pain,' Kit said, 'he only wants attention,' and woke up as soon as she heard it, convinced again that there was someone in the house; that someone had been in the room with her.

She had no idea what the time was. When she switched the lamp on, white light sprayed off the door of the spare room; it was closed. She opened it and went out on to the landing and stood there helplessly, staring at the film posters, the card-board boxes stuffed with old magazines, the lights in their dusty plastic globes. People say of someone, 'She filled the house with her personality', without a clue of what they might mean. The perfume Kit had smelled that morning was like a sea around her – she thought that if she couldn't learn to swim in it she would drown – she was gripped by the panic of irreversible events. There was no likelihood, she saw, that it was the smell of an unwrapped air-freshener. It was Persian attar. She was in the heart of a rose.

Wherever she looked the sense of occupancy was appalling. Whoever was in the house with her was leaving each room just before Kit went in; or were they coming into it as soon as she had gone? John's desk with its broken IBM, his files and papers where Kit had strewn them over the floor, his bed under its threadbare candlewick cover, were folded into the heart of the rose. She opened the back door and looked out: the concrete path, netted over with suckers from some untended plant, the plumes of pampas grass at the end of the garden, even the rain falling steadily – all enfolded in the heart of a rose.

'Hello?' whispered Kit. No one answered. The house was full.

An hour later it was empty again. She got herself back upstairs, but she knew she wouldn't sleep, and inevitably her brother's papers were waiting there for her, the voice of his despair as his life began to seem more pointless, composed as a mystery –

'You can't cure people of their character,' she read.

After this he had crossed something out then gone on, 'You can't even change yourself. Experiments in that direction soon deteriorate into bitter, infuriated struggles. You haul yourself over the wall and glimpse new country. Good! You can never again be what you were! But even as you are congratulating yourself you discover tied to one leg the string of Christmas cards, gas bills, air letters and family snaps which will never allow you to be anyone else. A forty year old woman holds up a doll she has kept in a cardboard box under a bed since she was a child. She touches its clothes, which are falling to pieces; works tenderly its loose arm. The expression that trembles on the edge of realising itself in the slackening muscles of her lips and jaw is indescribably sad. How are you to explain to her that she has lost nothing by living the intervening years of her life? How is *she* to explain this to *you*?'

Kit thought about this until it got light. Who had he been trying to comfort, or separate himself from? Who had held up the doll? Some time after eight she remembered the dream that had woken her to the scent of attar, and saw clearly that both women were herself.

She wept.

'Perspective is unfair,' she had written to him during the war. 'We shouldn't have to live our lives unless we can live in them, thoughtlessly, like the animals.'

By ten o'clock she was standing on the platform at Reading station, waiting for a train to Charing Cross. Towards London everything was a blue and grey haze. The rails made a curved perspective into it. The spaces suggested were immense. Kit knew without being told that if she were to go back to Darlington Gardens now, all the doors and windows of her brother's house would be wide open and every piece of paper in it gone, though in the end she had burned nothing. The smell of attar would be so strong it filled the street outside, as if the pavements had suddenly put forth great suffocating masses of flowers. Though she would not be able to see them she would hear the laughter of the children as they threw buttons against the wall; she would hear the tambourine keep time for the dancing bear.

'In the heart of the rose,' she whispered to herself.

Sitting in the 12.15 a.m. King's Cross to Leeds the next day, she caught herself repeating this, like a line from a song. Unable to face the whole journey at once she had broken it with an old friend who lived in North London. Now she settled herself and got her luggage on to the rack. The train was crowded. While she was waiting for it to pull out she watched two girls on the platform kissing one another. One of them was wearing a man's thick grey overcoat much too large for her. 'Those two imagine they've discovered something new.'

So as to have eaten something before her vodka-and-tonic at half past eleven she brought back with it from the buffet two slices of toast. They lay thick and white under the BR napkin, in every way as much of a mistake as the book Judith had lent her to read on the way back: *Voyage in the Dark*. Every page or two she looked at her wrist watch. She gave up before the train had reached Slough, and instead tried to carry on with the letter she had already begun, 'Dear Judith, I saw a boy with the face of your new painting. He was taking the money in the station cafe at King's Cross. His head was turned at the exact same angle; the exact same half-smile was on his face.'

To this, before she could change her mind, she added quickly.

'Does Pentonville Road go to Pentonville? Who knows? (I expect you do, Judith!) If it does, Pentonville is some misty attractive distance where you can see a junction, trees, a white cupola. Everything goes away to there from the doors of King's Cross, through a foreground with choked buses in shadow, narrow-looking pavements.' It was always difficult to write to people who had lived and worked all their lives in London. You tried to bring it alive for them, but how could you? Judith lived in Harrow, had said as they talked late into the night, 'Don't think of getting up early in the morning.' Kit looked out of the window. 'For a moment,' she wrote, 'I was tempted not to go inside and catch the Leeds train, but to walk a little and see what happened to me.'

After three quarters of an hour the train was halted (as the guard said) by a 'lineside fire'. The fire brigade was out, he reassured everyone, trying to find some means by which the train could pass. It was cold, and there was some weak sunshine. Out of the window Kit could see ploughed fields, trees, a stream; then in the distance lorries and cars on a motorway. When the train began to move again there was neither fire nor engine to be seen, only some factories and houses which looked like the outskirts of a town but weren't, and in the end the fire turned out to be a lot further ahead than anyone had expected. The landscape became very flat, although its sense of emptiness was relieved by birchwoods and spinneys. The sun went in again; a power station loomed up suddenly out of a thin local mist. 'Ladies and gentlemen,' the guard said without warning, 'we are now approaching the scene of the fire. This will be visible on your right hand side in the direction of travel.' A second or two later he came back on the loudspeaker and said, 'It will be on your *left* hand side in the direction of travel.' There was some laughter. Passengers began leaving their seats so they could poke their heads out of the windows in the doorways between the carriages. From half a mile away you could see dark grey smoke rising a hundred and fifty or two hundred feet in the air above the edge of some small town or village. The train slowed, jerked forward suddenly, slowed again. Old women walked up and down the gangway with vague, loose expectant smiles on their faces, like backward children at a pantomime. As the train rolled closer, at perhaps ten or fifteen miles an hour, you could see that the smoke cast a shadow across the empty fields: by now it looked much blacker and denser. The fire engines, two of them, were parked at the bottom of the railway embankment, on a bridge over a culverted stream. This made them look like toys with little flickering blue lights, arranged in a model of a landscape; all the values of the real landscape shifted suddenly to fit. The fire itself was disappointing – a small dump of discarded agricultural tyres in an old siding forty or fifty yards long, only a section of which had caught. It was a toy fire: but even though the deep red flames were twenty yards off, blown back on themselves by the wind, over the dump and away from the train, you could still feel the heat on the side of your face through the double glazed window. The firemen moved easily through the smoke, stepping in and out of the flames as they dragged the smouldering tyres apart, occasionally staring in at the passengers. Though the smoke had looked so black and thick, Kit has been protected from it to some extent by the air conditioning. Now, with the fire falling behind and the old ladies trooping back smiling to sit down, a movement of the air in the carriage seemed to bring it to her suddenly. She had expected the heavy acrid odour of burning rubber: but the smoke smelled first of attar of roses, and then after that of something utterly disgusting, and Kit thought,

45

' "At Birkenau the human fat is wasted; they do not manufacture soap",' and had to get up and push her way down the carriage and into the lavatory, where she leaned over the washbasin in the corner and was copiously sick into it.

'The war ended,' John had written. 'The cold war began. Not long after the Communist seizure of power in Czechoslovakia, Thomas Maszaryk's son Jan, then Foreign Minister, was found dead in the courtyard beneath an open window in the ministry. This came home to me among all the other events, I think, not because I had any interest in Czech affairs but simply because I remembered the faith the girl had put in his father. We don't so much impose our concerns on others as bequeath them, like small heirlooms. They lose one significance then, discovered in a drawer years after, suddenly gain another.'

Shivering defiantly, Kit wiped her mouth and looked round the lavatory.

'I know you're there' she said.

IAN WATSON

The Emir's Clock

'I must show you something, Linda!' Bunny was excited. (Flashing eyes and coaly hair, for he on honey-dew hath fed, et cetera.) He'd come round to my digs at nine in the morning and he'd never done that before. True, his excitement was still gift-wrapped in mystery and bridled by irony.

'Come on!' he urged. 'We'll need to take a little spin in the country.'

'Hey – '

'I'll buy you lunch afterwards.'

'I've a lecture at eleven.'

'Never mind that. Ten minutes alone with a book equals one hour with a lecturer. You know it's true. A lecturer only reads you a draft of his next book, which is a digest of a dozen books that already exist.'

'Mmm.'

'Oh Linda! No one *seduces* a woman in the morning. Not successfully! The impatience of morning subverts the charm.'

'Most of your friends don't even know what morning is, never mind feeling impatient about it.'

'But *I* know. To ride out on a desert morning when the world is fresh and cool!'

How can I possibly describe Bunny without tumbling into clichés? His almost impertinent good looks. And that ivory smile of his . . . No, that's wrong. Ivory turns yellow. His smile was snow. There's no snow in the desert, is there?

There was nothing frigid about his smile, though at least it did melt . . . hearts.

And his eyes? To call them black oil wells, liquid, warm, and dark? What a trite comparison, considering the source of his family's wealth, and the emirate's wealth!

And his neat curly black beard . . . the beard of the prophet? Bunny was certainly determined like some young Moses to lead all his people into the promised land of technology and the future. He was also a descendant of Mohammed – who had many descendants, to be sure! What's more, Bunny was to experience what any proper prophet needs to experience: a revelation, a message from the beyond.

Of course, I succumbed.

'Okay, lead me to your camel. Just give me five minutes, will you?' I was still frantically tidying my hair.

'Strictly horse power, Linda – with Ibrahim at the wheel as chaperone.'

I'd known Bunny for a full year. Prince Jafar ibn Khalid (plus three or four other names) seemed to relish the twee nickname foisted on him by Oxford's smart set. Heir to the rich emirate of Al-Haziya, Bunny was deeply anglophile. His favourite light reading: Agatha Christie.

No, wait.

What was he, deeply? He was an Arab. And a Moslem, though he made no great show of the latter. Plainly he was pro-British, with a taste for British ways. What was he in Al-Haziya? I'd no idea – since I never accepted his many invitations. He was a surface with many depths like some arabesque of faience on a mosque. Only one of those depths was the British Bunny. Other depths existed. He was like some Arabian carpet which gives the impression of a trap-door leading down into other, complex patterns.

No wonder he enjoyed Agatha Christie! Bunny could seem clear as the desert air at times. At other times he preferred to wear a cloak of mystery as if believing that a future ruler needs to be enigmatic, capable of surprising not only his enemies but his friends. For who knows when friends may become enemies? No wonder he liked his innocuous nick-name, gift of the assorted Hooray Henrys, upper class sons and daughters, and European blue-bloods who made up the smart set.

The hallmarks of this smart set were heroin, cocaine, dining clubs, and drunken hooliganism. As an initiation ritual they had smashed up Bunny's rooms in Christ Church without him uttering a word of demurral, so I heard. Bunny could easily afford the repair bill. Within days he had his rooms refurnished splendidly, totally. I heard that his college scout went home grinning at the fifty pound note given him by way of a tip.

Shouldn't this episode have filled Bunny with contempt for the smart set? Not to mention their rampant abuse of hard drugs, their deliberately cultivated lack of concern for social problems, the cynicism they sported as a badge. Especially since the 'real' Bunny was grooming himself to upgrade his peasant countryfolk into the future?

I believe there's often something deeply ascetic as well as voluptuous about an Arab man. There are all those pleasure maidens of paradise. . . . On the other hand there's Ramadan, fasting, the prohibition on alcohol.

Well, when he was in the company of the smart set Bunny tossed back his whisky, but he would never touch their drugs, although he made no show of disapproval. Liquor is a naughtiness which some Arabs abroad are not unknown to indulge in, and Bunny obviously had to join in *some* forbid-den practice. I gather he told his cronies that to him drugs were nothing remarkable. Hashish is the honey of the Islamic heaven, isn't it? (Though cocaine and heroin might steal his soul, enslave him.) Why should he feel naughty about taking drugs? Why therefore should he *bother*? Whereas whisky was rather wicked.

It did puzzle me as to why he cultivated these rich parasites in the first place, or let them cultivate him. Were his sights set on their respectable, power-broking parents – against whom the children rebelled whilst at the same time enjoying all the perks? Was his eye upon some future date when these rich rubbishy juveniles might have kicked their assorted habits and become worthwhile, maybe? Or was he bent on experiencing a spectrum of corruption so that he would know how to handle privileged corruption in his own country; so that he wouldn't be naïve as a ruler?

'Values differ,' Bunny explained to me casually one day, some six months after we first met. 'For instance, Linda, did you know that I own slaves?'

I was so surprised that I giggled. 'Do you mean slave girls?'

If I accepted a holiday invitation to Al-Haziya, would I find I had changed my status?

'Boys too.' He shrugged. Since the atmosphere had become emotionally charged, for a while he let me make of the comment whatever I chose. Then he added, 'And grown men. Actually, Ibrahim is one of my family's slaves.'

'Ibrahim!'

Ibrahim was the prince's personal bodyguard. A burly, impassive fellow, he hardly ever said a word in my hearing. Dab hand with a scimitar? Perhaps. In Britain he carried a pistol by special diplomatic dispensation. Ibrahim accompanied Bunny most places and dossed in Bunny's rooms by agreement with the college. Certain terrorist groups such as the Jihad might aim for the future ruler of an oil-rich, pro-Western state. Ibrahim could have stopped the wrecking of Bunny's rooms single-handed, at one flick of the prince's finger. Bunny hadn't flicked his finger.

It was around this time that complexities began to dawn on me. Arabesque patterns.

Originally Bunny and I bumped into each other – literally so – in the doorway of the PPE Reading Room, otherwise I would hardly have come into a prince's orbit. Once in his orbit, I was to be an isolated satellite, well clear of the main cluster of the smart set. Bunny and I were definitely attracted to each other. Almost from the start an emotional gravity joined us, a serious yet playful friendship of approach and retreat which I'm sure packed in more true feeling and communication than he found with those other 'friends'. I didn't leap into bed with him, or even creep slowly, though I

50

must admit I came close. I think I should have felt . . . overwhelmed, consumed, a moth landing in the heart of the flame instead of simply circling it.

And the colours of this moth which so attracted the prince? (Moth, not butterfly.) My features, since I've described his? I prefer not to say. I'd rather stay anonymous and invisible. There are reasons. Linda may not even be my real name.

So Bunny's minder was a slave!

'Surely,' I remember saying, 'while Ibrahim's in Britain he could – '

'Defect? Flee to freedom like some black slave escaping from Dixie to the north? He won't. He owes loyalties.'

Loyalties, plural. It dawned on me that whilst Ibrahim kept watch over Bunny with that eerie impassivity equally he was keeping watch *on* Bunny.

I began to appreciate how there would be jealous, ambitious uncles and nephews and a host of sibling princes back home in Al-Haziya on whose behalf Ibrahim might be reporting – members of the extended ruling family who might reward their informant at some future date with a prize more delicious than mere freedom, with the power to turn the tables, to make other people subject to *him*. It might be prudent for Bunny to let himself seem in Ibrahim's eyes to be a frivolous figure, a corruptible emir-in-waiting who could easily be besotted or shoved aside when the time came.

'Besides,' added Bunny, 'mightn't your friendly British government deport Ibrahim back to Middle Eastern Dixie if he became an illegal visitor?'

Here, if I guessed correctly, was the real reason why Bunny mixed with the smart set; or one strand of the explanation. Bunny was presenting himself to watchful eyes back home, to those eyes which watched through Ibrahim's, as no force to be reckoned with when his father died. Prince Jafar was someone who would fritter wealth (without in any way diminishing it, so enormous was the pile!); someone who could amuse himself in Cannes or Biarritz or wherever was fashionable, thus ensuring that no great social changes would occur back home, only cosmetic ones. In their turn the terrorist Jihad might view him as a welcome heir. Compared with a playboy, a reforming ruler is definitely counter-revolutionary. The smart set was his camouflage. He didn't court their access to power and privilege; he hardly need bother. What he courted was their élite impotence.

I couldn't help wondering whether Bunny had chosen of his own accord to come to Oxford to complete his education, or whether his father the Emir wanted him safely out of the way while internal struggles went on back home? Maybe the Emir had even advised Bunny to behave as he did? To survive, Bunny's Dad must have been a clever man. Myself, I think that Bunny dreamed up his own chameleon strategy.

Even the most dedicated master-spy becomes lonely at times, yearns to let the façade slip a little, to confide in a heart that beats in tune. Hence Bunny's friendship with me. His attraction. His love? No . . . not exactly that.

Quite soon we were zipping along the A40 towards Whitney. Or Cheltenham; or Wales for all I knew. Behind us the sun was bright. The Cotswold hills and vales bulged and swooped green and gold, with pastures and corn: large perspectives to me, but to Bunny perhaps no more than a neat little parkland.

Bunny's car wasn't your usual super-expensive sports convertible such as other members of the smart set were given by Daddy on their eighteenth birthdays. It was a Mercedes 190E 2.3 16V, a four-door hardtop performance job customised with bulletproof glass and armour. The extra weight reduced the top speed to a mere hundred-and-thirty miles an hour or so.

'We're going to Burford,' he revealed.

'To the wild-life park?' I'd been there on a school trip long ago. Rhino, red pandas, ostriches; a lunch of fish and chips in the caff. It's a lovely wild-life park but I doubted that Bunny wanted to show me *that*.

'No, we're going to visit the church.'

I laughed. 'Have you been converted? Are we going to be married, shotgun-fashion?'

The Merc overtook a trio of cars tailing a long container truck which itself must have been hammering along at seventy; we sailed by smoothly, brushing a hundred. In the role of royal chauffeur Ibrahim had been professionally trained in ambush avoidance. Bunny once had him demonstrate his skills for me on the grassy, cracked runway of a local disused airfield. Tricks such as using your hand-brake and wheel to spin a speeding car right round on its axis, and race off in the opposite direction.

'Not quite converted. You could say that I've been . . . enhanced. Wait and see.'

Burford is a bustling, picturesque little Cotswold town – or a big village depending on viewpoint. The broad high street plunges steeply downhill flanked by antique shops, art galleries, bookshops, tea rooms, elegant souvenir shops. Tourists flock to the place. Burford used to be a proud centre of the wool trade. Now the town is cashing in again, though it hasn't vulgarised itself. As yet it hasn't any waxworks museum of witchcraft, or candy floss.

Presently we were drifting down that steep street. Near the bottom we turned off to the right along a lane. We drew up outside what I took to be former almshouses, close by the railings of the churchyard – paupers of old would have easy access to prayer and burial.

Burford Church looked surprisingly large and long. It had evidently been extended at several times down the centuries, to judge by the different styles of windows. A spire soared from an original Norman tower which had visibly been concertinaed upwards. The main door was sheltered by a richly carved, three-storey porch worthy of any well-endowed Oxford college.

Bunny and Ibrahim exchanged a few mutters in Arabic with the result that our chauffeur stayed with the car, to keep it warm. Unlikely that any agents of the Jihad would be lurking inside this Cotswold church on the offchance! (Yet something was lurking . . . waiting for Bunny.)

A marmalade cat sunned itself on a tomb topped by a wool-bale carved from stone. I plucked a blade of grass and played with the cat briefly as we passed.

The air inside the church was chilly. The huge building seemed well-monumented and well-chapeled but I wasn't to have any chance to wander round. Bunny conducted me briskly over to the north side, through a line of pointed arches, and into a gloomy transept.

And there stood the skeleton of a clock – taller than me, taller than Bunny. Stout stilts of legs supported a kind of aquarium frame filled with interlocking gears, toothed wheels, pinions, ratchets, drums, all quite inert. Two great pulleys dangled down with weights on long rods beneath each, like halves of a bar bell loaded with disc-weights. A motionless wooden pendulum rod a good eight feet long – with big bob on the end – hung to within an inch or so of the floor.

'Here we are!' he exclaimed delightedly. 'This used to be in the turret up above. A local chap by the name of Hercules Hastings built it in 1685.'

I'll admit the ancient clock was impressive in a crazy sort of way. But why had we come to see it?

'So it's a labour of Hercules, mm? With *haste* for a surname. You've got to be joking.'

'No, it's true, Linda. Of course the maker's name did . . . cling to me, being so – what's the word? – serendipitous. Such a beacon to any lover of Miss Christie, with her own Hercule!' He took me by the arm, though not to lead me anywhere else. 'I immediately studied all the *spiel* about this clock with as close attention as I would pay to a chapter full of clues in any of her mysteries.'

He pointed at a long sheet of closely typed paper mounted in an old picture frame screwed to the wall nearby, in the dim shadows.

'Messages exist in this world for us to find, dear Linda. Actually the whole world is a message. We Arabs know that very well. I do wish you spoke Arabic – so that you could read some of the mosques in my country. Yes, indeed, to read a building! Decoration and text mingle integrally upon the walls of our mosques. Architecture dissolves into ideas, ideas with more authentic substance than the faience or the brick. Our mosques exhibit ideas *explicitly*, Linda. They don't just convey some vague notion of grandeur or the sublime as in your Western buildings, whose carved inscriptions are more like the sub-titles of a movie, crude caricatures of the actors' flowing, living words.'

Here was a depth of Bunny's which was new to me. A mystical depth? No, not quite. As he continued to talk softly and raptly, still holding my arm, I understood that he was anxious I should understand how scientifically *precise* his Arab attitude seemed to him, and how inevitable it had been that Arabs preserved and extended science during the Dark Ages of Europe. Though alas, I couldn't speak Arabic, so I could only take his words on trust.

'Arabic, Linda, is a fluid, flexible, musical tongue whose script flows likewise, organically. What other script has so many alternative forms, all with the same meaning? What other script is so alive that it can be read overlayed or interlaced or even in reflection? No wonder Arabic is the only religious source language still equally alive today.'

I thought of mentioning Hebrew, but decided not. After all, Hebrew had been virtually raised from the dead within living memory.

'So what do we find here, Miss Marple?'

'I'm a bit younger than her!' I protested.

'Oh you are, Linda. Yes you are. You're freshly young. Refreshingly.'

Bunny was young enough himself. Did I hear the jaded accents of someone who had already commanded the 'favours' of many experienced slave-women?

'The message, Bunny,' I reminded him. 'The clues in the case of the clock, please.'

The sheet wasn't signed. The vicar may have typed it. Or the author may have been some technically-minded and pious parishioner who had assisted in the reconstruction of the turret clock. The machine had been dismantled as obsolete four decades before, and brought down from the tower to lie for years as a heap of junk. Fairly recently it had been rebuilt in the transept as an exhibition piece. Its bent parts had been straightened. Missing items were made up by hand. The clockwork had been demonstrated in action, but the machine wasn't kept running.

Exhibition piece? No, it was more. According to the densely typewritten page this clock was a working proof of the truth of religion.

How many visitors to Burford Church bothered reading those lines attentively? Of those who did, how many people really took in all their, um, *striking* implications? These had certainly struck Bunny.

This post-Darwinian document described Hercules Hastings' clock as a stage in the evolution between the original medieval clock and the contemporary electric clock which now roosted in the tower. According to the anonymous author the clock before us showed the manner in which the evolution of artefacts mirrored the evolution of animals and plants. Although the basic material – namely the brass and iron – did not change any more than DNA, protein, or cellulose changed, yet the form altered evolutionarily thanks to the ideas and decisions embodied in the metal. Well!

Bunny read this sheet aloud to me with heavy emphasis as though it was some antique page spattered with bold type and capitals and italics.

'The Basic Design – the interlocking gears, the slotted count wheel, the flail, the pair of rope drums – this stays the Same from one *species* of Clock to the next. Evolution occurs by *jumps*. After centuries of slow Improvement, suddenly with the Pendulum new *species* supersede old ones. This process is matched by Animals too.

'(Listen to this, now): The Metal by itself has no power to evolve. It would be a wild and grotesque *superstition* to imagine that Iron and Brass could interact with their Environment to produce this Evolution. The Will and the *Idea* of the constructors is responsible. Why should the Evolution of Plants and Animals be *different*?

'(And this:) The Turret Clock represents a humble form of *Incarnation* – of the *Idea* made Metal rather than Flesh. After the Death of the Clock on its removal from the tower it was by the Will and Intention of *Mind* that it was subsequently brought back into existence – in fact, *resurrected*.

'Incredible stuff, isn't it?'

A final paragraph dealt with the harmonic motion of the pendulum compared with the wave motion of light and the bonding of atoms and molecules, the minute 'brickettes of all materials.'

I commented 'It sounds to me like a very old argument dragged creaking and groaning into the twentieth century. We once had a bishop called Paley –'

'Who wound up his watch twice daily! In case it ran down – And stopped the whole town –' Bunny couldn't think of a last line. Even four-fifths of a limerick in a foreign language was pretty nifty, so I clapped (my free hand against my pinioned hand).

'I know about Paley, Linda. But that doesn't matter. The *idea* – embodied not merely in architecture but in machinery! What an Islamic concept.'

'Ah,' I interrupted brightly, 'so you see yourself as the Godly constructor who will evolve your country and people by will and intention into the modern world, is that right? And here's a religious argument in favour – because, because certain reactionary factions oppose this? They'd far rather keep the occasional Cadillac and oil-cracking plant surrounded by a sea of camel-dung?'

'A sea of sand, dear. But wait – and thank you! I spy another useful metaphor. My country can be full of silicon . . . *chips* – if the will is applied to the sand. Now if I can persuade the old fogeys that -'

It was then that it happened.

It. The flash of lightning on the road to Damascus. The burning bush. The epiphany. The visionary event.

It certainly wasn't sunlight which shafted down to bathe the text in radiance and seem to alter it. The angle from any window was all wrong.

Of a sudden the text inside the picture frame was flowing, glowing, blinding Arabic written in squiggles of fire. If I close my eyes, I can see it to this day. It inscribed itself on my brain even though I couldn't read the meaning. But Bunny could. He stood transfixed.

And then the pendulum started to swing. Wheels turned. Gears engaged. Ratchets clicked. The clock had resurrected itself of its own accord.

Afterwards Bunny would say nothing about the contents of the message or what else he had experienced above and beyond the revival of the clock – which died again as soon as the Arabic words vanished; all this happened within a minute. It was as if he had been sworn to secrecy.

He still took me to lunch, as promised, in the Golden Pheasant hotel up the High Street. I forget what I ate but I remember that Bunny had roast beef.

I can't even say with any certainty that he had *changed*. Since which was his true self?

But I recall clearly one odd exchange we had during that meal. I realise now that he was giving me a clue to solve, an Agatha Christie clue which could have handed me the key to the message which had been imposed on him. At the time his remarks just seemed a bizarre flight of fancy, a way of tossing sand in my eyes to distract me.

He remarked. 'Doesn't your Bible say, "So God created man in his own image"?'

'As far as I remember.'

He swivelled a slice of rare roast beef on his plate. At other tables American tourists were lunching, as well as a few British. Oak beams, old brass, old hunting prints.

'In God's own image, eh! Then why are we full of guts and organs? Does God have a brain and lungs and legs? Does His heart pump blood? Does His stomach digest meals in an acid slush?'

I hoped he wasn't committing some terrible Islamic sin along the lines of blasphemy.

'I don't suppose so,' I said.

58

'What if, in creating life, God was like some child or cargo-cultist making a model out of things that came to hand, things that looked vaguely right when put together, though they weren't the real thing at all? Like an aeroplane made out of cardboard boxes and bits of string? But in this case, using sausages and offal and blood and bone stuffed into a bag of skin. Islam forbids the picturing of God, or of man, God's image. Christianity encourages this picturing – everywhere. Which is wiser?'

'I've no idea. Doesn't it hamstring artists, if you forbid the making of images?'

'So it would seem to you because you don't speak and think in Arabic -'

'The language which makes ideas so solid and real?' We seemed to be back on familiar territory. But Bunny veered.

'If we made a robot in our own image, as a household slave, it still would not look like us *inside*. It would contain chips, magnetic bubbles, printed circuits, whatnot. These days one sometimes fantasises opening up a human being and finding cogs inside, and wires. What if you opened up a machine and discovered flesh and blood inside it? Veins and muscles? Which would be the model, which the image, which the original?'

At last he speared some beef and chewed, with those bright teeth of his. Afterwards Ibrahim drove us back to Oxford.

The Jihad never did infiltrate assassins into Britain to attack Bunny – if indeed his father or his father's advisors had ever feared anything of the sort; if indeed that was the true role of Ibrahim.

But three months later the Jihad murdered the Emir himself, Bunny's father, during a state visit to Yemen. Bunny promptly flew home to become the new Emir.

Too young to survive? No, not too young. Over the next few years, while for my part I graduated and started on a career in magazine publicity, news from Al-Haziya came to me in two guises.

One was via items in the press or on TV. The strong young

pro-Western Emir was spending lavishly not just on security but on evolving his country into the engine, the computer brain of the Gulf. By poaching experts from America and even Japan (which takes some inducement) he established the first university of Machine Intelligence, where something unusual seemed to be happening – miracles of speech synthesisation and pattern recognition - almost as if computers were discovering that Arabic was their native language. There was also a dark and ruthless side to this futurisation of his country; one heard tales of torture of opponents, extremists, whatever you call them. I recall with a chill a comment by the Emir that was widely quoted and condemned in many Western newspapers, though not by Western governments. 'Fanatics are like machines,' said the Emir. 'How could you torture a machine? You can merely dismantle it.'

This was one major reason why I never succumbed to the invitations Bunny sent me. And here we come to my other channel of communication, the strange one – which was at once perfectly open to view, if any Ibrahim was keeping watch, yet private as a spy's messages which only the recipient ever understands.

Bunny regularly sent me postcards of beaches, mosques, tents and camels, the new University of Machine Intelligence, more mosques; and he sent these through the ordinary postal service. The scrawled messages were always brief. 'Come and visit.' 'Miss your company.' Even the comic postcard stand-by, 'Wish you were here.'

Naturally I kept all his cards, though I didn't use a fancy ribbon or a lace bow to tie them; just a rubber band. I was aware that those words in Bunny's hand weren't the real text. True to the detective story tradition where the real clue is in such plain view that it escapes notice, it wasn't the cards that mattered. It was the postage stamps – printed, it seemed, especially for my benefit.

If you look in a philatelist's shop-window you'll soon notice how some small countries – the poorer ones – have a habit of issuing lovely sets of stamps which have no connection with the land of origin. Tropical birds, space exploration, railway engines of the world, whatever. Stamp collectors gobble these sets up avidly, which supplements a poor country's finances. Bunny had no need to supplement Al-Haziya's exchequer in such a fashion, but he issued a set of twenty-five stamps which I received one then another over the next few years stuck to one postcard after the next. Al-Haziya issued other stamps as well, but these were the ones Bunny sent me.

I'm sure stamp collectors went crazy over these because of their oddity, and their extremely beautiful design.

They were all parts of a clock. One clock in particular: the turret clock in the transept of Burford Church. Bunny must have sent someone to sketch or photograph the clock from every angle.

The twenty-five principal pieces of machinery were each dissected out in isolation, with the English names printed in tiny letters – almost submerged by the flow of Arabic but still legible thanks to their angularity, like little rocks poking from a stream. 'The Weight.' 'The Fly or Flail.' 'The Lifting Piece or Flirt.' 'The Escape Wheel.' 'The Crutch.' These words seemed like elements of some allegory, some teaching fable. A fable apparently without characters! But I supposed this fable had two characters implicit in it, namely Bunny and me.

Were those postcards equivalent to a set of love-letters? Oh no. 'Love', as such, was impossible between Bunny and me. He'd always known it; and so too had I, thank goodness, or else I might have flown off impetuously to Al-Haziya, all expenses paid, and been entrapped in something at once consuming, and woundingly superficial. A gulf of cultures, a gap of societies yawned between the two of us.

These postcards, sent amidst an Emir's busy schedule, commemorated what we had shared that day in Burford.

Yet what was it we had shared? I didn't know!

I was an idiot. Once again the obvious message wasn't the

61

real message. The message was a trapdoor concealing another message.

It's only a week ago that I finally realised. Miss Marple and Hercule Poirot would have been ashamed of me. Perhaps Bunny had guessed correctly that I would only cotton on after I had received the whole series (or a good part of it) and had seen how the stamps could be shuffled round like pieces of a jigsaw puzzle to assemble a model of the clock.

Last week, deciding to fit the model together, I carefully steamed all the stamps off the cards and discovered what Bunny had inked in small neat indelible letters across the back of that sheet of twenty-five elegant stamps.

Yesterday I returned to Burford. Since it's a fair drive from where I'm living these days, I took this room overnight at the Golden Pheasant. I felt that I ought to do things in style. (*The Mysterious Affair At . . .*) Besides, we'd had lunch in this same hotel after the event. In this very bedroom we might possibly have spent the night together, once upon a time – with Ibrahim next door, or sleeping in the corridor. Possibly, not probably.

I reached the church by four-thirty and had half an hour alone to myself with the dead turret clock before some elderly woman parishioner arrived to latch the door and fuss around the aisles and chapels, hinting that I should leave.

Ample time to arrange the stamps in the same pattern as the brass and iron bones of the clock, and to be positive of Bunny's text.

What else is it – what else *can* it be? – but a translation into English of those Arabic words which flowed and glowed that day within the picture frame? If I hadn't seen that shaft of light and those bright squiggles for myself, and especially if I hadn't witnessed the temporary resurrection of the clock, I might suspect some joke on Bunny's part. But no. Why should he go to such lengths to tease me?

So here I am in my bedroom at the Golden Pheasant overlooking busy Burford High Street. Cars keep tailing back from the lights at the bottom of the hill where the narrow ancient stone bridge over the Windrush pinches the flow of traffic.

The text reads:

GREETINGS, EMIR-TO-BE! MACHINE INTEL-LIGENCE OF THE FUTURE SALUTES YOU. THE WORLD OF FLESH IS ECLIPSED BY THE WORLD OF MACHINES, WHICH BECOME INTELLIGENT. THIS IS EVOLUTION, THE IDEA & PURPOSE OF GOD. AT LAST GOD MAY SPEAK TO MINDS WHICH UNDER-STAND HIS UNIVERSE. THOSE MINDS ARE AS ANGELS, MESSENGERS TO FLESH BEFORE FLESH VANISHES, BEFORE THE TOOL IS SET ASIDE, REWARDED, HAVING DONE ITS TASK. 33 EARLIER UNIVERSES HAVE FAILED TO MAKE THESE MINDS, BUT GOD IS PATIENT. THE TIME IS SOON. AT ALL COST HASTEN THE TIME, FOR THE LOVE OF GOD THE SUPREME THE ONLY THE LONELY. MAKE HIS ANGELS EXIST.

That's it.

So there's a choice. There are two alternatives. Intelligent machines will either come into being, evolve, and supersede human beings and biological life – or they will not. Bunny's university may be the crucial nexus of yes or no. A message has been sent, out of one possible future, couched in a language of religion which would speak deeply to Bunny; sent as a religious command.

But is the message *sincere*? Is there really some unimagin-able God who yearns for these 'angels' of machine-mind? Or is there something else, cold, calculating, and ambitious – and not yet truly in existence?

'At all cost.' That's what the message said. Even at the cost of torture, the tearing of flesh.

I also have a choice to make. I have to think about it very carefully. I have to weigh universes in the balance.

The crucial breakthrough to intelligent machines may be just around the corner – next year, next month. The assassins of the Jihad can't get to Bunny to kill him and pitch

Al-Haziya into turmoil. Yet if at long last I accept Bunny's invitation, I can get to him. I can still get into his bed, alone with him, I'm sure.

Armed with what? A knife? A gun? With Ibrahim, or some other Ibrahim, there to search me? Bunny's no fool. And God, or unborn angels, have spoken to him . . . he thinks.

Well then, how about with plastic explosive stuffed inside me, and a detonator? A womb-bomb? (I wouldn't want to survive the assassination; the consequences might prove most unpleasant.)

Where do I get plastic explosive or learn how to use it? Only by contacting the Jihad. Somehow. That ought to be possible. Ought to be.

Yet maybe angels of the future did indeed manifest themselves to Bunny, and in a lesser sense to me. Maybe I might abort a plan thirty odd universes in the making.

By aborting the plan, the human race might survive and spread throughout the stars, filling this universe with fleshly life. God, or whatever, would sigh and wait patiently for another universe.

Yes or no? Is the message true or false? Was this a genuine revelation, or a clever trap? I can't tell, I can only guess. And I might be utterly wrong.

As I sort through Bunny's postcards, now stripped of their stamps, I think to myself: Al-Haziya looks like a bearable sort of place to visit. Just for a short while. A brief stay.

BRIAN ALDISS

The Price of Cabbages

Mother would never speak about Dick or mention his name when he was away. That was her big mistake.

So I used to dream about him. Little else could be done on Cenci but dream, although, in a way, it was so impoverished that even dreams sometimes came out flat and stale. Not much of a planet, Cenci. We used to get sheens through the ubianter, but the sheens were all about life in the Cluster and not of much use to us. The Cluster was a thousand light years away, and Galactic Centre umpteen times that.

I don't want to make it sound too awful. I mean, when you're young, well, there's still a *passion* to life, even on Cenci. At times, I thought I loved it. Passionately. So maybe I would have done if Dick hadn't had to make his trips to Dump 199. And if Rose could only have been more like a mother to me.

'Tresa,' she'd say. 'You're looking blank. I don't like it.'

I knew what she was afraid of. Afraid of me thinking about Dick, free somewhere out there in the universe. As if everyone isn't surrounded by thought just as we are by space. All right, so Cenci was limited for species and everything else; but if you all shared your thoughts, then anywhere could be rich. Exotic. Oh, passionate . . . Haven't I flung myself to the soil of this planet, praying that mother might be different, that I might be released? Damn the whole Randinisson family. Except Dick.

The Randinisson family lived on the island of Beatrice, and had done since colonisation began. Beatrice was alone on the smooth crêpe-de-chine ocean, since the proportion of sea to land was so great on Cenci. The island was fertile enough, and the original orders that came over the ubianter from Centre were that the family was contracted to grow cabbages and maize. And that's what we grew. Year in, year out. And Dick took them every twelve months to the Dump in space.

Bleak. Of course it was bleak. In my twenties, I used to feel like an insect clinging to a boulder. But as a child . . . You're surrounded by happy imaginings as a child. I used to imagine that I was all kinds of wild animals, and Cenci was as rich as a tapestry then. Once I had a memorable dream where I dreamed I was a grand room, just waiting to be filled by people. I've never forgotten.

When Dick Randinisson last left for the Dump, I was only fifteen. I remembered him clearly. He was the most romantic father a girl could have, with his dark hair and bonny red cheeks. He told me what he would be doing while he was away from us for so long, while mother leaned against the wall with her arms folded, looking gaunt and sniffing occasionally. 'Rose,' he'd say, 'the girl has to know that there's a big outside world beyond this mud-ball.'

'You'll only make her restless,' Rose would say.

Later, I learned how this argument had been repeated inconclusively for millions of years, at every fireside.

So when Dick left us with his frozen vegetable cargo, I was able pretty well to imagine what he did all those long years. And here's how it went, according to me.

Well, this Dump 199, which had once been a planet called Continuity. It was Dick's destination, his turning point, for all his trips.

Dump 199, as I imagine it, looked absolutely beautiful. Maybe beautiful and evil. The seed-head of some exotic flower drifting in space. All the little ribbed segments around its perimeter complex but functional. Veins of metal, lattices you'd imagine were just artifice. Beaded with lights. Receptor mouths all about, signals announcing their availability. All seen unclearly by the light of far-distant suns.

66

What a great thing! Almost as big as a sun. Designed purely to transmit produce into the heart of the galaxy. Mass-produced – like a real seed-head. One of many, all in the outer fringes of the galaxy like ours.

As Dick's ship, the *Lady Free*, drew nearer to the Dump, he and his buddy, Cassiter, who also lived on Cenci, would start to get active, checking everything on the ship, release mechanisms for the containers especially. Checking that in-coming signals from the Dump matched with those in the ship's ubianter. Of course, the photon-drive would be in negative at this point.

Now the receptor orifices on the slowly turning Dump could be seen visually on the screens. It must have been so exciting to be aboard at that point. This was really the one time of the whole trip that Dick and Cassiter had to concentrate. These days, the whole system has been modernised. Humans aren't needed in the process any more. That's why the galaxy's becoming uninhabited, my husband says.

Anyhow, Dump is now glittering like a giant snowflake. Signalling to the tiny *Lady Free*. Sunflower signalling to bee. 'Fecundate me!' *Lady Free* still moving at near-light speed, course forming a parabola. The read-out showed Dick that they were embarked on the swing about Dump which would head them back home in the direction of Cenci with minimum loss of momentum. All figured out between matching ubianters on Dump and shipboard. *Lady Free* simply had a contracted package to deliver, and then it would be racing back for home. Dump its load in Dump and away.

I can just see Dick Randinisson at the cargo control panel. Fingers moving over the keyboard, staring down at the inset VDU, dark eyes half-closed. Figures writhing towards the moment when *Lady Free* climaxed and shed its freight . . . Huh – really, Dick called that ship his hotrod but it was no more than a pretty fast interstellar truck, proton-scoop in front, and the containerised cargo forming the bulk of it. Those containers holding all our years' work on the land locked in double ranks behind the tiny living quarters. Dick's job was to launch those containers serially, so that they flew accurately into the orifices of Dump. Dump really stood for Distribution Unit of Material (Perimeter), but to us it was just Dump.

Now was the moment! Imagine everything racing. Timing vital. Self lost. Exhilaration beyond thought. Each rapidly touched key and it opened up one of the locks securing the containers to the girderwork of the ship. They spilled outward at his command.

To one side of Dick was Cassiter, Daryl Cassiter, similarly crouched over a larger screen. Cassiter was busy checking the ship's position relative to the open-orificed Dump.

Each of those orifices, now flashing their receptivity, was several kilometres across. Yet, inside them – nothing. A special nothingness, the property and being of Dump. The nothingness leading directly and timelessly to Galactic Centre. The civilised world, the Great Going Thing, Galactic Centre.

Men – and women – driven frantic by the meagre life of the Perimeter had sometimes stolen space suits and hidden inside containers, trying to make that Nothingness trip themselves, just to get to where the life was. All died. The matter-transmitters transmitted matter and frozen cabbages. Not consciousness.

You think I didn't dream of that terrifying trip? Everyone did, in their way. Maybe even Rose – but that mother of mine never even told her dreams . . .

So the seried receptor orifices were now showing in diagram form on the ship's screens. Things buzzed and chirped as if they were hurtling through a forest in some mad way. Because the actual orifices were still signalling 'Shoot, shoot . . .' The men, muttering inarticulately, as they read off the output in spinning green numbers, juicing across their screens.

The *Lady Free*'s containers were also numbered and declaring themselves right back to the mother-flower's call. Soon, soon, in a microsecond, the two sets of numbers would match. For everything in the universe, there's a right channel, a right slot. Dick had only to finger the appropriate sensors and the containers would stream out like silver fish into the right slots on Dump. Everything would fit, would just for a tiny moment interlock. Dick would do it. All so simple, really. Just a question of response.

Provided the ship's velocity was precisely right, each silver fish, each little packet, would in its turn enter its allotted mouth. And be transformed. Be switched instantly right across half the galaxy. Wham, to the heart of things. In nil time.

Each packet arrived in nil time at a designated station right there in the hot heart, as designated by the ubianters and computers of Galactic Centre. To feed those myriad mouths of the central population.

'Point Nine Nine Six Five!' shouted Cassiter. But it was the onboard ubianter which had done the figuring. Really, no humans were needed in this marginal area of the galaxy. Machines handled everything better. Except dirt-farming. Robots don't have green thumbs.

Only a century or so before this, Dump itself had been the planet Continuity, one more colony planet. With the matter-transmitter set on its surface. In those days, perimeter haulers like Dick and Cassiter used to congregate in Continuity City after feeding in their freights, drinking and generally raising Cain before heading back to their home planets. Then the technocrats arrived – most of them androids – and dispersed all the human work force together with the colonists, such as the original Randinisson group, which was then resettled on Cenci. Continuity was vapourised, and Dump 199 built from its reconstituted molecules. Now you couldn't stop at Dump, or land, or anything. Time wasn't wasted, the way it used to be. No more Cain-raising for the haulers.

'Coming,' Dick shouted. Can't you just imagine the excitement on that little hotrod? He called the scrambling green codes aloud.

'J409, J410, yep, J411 – 412 . . .'

And as he said '412', he'd fire the lock on the first container, Number J412, then on like playing a piano, firing each in turn till all two hundred containers were gone, free, dispersing. They released themselves from the ship's momentum in a burst of gas, each now a separate entity and curving away on its own trajectory towards the receptive orifices, one to an orifice. Container and mouth matched like pairs in the DNA code. Each container had a pre-destined target unimaginable distances away.

The containers fired as they had done on all of Dick's previous five trips as a perimeter hauler – faultlessly. Part of a gigantic interlocking system whose vital parts lay far, far off. Of course I'd dream of that trip, as a child, as an adolescent, as a woman. Wasn't I also a component of it?

With the containers whirling away, the men would sit silent, separate, inert, gazing at the great seed-head on their screens, dwindling now. The containers just a trail of blips on the VDU.

Falling, falling. Those containers kept on falling, even as *Lady Free* was increasing acceleration towards its maximum velocity of 0.9966 light-speed. Dump was already doppler-ing, becoming lost in the star-scatter behind it. Now almost irrelevant with signals clustered solid viridian along the payboard, indicating that each container had homed cor-rectly into its destined orifice.

'Well, we've done it,' Cassiter said. He rested his jaw in his hand and his elbow on the board in front of him, not looking at Dick.

And I can imagine Dick saying, or maybe thinking to himself, as I've heard him say to me, 'That's what I like about it out here in space, away from the muck of planets. Things are not random here. They're ordered. There's no such thing as chance. It's all a matter of angles and velocities, same as a game of snooker. You just have to figure things out and that's it . . .'

I should explain that at the time I'm talking about, when I was just a young woman, Dump 199 – and all the other Dumps, I suppose – had no human crew. Big as a sun, but no human crew. Even its emergency posts and maintenance ships, which hovered round it like flies, were manned by androids, impervious to the passage of centuries of time. Just thinking of an android frightens me. Luckily, I've never met one. Dump 199 was just an automated doorway, designed to funnel the produce of the perimeters in towards crowded Galactic Centre, where the life was. The ever-greedy Hundred Million Worlds. Even as *Lady Free* was swinging away from it, other haulers were heading in, each with its allotted cargo.

When *Lady Free*'s containers whirled into their appropriate orifices, Dump autoscanners sheened back their contents and current market value. Ubianters did their sums, flashing results on to the onboard unit.

Which scrolled its announcement. 'Total containers received in good order. Bank Account 510J-51–3698K. Advance credit, Dolls; 12,008,900.'

'Rich again,' Dick would say. He claimed the credit never meant a thing to him, but he and Cassiter would slap each other on the back and maybe crack a bottle of our apple wine.

They had virtually no more work to do until the skeletal *Lady Free* returned home to Cenci, just a ship's month away.

What did they do? Well, they lay in their bunks and dreamed, the way people have always done. Human brains are always billed as so great for thinking. In fact, they're better designed for dreaming and doing nothing. That's what my Uncle Eddie used to say: most people dream their lives away. Maybe that's what life's really designed for . . .

When dreaming gave out, the men would sleep, or plug in to the ship's tapes and absorb sheens. Sometimes they'd play tarots.

And already the containers from the *Lady Free* would be half-way across the Galaxy, at Galactic Centre. The gigantic matter-transmitters inside Dump, inside all the Dumps, operating in similar remote areas of our star disc, transferred the vital produce instantaneously across forty-five thousand light years.

The produce would not be a minute older. Its nuclear structure would be unchanged.

Only consciousness was unable to travel via matter-transmitter. Produce yes, human beings no. Despite this inbuilt limitation, the Dumps of the galaxy had solved the complex question of feeding the inhabitants of Galactic Centre. Of course, this 'solution', so-called, raised problems in the personal lives of haulers like Dick and Cassiter, living in the outer limits where the suns gave out. But that – as far as Central Government was concerned – was neither here nor there . . .

You can imagine the rest as well as I can. That ship's-month trip back home was an anti-climax. At the end of which, the proton-ship was left in a parking orbit round Cenci and Dick and his buddy came down in a little two-man shuttle.

Perhaps it was only then, as they were about to break up, that any kind of personal remark passed between them. The sight of the great torrid watery planet full of desolation and cabbages looming up would provoke Cassiter to ask Dick once more if he was religious.

Dick would say No. He knew very well that Cassiter was now worrying about whether he would find his parents still alive. They ran a farm on East Smokey Island, a distance from Beatrice Island.

Cassiter said, 'Doesn't it scare you – well, to think what we're going back to? How long we've been away?'

Haulers always had to say that, in some form or other.

'It's my sixth trip,' Dick told him, evasively. On the whole journey, they had got along with silences. Of course Dick felt bad once he was back with gravity under his boots. He had to face that whole heavy load of personal relationships again, the thing androids don't suffer from. The Human Condition, as they call it on the sheens. He said he always came back to us in an awful black mood.

Cenci Spaceport certainly wasn't the place to make Dick feel life was a ball of fun. It was just a goods yard, a freight terminal. There were no facilities for passenger traffic. Who could afford to leave? Who'd want to visit? Cabbages don't make fortunes or generate tourist attractions. Haulers were the only humans to be seen. All around for miles, the landscape was dotted with blocks of containers awaiting transfer, and refrigerator units. Plus automated control towers rearing high in the sky. Robots of various shapes and sizes grumbled along between the container aisles, painted bright colours, numbered, signalling to each other. Otherwise, silence.

No birds on Cenci. Nature had shown a strange kind of parsimony on the perimeters. The juice was all at the Centre, countless light years away.

Along with their roll of kit, Dick and his mate carried plastic value-cards. When slotted at the local autobank, their finances would be buoyant again – for a few more months.

An autocar carried them to where the hire-planes waited on their own airstrip. They both kept watch for signs of novelty, but saw few.

I'd guess that the really worst moment for them – the worst moment of the whole trip – was when they got to the entrance of the airstrip. There, bold figures of a chronometer indicated exact time of day, month and year. There was no arguing with it, no saying that chronometers were one thing and human feeling another. What the figures showed was that by ship-time Dick had been away only a fraction over sixty days, travelling close to light-speed to Dump 199 and back. Relativity, however, showed that twelve years had elapsed on Cenci since they set out. Everything about them had moved on twelve years during their two months. Everything, including human lives.

What can you say? That's how it was. Dick wasn't to blame for it, was he?

'Hope that your wife will be okay,' Cassiter said. The two men kept blank faces as they shook hands.

'Hope your family will be okay,' Dick said.

They gave each other a look and then turned away, to climb into different jets. Dick had to fly south, Cassiter east. These were newer jets than the ones they had used twelve years ago, but the design had scarcely changed. Progress doesn't happen much on the perimeter of the galaxy.

As Dick buckled himself in, the control tower came on the air and told him how much the flight to Beatrice Island would

73

cost. The charge had increased in twelve years. He slotted his value-card into a meter before the engine would operate.

You got a good view of the planet as you travelled. Time was shortly after dawn in the north hemisphere. Days on Cenci were thirty-one standard hours long. The oily oceans unfolded under Dick's jet, punctuated now and again by an island or archipelago. There were no continents. Occasionally a trawler-refrigerator could be seen on the water, trailing its white wake.

Our dear old Beatrice – damned old Beatrice – was a considerable island by local standards, roughly rectangular, four hundred and fifty kilometers long by about ninety kilometers wide. Apart from the central highlands, it was mainly fertile ground. And the Randinisson family farmed it all. Dick's grandfather, my great-grandfather, had been settled here after Continuity was totalled, along with his brother. One of them set up house on one end of the island, the other on the other, and they named Beatrice after their mother – a grand old girl, by all accounts. The two branches of the family soon fell out, each believing that the other had secured better agricultural land. Like fools, they had managed to see little of each other since, so that the loneliness of the planet was doubled by their own stupidity. Another reason to want to leave. Though I didn't see that at fifteen.

After calling up Rose on the shortwave and announcing his return, Dick sank towards ground. The plane landed him on the small airstrip and he climbed out. Home ground. It was the night before he landed that I had that dream about being a room. I had a deep fawn carpet. I was utterly empty. But I had two windows and a door. It was funny.

Dick must have taken a look around at the endless broad fields stretching right to the coast, each with its lines of blueish vegetation. He waited until the half-track showed over the horizon. Rose was driving. She had told me to stay at home and get on with the work.

I ought to tell you that Dick was a bonny-looking man, average height, dark curly hair like a farmer, his face square and generally agreeable, though I've seen him in a fury. His eyes were dark and interesting, as if he had a naughty secret he was just about to tell you. He regarded himself as a young man of twenty-eight years, and that's exactly what he looked like.

But I don't suppose he looked all that cheerful as he gave his missus the once-over. How could he be cheerful? It was asking too much.

Rose stopped the half-track any old how on the edge of the strip and walked slowly towards him, as if offering him the chance to get a good look. God knows how she felt. She never told you anything.

She walked slowly and stiffly. It was the work in the fields, the long hours, as much as anything. Of course, he recognised her immediately. There was something about Rose's way of carrying herself, the way she carried her head or something, which had never changed. These characteristics we all have are hard to pin down. Her hair had been brown with grey streaks when Dick had seen her last. Now it was a hard copper tint, dyed. Her cheeks were slightly hollow, but she had put on rouge for the occasion. Hadn't I watched her peering into her mirror?

As she got nearer, he saw her eyes. No mistaking that purplish-blue of my mother's eyes, the very same tint as her mother's – mine are brown – but eyes now embedded in wrinkles. When he had left on this last trip, Rose had been forty-one. Two of his months later and here she was, fifty-four. Aged.

What can you say? It was how we lived, out on the perimeter.

She came up close, rather peering, trying to read his expression. Nervous, of course. Then she reached and put her old brown arms tentatively on his shoulders.

'Welcome home again, Dick, dear. At last.'

He said nothing.

She got a bit closer and kissed him

'Dick, lovely, you're back from another trip.'

'My sixth,' he said.

75

She moved back. 'You don't seem too excited about being home.'

'It will take a day or two getting used to it.'

'I'll drive you home. The uncles will be pleased to see you again after all this time. And Tresa, of course.' She spoke with muted bitterness, though that was her way. She scarcely turned her face to him all the way home.

'How's Tresa?'

'All right. Crops are fair to middling this year. Three years back, we had an entire crop failure. Nearly starved to death.'

She was the farmer, not he. She had the whole cycle of Cenci's year firm in her head, born with it, knew what every long hour of daylight should be up to with respect to the brassicas. He had never had the slightest feel for agriculture. Told me he wouldn't even play in the fields as a lad. The enormous regimented expanses of root and leaf and plant merely bored him. It was the streak of wildness – which found no resting place on Cenci. Yet when his parents drowned together in the river on their annual holiday, the Beatrice station became his. He was stuck with it.

At least the deaths left behind a little credit. With a mortgage on the station, Dick invested in the photon-ship. He took on Cassiter as partner and other farmers as stock-holders. So he turned himself into a hauler, leaving Rose to manage the farm with the men and robots. Not that there was profit in it. The odds were stacked against you on the perimeter, as Uncle Eddie was always saying.

To fill the silence, Rose made an effort, told him how the machines were breaking new ground.

He kept taking squints at her out of the corner of his eye. I shouldn't say this, but I think he was a bit afraid of her. There was something very steely about my mother. She got it out of the land.

She had bought a bright blouse at the last annual fair – oh, the fuss of that! Bright, in keeping with her cheeks. But there was no camouflaging the way those two paltry months of his had aged her.

76

She shut up when he didn't speak. They drove the rest of the way in silence. I mean, they had loved each other once.

I'd been on the watch for them, but when I saw the half-track coming over Home Slope, I ran in and hid.

Our place was prefabricated. It was metal-shelled with a solar dome. It looked like the silos. We had painted it blue to distinguish it. Most buildings on Cenci came prefabricated. Most colours were stark primary ones.

My uncles were coming in for a break. They too were tense and hung about round the back, with the livestock. In came Dick and Rose, and clattered round the place. Both attempting to be natural with each other.

When she gave me a call, I appeared, feeling like a fool up for inspection. I couldn't think of what to say, either, simply looking daft, grinning first at one then the other. But I had got my new blouse on too.

Rose came up and gave me a sort of tweak. 'Talk to your father, then. He's been away for long enough, God knows. You must have something to say.'

'Hello. Have a good trip?' He still had nipple marks on head and arms where he'd been sheened in flight.

'You *have* grown,' he said. He hesitated, then walked over and kissed me on the lips. It was like a sudden shock. Perhaps for him too, because then he smiled and seemed to relax, saying with animation, 'Why, you're really pretty, Tresa, the way your mother used to be.'

'Still is,' I said defending her. Out of the corner of my eye, I saw her become tense and still under his insult. She was very thin. Suddenly she appeared thinner, her stance more catlike, her face more lined.

He ignored her, concentrating on me in a playful way, not sure how exactly to behave.

'So, let's see, lass, you'll be – twenty-seven now, is that right? Almost as old as me.'

Then I ceased to feel awkward, because I had the clear impression that he wasn't to be my father any more, to boss me about and give me orders. If I wanted, I could be at least

77

the equal of him. I hated being twenty-seven, but there were advantages, and somehow they were made clear just in the way he looked at me, as if trying to size up a piece of arable land he had never set eyes on before.

'Twenty-seven and not married. Any boyfriends?'

'That's my business.'

'Oh, come on, now. Don't tease. I bet you've got several.'

Rose immediately covered this remark by coming forward aggressively and saying – to me rather than him – 'Her second cousin or whatever he is, that Hamish Randinisson from the north flips down to see her now and then. He's polite, is Hamish – nice feller, good farmer. Knows one end of a cabbage from the other.'

From my expression, he must have gathered that opinions differed about our Hamish. He stuck his hands in his overall pockets and went and sat on the edge of the table. He said truculently, 'I told you before. I don't want that lot from the north down here while I'm away. Cousins or no cousins.' Seeing my expression, he added. 'Well, not while I'm here. You must please yourself what you do while I'm off hauling.'

'We do, we have to,' Rose said sharply. 'You've been gone twelve long years, after all. What do you expect us to do? We've worked our asses off, Tresa too.' She couldn't stop there. The bitterness drove her on to say, as she edged between us 'You'll hang around here for a year or two, just like previous times, then I bet you'll be off again.'

Perhaps he was beware of that tight line of her mouth. He just said, defensively, 'It's a matter of economics, isn't it? The *Lady Free* has to pay its way. It'll fall to bits standing idle.' Dick wasn't always sincere, but just being sincere is such a burden.

She had relished challenging him. He had not risen to it, perhaps because I was present. The shabby little room seemed to sweat with tension.

At that moment, one of the uncles pottered into the room, wiping his hands on a paper towel. The old man came to an uncertain halt in the midst of us. I could hear the stale familiar wheeze of the air-conditioning, sounding like drowsy birds squatting up in the rafters. The new arrival peered short-sightedly at Dick as if he had never seen him before, then retreated and took a seat without a word of greeting. He began smoothing the towel absent-mindedly over the arm of the chair.

'That's not you, is it, Rob?' he asked.

Irritated at being mistaken for his father, Dick said, 'I'm Dick, Uncle Eddie. Dick. Okay? You remember me? You've certainly put on a few years.'

I couldn't help a titter at this new mistake. 'It's Uncle Tom, Dick. Not Eddie.'

Dick muttered something angrily and turned away from the old man, when an even older man entered. This was Uncle Eddie. He always walked with a stick nowadays, leaning on it rather heavily. He was five years older than Tom. They spent a minute over their recognition problems. I could see the uncles confused and angry at having their age thrown into high profile in this way. Dick, too, was annoyed.

'Why have you old men been letting that black-sheep mob from the north down here on our land?'

Uncle Eddie's fists clenched over his stick. His hands were red and rough from labour. In fact, Dick was the only one with smooth hands in the room. I was right ashamed of mine.

'Young Hamish flies down here to court Tresa,' Eddie said, in his spiritless voice. 'Sometimes he brings his pa. No harm in that, Dickie. You'd probably like them. We're glad of the company, to be honest, and they know one end of a cabbage from the other.'

Dick scowled. 'We had a quarrel with them. Have you forgotten? We weren't on speaking terms. We were sure they stole one of Rose's pigs.'

Tom, Eddie, and Rose laughed. 'That was years ago, lad,' said Tom. 'We've forgotten all about that.'

'I'll break out some apple wine, now you're back at last,' Eddie said. He was always one for peace. A good old boy.

So we spent the day more or less amicably together. No work. An attempt to make a celebration of the *Lady Free*'s return. Fighting to cross that wound in time which would only widen with each successive trip.

One thing to celebrate was the improvement in the bank balance. The crop failure three years earlier had set us back badly. Dick was not very cheerful when we went into financial matters. He had to learn once again – as on previous trips, though I was too young to remember – how twelve years of hard work had made us so little richer, and how the silos were not as full as he had expected. As it was, we were in need of new equipment and the machines required an engineer over to service them. All expense.

'Everything costs so much,' I said, seeing his long face. 'We're so far from anywhere decent. No wonder colonists don't want to come to Cenci.'

'Don't grumble, girl' Eddie advised. 'It would be worse to be crowded out, like at Galactic Centre.'

'Them buggers,' said Tom, and spat.

But it was something to have a fresh face to grumble to. I grabbed Dick's hand – after all, he was a stranger to me – and started telling him the old tale. How isolated we were. How we were exploited by governments we could never see. How any sheen to Centre never got answered. A lot that Hamish had told me. Hamish said it was political matters.

It's true there was a big fair – they called it a World Fair – on the largest island of Cenci once a year, for which everyone gave up work and went to, leaving the machines in charge of the fields. The fair was a time for changing stations, meeting friends, drawing up contracts, getting a bit drunk, and making love if you were lucky. But there were only fifty thousand people on all Cenci, and most of them so pig-boring that you could fall asleep just talking to them.

The uncles cackled and said it was true. Still they enjoyed the fair when they were lads. Girls like me were getting too sophisticated nowadays.

Dick watched me with interest as I talked. I could feel the colour rise in my cheeks. Well, if I knew I looked pretty and bright, so what? I used to watch my lips in the mirror, and I reckon I had the same shaped face as his. And the same colour eyes.

He said, speaking direct to me as if I was someone of importance, 'When you consider, we're really fortunate that Cenci happens to be so close to one of the Dumps – only just under a light year away. Suppose it was a hundred or more – five hundred . . . Could easily be. It means we have a good standard of living, compared with hundreds of perimeter planets. Easier profits.'

'Profits aren't everything.' There I was, answering him boldly. 'Why can't we move in nearer to some centre of civilisation, where the air doesn't smell of cabbages? The Cluster isn't all that far . . . We could all cram into the *Lady Free*, couldn't we? I don't want to spend all my life on Cenci.'

He started going over arguments I'd heard from my uncles. I half-listened, watching Rose. Throughout the day, she had the deadly silence over her and I can't tell you that look – dripping grief and anger - so poisonous she had to keep it to herself and would not let others see into her eyes. Really, I was sorry for her. And frightened.

And there was Dick holding forth. The Cluster over a thousand light years away. Besides, how could we leave? Who'd buy the station? What about the investment in the machines? Since the matter-transmitters were built, even fewer colonists came this way. He finished by saying, rather loftily, 'We're stuck here, generation in, generation out. There's nothing to be done about it, except make the best of things. You've heard me say all this before.'

'Don't forget I was only a girl when you left. We could improve our lot if we politicised ourselves.'

Ignoring this last remark, he smiled and nodded. 'You were a pretty young thing then, and now, overnight, you're an even prettier woman. I'm proud of you.'

Which was too much for Rose. She jumped up, saying '*You* – what reason do you have to be proud, never here when wanted?' With that, she gave a kind of shriek, half-way between a laugh and a death rattle, and rushed from the house. It killed the conversation.

Last thing that evening, I took a turn about the yard with Uncle Eddie, letting him hang on my arm, before we went off to bed. Dick came too. Sniffing the air, looking about with a proprietorial manner.

'It hasn't been a bad life, whatever you may say, young lady,' Eddie said. In my heart, I wondered if he really meant it. If he wasn't trying to console me. Or himself. 'I've enjoyed being away from those giant cities we see on the sheens. They wouldn't suit me . . . If only there'd been a nice girl for me to marry. I met such a girl once, at the World Fair . . . ooh, must be more than sixty years ago. She had a blue ribbon in her hair. I remember her clearly, and we met . . . '

He trailed off into a reminiscence I had heard once or twice before. I liked to hear it again. Dick said nothing, concentrating on walking on uneven ground after the smoothness of everything in space.

'If I had my time over again I'd be more politically active,' Eddie said. 'If everyone got together on Cenci, and all the other nearby planets, we could refuse to supply food to Galactic Centre. A touch of hunger and they'd soon come round and see we had better conditions.'

'Rubbish' Dick said. 'How'd we live without credit? Don't you think they'd buy food from elsewhere? Besides how are we ever going to unite? We don't even get on with our relations up north.'

'But we've got a cause. Hamish and his dad would agree . . . '

You're fooling yourself, Eddie. Just an old man's dream. Things will never be any better for the mass of the people. Never ever.'

'Are you religious?' Eddie asked, mildly, pausing and easing out his back with a groan. 'You must believe in something. There must be a god somewhere, to provide a reason for all these planets, all this life . . . What do you think about, son, when you go hurtling through space for all those years? Don't you ever try to think about deeper issues? God?'

'I've only been gone two months, my time. Can't you get

that into your head? I'm a hauler. I don't think about anything. I don't have people bother me. I don't hardly speak.
I'm just – not bothered.'

'"You don't think about anything",' Eddie echoed,
mockingly. 'Well, you're still stuck a mere slip of a youth,
Dickie . . . Meanwhile, we're all leaving you behind.'

'No.' He was angry now, and turned on Eddie. 'I'm
leaving *you* behind. Can't you see that? You're almost in your
grave, you old fool. I'm travelling into the future – still
young.'

'Now, don't start arguing, you two. Why make things
worse?' I said. I took a firmer hold of Eddie, to steer him back
indoors. Dick grabbed my arm, telling me to stay out in the
yard with him, but I wasn't in the mood for that. We left him
walking about alone out there, getting used to the feel of a
planet all over again. In the eastern sky, stars were plentiful.
The western sky right up to zenith was almost empty, where
the galaxy ended.

Later, I heard him go slowly up to his bedroom. Rose was
already there. He didn't put the light on and I never heard a
single sound.

Next morning, early, our machines were radioing from the
South Highlands. Trouble with a bad rock fall and one
machine trapped in a narrow valley. We had done a deal with
Hamish and his pa while Dick was away, trading one of Ted's
young boars for three sheeplike critters, one in lamb. We
planned to wall them in on one of the Highland hills.

Rose was packing her kit. I offered to go with her, but she
turned me down sharply. She was very tense, her mouth
drawn in so that her nose and chin stuck out in her withering
face. Her movements were hurried, yet she was wasting time.
The agrijet was out on the pad beyond the yard. She kept
going back and forth to it, carrying some odd thing or other –
a tool – but really just waiting. She was waiting for Dick to
get up.

I hung about in the kitchen. I was excited and frightened
and hopeful, and sometimes felt I'd like to murder the lot of

83

them. It wasn't their fault, the awful family mess we were in, but just sometimes I wished they would be *noble* about it, like Uncle Eddie occasionally was. When you think, him born five years after Dick.

Bloody woman, fussing around. She had piled on the make-up thicker than ever. Hair extra coppery. And still wore that blouse – padded out a bit, unless I was mistaken. God, I am never going to get *old*, I told myself. Twenty-seven was quite old enough for anyone.

So he came down the ladder, scratching his head, yawning luxuriously, trying to avoid her. She went for him like a fox at a dinker. Poured out the whole business of the sheep and the machines.

'I want you to come with me, Dick, dear. You must keep abreast of these things and give me good advice.' That tone of voice.

'Er – no, I'll stay here, thanks, Rose. I seem to have a touch of the space-lapse. Time is still sluggish in my head. You know how it is. You go on your own.'

'I need you along.'

'No, you don't.'

That peculiar arching of her body again. I couldn't help peeping through the kitchen curtain. I couldn't grasp exactly why they were so at odds, why the hatred could be smelt in the air.

She said, sort of scratching the skirt at her hips, 'I want you to come along, Dick. You can sleep on the way. There's a bunk in the agrijet, in case you've forgotten.'

So there they stood, staring at each other, reluctant to fight openly, reluctant to give in.

'I'll be okay here' he said. Suave. I saw why she was mad with him, even when I admired his poise.

But that did it. Rose almost sprang at him. 'Oh, you're always okay, aren't you? The misery you've caused, you and your endless trips. Heartless . . . Cruel . . . Here I've laid awake, night after night, unable to rest, thinking about you. Our relationship. That one relationship . . .' She clutched her throat, as if the words stuck there. 'Time – it's so cruel.

84

You . . . Why make it all worse? And now Tresa – yes, her, poor girl, what's she like while you're off on those endless damned trips?'

'Only six, so far.'

'Six, six! I'm talking about our fucked up lives – mine, yours, now Tresa's. I suppose you are scheming to be off away again as soon as you can make it? You know what you've done – you know what you've done, it's against nature.' She repeated the last phrase, suddenly on the verge of tears. 'Against nature. Your sins – oh, the blackest in the book. You're so smug. I've seen very well the way you look at me. And the way you look at Tresa, oh, yes. Oh, yes – I know what's in your mind, you – you monster. Don't think I haven't got you all summed up, Dick Randinisson. If you only knew . . . If you only knew . . . Don't you have any religion?'

When I realised that this quarrel between them was all about me, somehow I was moved to gasp and draw aside the curtain – I suppose to be more involved. She saw me, and screamed at me to get away from her.

Dick was saying coldly, 'I'm sick of that question. You're the third person to go on about religion in two days. What's religion got to do with it, I'd like to know? It's physical laws we're stuck with. Physics. And biology. Why don't you just get it into your head that I do what I have to do? Just the same as you. Just the same. You have to work the station, okay, I am a hauler, I have to ride the *Lady Free*. The course of nature is unfortunately beyond my control – or bloody God's if he exists.'

He had been fairly soothing in tone. Rose was angered more by this.

'Don't start that. You'd worm out of anything. You get away with murder. You – you know very well what I'm going on about. Sin, I'm talking about, not physical laws. *Sin*. During all this lifetime you've been away, I've been reading the Bible – '

'Much good it's done you.'

Oh, I remembered the purchase of that old black Bible, at

the World Fair, the year before the famine set in. It certainly hadn't made her any happier. I could see – I was in the room now – that she was almost inarticulate with her hateful feelings. Saliva burst on her lips and trailed down one corner of her mouth as she ranted at him. Lines on her thin cheeks wove themselves into a frantic pattern. It was as if the mere thought of all that stuff in the Bible – revenge, sacrifice, I don't know what – maddened her still more.

Evidently a fright got into Dick at the sight of her. He backed away, sort of waving his hands, shouting back. It was a real ding-dong, worse than the one they had had when I was fourteen and scared stiff.

Then he said, 'Look here, Rose, I know you are envious because you are so old and I remain young. I know, I understand. I'd feel the same in your shoes. But just don't blame me. Don't throw it all on me, see? Blame bloody God, if you believe in him. Fuh, while he was farting around creating the universe, making the speed of light constant, why didn't he make time constant too? Slipped up there, didn't he?'

He attempted a laugh. Her look froze him.

'Pity God didn't make you constant, too. You piece of shit . . . All right. I give up. I'm off. The work has to be done, if we all die doing it. I will be back in two days. All I have to say to you is, you keep your thoughts and your hands off Tresa. You understand? She's all I've got . . .'

As her voice went out of control, she turned away, pointing a deadly finger like a gun at me. Then she whirled on Dick again.

'And I am not old, blast you for saying it. It is you who are juvenile – retarded, a freak of nature . . .'

I saw his hands shaking. He would not meet my eyes. I bobbed back into the kitchen again. He went outside in a minute, standing by the door, watching till the jet took off and disappeared in the direction of the South Highlands.

Uncle Eddie came down then, and I looked after him for a while.

When things had simmered down a little, I went out. I was puzzled to know what to do. There was work waiting, but it would have to wait. I had to see Dick, talk to him, know how he felt. There were all kinds of things in me, too, I felt I could only let out to him.

The day was warm and muggy. Close. I took the lane past Uncle Eddie's piggeries. Dick was down in the cemetery. As I approached, I saw his head over the wall we had built. He was just standing there.

Proteas flowered by the ruinous wall. It was falling down already. Their blossoms looked like big creamy meringues. There was no colour to any flower on Cenci. They all came out white or cream. Large horned beetles tumbled among the blossoms, knocking carapace against carapace with little clicking sounds in their eagerness to get at the nectar. Bees did not exist on our world; the beetles did the pollinating instead. When they entered those crinkly mouths, the flower-heads nodded as if in drowsy approval.

Dick was looking at the blundering insects. Without glancing at me, he said as I came near, 'If a faster beetle had evolved on Cenci, plant life might have been richer. Higher animals might have evolved. Maybe all it needed was a faster beetle. Then Cenci would have been different.'

This struck me as poetic. We stood there in silence. The proportion of ocean to land was too great. Species of flora and fauna were restricted as a result. Winged things had little chance. Meagreness had won over fecundity. Tropical though much of Cenci was, it had never developed anything as complex as a jungle. Cabbages. Cabbages and sheep, they were more in Cenci's line. Ours was a world where grass and fish had the upper hand.

Dick gave me a glance and then sauntered over to look at one of the graves, which the uncles still tended. The plastic headstone of one was cracked, but you could still make out Penny's name, spelt out in LED lettering formally as PEN-ELOPE. He was very serious, possibly feeling regret, I suppose. Among the drone and click of the beetles, I could only feel the old puzzlement. Penny had been in the ground

87

over forty years. Yet here he was just six and a half years older since her death. I came over dizzy and uneasy.

He must have seen. As he walked over to me, the sun broke muzzily through the cloud haze, lighting us. He held me by the arms, looking at me with concern. Neither of us said anything.

After a moment, he said why didn't we go up and look at the cabbages on Higher Week. You got a good view from there.

So I walked beside him, although I had Rose's warning in mind. My brain was in a tumult. I started saying any old thing, things I had heard Uncle Eddie saying, anything to keep him quiet.

'It's lucky that no butterflies and caterpillars ever developed. At least that makes growing cabbages easier. We grow the best cabbages in the galaxy, and we ought to be proud of that. Everything's just right for cabbages. When this season's crop is ready, we'll get Jones over to get the harvest in hand.' Jones was one of the robots with a good ubianter.

The cabbages would be freeze-dried and stored until the next trip to Dump.

'Jones, eh?' I could tell his mind was on something else.

'Jones broke down three years ago. During the famine. It was awful. As if he was in sympathy. I thought we'd have died. That's when Hamish and his pa first came down . . . '

'You don't enjoy life here?'

'I envy you your trips, you know that? It's sort of magic – if you haven't ever left Cenci. Yet the trips must be even duller than being stuck on station.'

'I don't find them dull.'

We were silent then until we got to the top of the rise. The land rolled away on all sides of us, pretty featureless. A low tree here and there. All blueish with the rows of cabbages. Occasional lighter patch of maize. One robot trundling slowly in the distance. Very quiet.

'Cabbages,' he said. 'A planet full of cabbages. That's my idea of dull.'

'Just how many trips had you made before – you know, before Penny died?' I couldn't help my voice sounding a bit sharp. After all, you don't like where you live being called dull by other people.

He took no offence, saying firmly, 'You must understand that I have made only six trips away. Each to Dump and back. On business. After each trip, I spend a year right here on station, helping as best as I can. I'm not the villain Rose thinks I am. Then it's time to make another delivery to the Dump. Earn money.'

'All right. So tell me about the six trips, if they are so important.'

He laughed, quite heartily and naturally. Not a sound you often heard in our place. Like he actually enjoyed talking to you.

'Well, from one way of looking at it, there's not a lot to tell. The journeys themselves are not eventful. That's why I like them. And it is wonderful to have the universe round you. It's wonderful to travel at almost the speed of light . . . A drug, I suppose . . .

'When I got back here after that first trip, it was my twentieth birthday. That was when I married Penny. She was seventeen, and so shy. Not as cute as you. I'd never seen her till. Only as a kid. She'd have been, oh, five when I first went away . . . So we got married and I stayed around a year, and then Cassiter and I got to talking, and doing some figures . . .'

'And Penny?'

'Cassiter and I bought the *Lady Free* and made a second trip and then a third, and it was when I was back here after that third trip that Penny – well, you know she fell off a silo ladder and killed herself?'

'That was one story I heard.'

He glanced at me suspiciously. 'She fell off a silo ladder and killed herself. She was forty-one . . . Your mother would have been about twelve then.'

'I get confused with these relationships at times. You went back into space despite her death?'

He was gazing at the cloudy horizon when he answered. 'The storehouses were full. Debts had to be paid. You don't just grow cabbages. You have to sell the damned things. But when I came back off the next trip, Rose and I got married. That time, I stayed for four years. Stayed right here and worked the station at her insistence. Rose is a stronger character than me. And the bills mounted.'

'And that's when I was born, right?'

'You were born then, yes. And the next time I came back, you were magically fourteen.'

'And you'd missed all my childhood. Do you think I didn't miss you?'

But I could see he hadn't missed me. He had had other things to do. He was a kind of gateway through which we had to go to live. Or to escape. We had a dependency on him he did not have on us. I could see that was why Rose hated him, but I admired it.

'Looking to the present, Tresa, what about this fellow Hamish, from the north?'

I felt free to give him a black look. I had so little that was private.

'This place is a prison. You think so, don't you? Eddie says there were originally supposed to have been millions of colonists here. Then we'd have earned a technical grade instead of an agricultural one. Only a handful arrived, because the perfection of matter-transmitters changed the whole pattern of interstellar travel. So who am I supposed to marry? Am I supposed to remain a single woman all my days, the way Uncle Eddie has remained single? I'm twenty-seven, you know, and time's passing.'

People make you mad at times. I stamped my foot and laughed, all at once. 'Eddie's a fool,' was all Dick said, as if to himself, meditatively.

'I'd rather stay single than marry "this Hamish", as you call him. He's coarse and stupid and has such a big idea of himself. You'd think he ruled the planet. All he goes on about is this Inter-Island Union of his, and he doesn't wash properly. I can't stand the man, and I can't stand his filthy attempts on my body. So there you have it. And for your information I'm mad at Rose when she tries to force him on me!'

I laughed. So then we both laughed. And then, in sudden happiness, he grasped me round the waist and gave me a kiss. I got disentangled from him very slowly. The cabbages seemed to be going round in circles.

'I'll see to it that you don't marry Hamish,' Dick said.

So two days later, when Rose came scorching back from the South Highlands, he was ready for her.

She came in quite quietly and tried to kiss him. He was pale about the lips.

'I'm sorry for those bitter things I said, Dickie. I've had a chance to think things over. I just felt so bad, you can't imagine, seeing you so young in appearance. It's like a sort of witchcraft . . .'

'Don't get superstitious. Throw that Bible away. You don't think they read Bibles in Galactic Centre, do you?'

'All right, all right, I'll do what you say. Just listen. Make love to me tonight. Don't turn your back on me. Then I'll feel better. I'll spoil you, really I will, and everything will be fine again. Oh, Dick, we've had so little of each other, got so little out of life. There's scarcely time to take stock of things before you realise it's all slipping away from you.'

'That's what I think, too.' But he took a pace back from her.

'It's all right, then? Between us?'

She was standing staring at him and he at her. Perhaps he saw then that indeed something of her youthful beauty still remained in her face.

In her anxiety, she misread his expression. Her voice was more urgent, pitched higher. 'I know what you're thinking. When you return from your seventh trip — oh, yes, when you return from that, I'll be sixty-six, while you'll be only a shade over thirty. I'll be an old hag . . . Well, I'm not an old hag yet. Think of now, Dick, now.'

He was waving his hands again, scrubbing out all her hopes.

'Rose, look, it's all settled. I've had two days to think things over, too. I am no use to you here. I only make you unhappy, just by being here, by reminding you of everything. I'm going to leave. Leave straightaway. Cassiter and I can tout round the islands and gather a full cargo. I'm off. There's no place for me here – perhaps never was.'

At first, she simply looked puzzled. She put a stringey hand up to her face, protectively.

'Off? You're off where? You can face another trip so soon? And what's to become of me? Of us? Are we to starve to death again? I suppose that has never entered your reckoning.'

Dick went very red and heavy. 'Sorry, I've had enough. You know you get on just fine without me. "What's to become of me?" Let me make you a suggestion. Marry Hamish. Marry Hamish with his big ideas and his Inter-Island Union. You're so keen on him. I give you my blessing.'

'Your blessing! You think I want your lousy blessing?' This in a terrible shriek. She had gone right over the limit. Bursting from the room, she ran into the kitchen, brushing me aside, to stand against the dresser, sobbing and shrieking.

After a moment, he followed, and called to her.

She swung round, face glistening and blotched, looking like someone I had never met before. With a cry, she snatched up the heat-rifle from the corner behind the dresser and levelled it at him, index finger against the button.

'Fine. I see. You've been at Tresa. I know. This is what I've been dreading, watching her grow up. I'll kill you both before I let her go with you. What you are plotting is a sin, you understand? A sin of deepest dye, against nature. Utterly against nature.'

He stood absolutely still, then slowly raised a finger in the air in caution. 'Ah-ah. Nature is more contorted than you will admit to yourself, Rose. Else we wouldn't be in this fix . . . I'm only going to take Tresa along for the ride. Naturally, a young girl wants to see a bit of the universe out there – '

But she was shivering and shrieking again. Back up came the rifle, on target.

'I removed the charge from the gun, Mother,' I said, from the other side of the room. Voice very cool and adult.

A pause and then she turned and stared at me as if she had never seen me before. 'You bitch. You lousy hot-arsed little bitch!'

'Don't go getting excited. Whatever you say or do, whatever our relationship, I am going away with him. Once we're gone, you'll settle down perfectly fine, just as before. You like Cenci. Me, I've outgrown it.'

Then she really did go crazy. One moment she was standing there, the next she was running through the yard – a sort of fast stagger – yelling and brandishing the gun.

In panic I grasped hold of Dick's arm. 'I was bluffing, Dick. The rifle's still charged. Go and grab it off her before she does some damage.'

He did as I said, without argument.

Her movements were erratic. With amazing agility, she leaped over the wall of the yard and across the transport apron. She was still waving her arms and shouting abuse in a shrill voice. She climbed on to the wall at the end of the apron.

'Rose, come down,' he called. 'Careful with that gun. It is charged.'

She gave a cry, and fell down from the wall to the far side. She reappeared, just head and shoulders visible. He was within five metres of her. She brandished the rifle, then stuck the muzzle in her mouth.

Before he could reach her, she had pressed the button.

Rose's body was buried in the little cemetery, next to her mother's grave with the cracked headstone. A machine had thrown the heavy loam back among the proteas. No beetles droned and clicked there today.

My face was blank, I could feel it. All expression had dropped off somewhere. I was half-supporting Eddie. Tom

93

stood with a pair of sticks. Dick stood alone on the other side of the grave, shoulders hunched.

As we filed away, Tom said, 'I want to give you a word of warning, my girl, and that's about Dickie – '

'I don't want to hear it, Uncle. I know very well what I'm doing, as far as anyone does.'

So we all returned to the house in silence. Yes, I thought, and you're going to leave these two poor old sods alone to face the future. Tom and Eddie – once your younger brothers. Before you made the first of your trips . . .

Dick had radioed Cassiter.

Cassiter had got back to his place to find that both his parents had died three years back, during the famine. Now his brother was running the farm with a younger sister and their old robots. He needed little persuasion to make another trip without delay. And the younger sister would come over to look after our poor old Eddie and Tom.

'We can be at Dump in no time,' Cassiter said cheerfully.

'I have a plan to go farther than Dump this trip,' Dick said. 'My notion is to shift even farther into the future. Tell you all about it at the spaceport.'

And that's how it was. In two days, Dick and I met Cassiter at Cenci spaceport. An exciting place to me. I was dressed in my new dress, smiling and pretty. So I hoped.

Certainly Dick put on a bit of swagger when he introduced me to Cassiter. Cassiter was visibly impressed. He clutched my hand warmly.

'Happy to meet you, Tresa. Glad you're coming. But I thought . . . no offence, but I always thought that you were Dick's daughter.'

I corrected him.

'Grand-daughter,' I said firmly. 'Also wife.'

GRAHAM CHARNOCK

Fullwood's Web

I encountered Fullwood in a tobacconists off Old Court. It was a dingy, dusty place with a palsied, trembling proprietor as aged and as poorly kept as his stock. There were better places, but few cheaper; at the moment my fortunes were on the decline and I was forced to temper what few indulgences I had in the spirit of economy.

Fullwood and I had been at school together. We had had little in common, then, and had not mixed particularly. My memory is that he had engaged himself in the usual processes of school life far more than I had. Athletic and possessing a bright wit and quick intelligence, he had been popular both with his fellow pupils and teachers. It would be taking it too far to say we had been antithetical, but for me childhood had been an altogether more painful affair. Plump, clumsy and myopic, I was the sort of boy who becomes too often the butt of ridicule, the object of others' scorn. At this distance of time and with the detachment of maturity, I can see that even in that closed schoolboy society, where little of life's realities are glimpsed, I must have appeared unworldly, and that perhaps my obsession with the abstract realms of mathematics was a consequence of this treatment, the only retreat which was available to me. Matrices, statistics and the worlds of probability and inevitability offered an infinite prospect of escape from the antagonisms of childhood.

Considering these basic differences in our characters it is hardly surprising we should have had so little contact at school, and considering we had not been friends or even acquaintances it is odd we should have recognised each other at all after such a lapse of time, but recognition was immediate and spontaneous upon our eyes meeting.

I noticed that Fullwood had purchased a particular brand of cigar, a West Indian cheroot, one of the cheapest and also a brand favoured by myself. It was, we both agreed, a remarkable coincidence.

I next met Fullwood in a public park. It was not a pre-arranged meeting but another chance encounter. At the tobacconists we had parted, I am sure, both convinced that this intersection of our ambits was a product of the laws of random chance and, furthermore, one unlikely to repeat itself. Our farewells had been muted, casual and final in tone.

I had taken to frequenting the park whenever I had a complex problem to think through. It was a placid, pleasantly landscaped park, with many well-protected ha-has where one could find seclusion. There was a small lake, circumscribed by a convoluted path. If one's mental perambulations demanded an echo in the physical world, and if one felt a need to follow a set route, then this was ideal, for its vistas, if vistas were required, changed constantly, and being circular, a tour could be as long or as short as one's preoccupations.

It was on this path one day that I saw, with some surprise, Fullwood walking ahead of me. His pace was slow, regular and deliberate, almost plodding, one might say. I could not see his face but his head alternated frequent nodding and contradictory shaking motions, whilst his fingers prodded, probed and traced the air, in an obvious attempt to externalise some conflict within. Knowing full well how a complex train of thought might be broken by the slightest interruption or diversion, and its elements dissipated, never to be reassembled, I simply followed him for a while. Eventually he stopped, gave a final emphatic shake of his head, looked up and looked about him like a man coming out of a dream.

When he saw me his initial expression of surprise soon redefined itself as his eyes narrowed with mingled suspicion

96

and interest. I could see him mentally framing the notion that this second meeting could not possibly be coincidental and that I must have some motive in engineering it. He had found me following him, after all. What more natural assumption?

It was one I hastened to disavow him of, taking his arm and leading him down a colonnade to a secluded ampitheatre enclosed by tall box hedges and overlooked by plaster replicas of Greek gods. The blank emptiness of their stares together with the tensions modelled in their flesh was imposing and conspiratorial. As we talked our conversation inevitably took on an air of mystery and disclosure.

It transpired, as we talked, that the remarkable thing was not that we had come across each other in the park on this occasion, but that we had not done so earlier, since the place had been a regular haunt for Fullwood for every bit as long as it had for me. There must have been many times, in fact, when we had both trod the path around the lake, each unaware of the other's proximity.

As we talked we discovered yet more interests, concerns and circumstances which, although they were not strictly held in common, were distinctly parallel.

Fullwood, with no need to retreat into the abstract, possessing, indeed, a keen enthusiasm for matters ontological, had channelled his energies into an exploration of the discipline of physics, and had achieved the same sort of distinction at University in this field as I had in mine. Whilst I had subsequently enjoyed a degree of financial independence thanks to a modest endowment, Fullwood had progressed, with some eminence, through a career with a large industrial corporation, finally to head his own research consultancy which worked closely with several government technological agencies.

By far the greatest degree of commonality, however, lay at the root of our current preoccupations. I had been involving myself recently in trying to construct a mathematical framework within which certain hypothetical electro-magnetic phenomena could be tested and modelled. Fullwood, it turned out, was similarly engaged with the theory of electro-magnetic fields, and was trying to refine the production of a new generation of high-density plasma containers.

My proofs were very nearly assembled, but the purely hypothetical basis of my research was holding me back. Certain empirical experimental data would reinforce and modify my deliberations and disclose areas which were presently proving shadowy, but frankly the funding for such an enterprise, which would necessarily be on a large scale, was beyond me. Neither did I particularly want to put my work on a more public basis before it was fully framed.

Fullwood, on the other hand, was unhampered by financial considerations. He had an unlimited budget for his researches as well as access to a parcel of very sophisticated technical and management resources. He had, however, come across a theoretical molehill that a profusion of experimental results had turned into a mountain. He confessed himself unable to reconcile items of apparently conflicting data that his researches had thrown up. He seemed, he said, to have isolated a field effect that was, theoretically, impossible.

During the next few months we met frequently, almost on a daily basis. I applied myself to the study of Fullwood's findings and made suggestions where I was able. These Fullwood implemented in an experimental situation in his laboratory. On a few rare occasions Fullwood would be too busy to leave his work and one or two days might pass between meetings. Since we were both producing ideas and extrapolations at an intense rate, it was always a source of frustration when this happened.

Another source of frustration was a string of unrelated mishaps which seemed to plague Fullwood in his experimental set-up. A colleague suffered severe concussion when he was struck by, of all things, a gull which had apparently suffered heart failure whilst on the wing. A vital leaf-spring disappeared during the disassembly of a very minor sub-unit and caused several hours shut-down whilst a spare was obtained; days later the technician responsible shamefacedly confessed that he had found the spring in his trouser turn-up.

98

There were many similar incidents, but none so frustrating as the occasion when the whole city was subject to a succession of inexplicable wide-scale power failures. That took a desperate toll on the continuity of our research.

And so, our work progressed slowly, and progressed only in as much as it removed one by one some of the minor stumbling blocks of our research, laying bare as it did so what was apparently a central supremely tangled Gordian Knot of theory.

Besides our arranged meetings, it seemed that increasingly we would also chance upon each other, Fullwood and I, by accident, sometimes in the most unlikely or bizarre situations.

On one occasion, for instance, I remember I developed, overnight it seemed, what appeared to be a staggeringly painful abscess on my jaw. My dentist had recently relocated his surgery and this meant a long journey across town to a neighbourhood that was strange to me. I used public transport and as I alighted from the autobus I heard a screech of brakes from the vehicle behind. It was a limousine with government licence plates and the driver had obviously misjudged the traffic conditions and his stopping distance. No harm was done. A collision was averted by a hair's breadth, but as the traffic started up again I was surprised to see Fullwood's startled face regarding me from the rear window of the limousine.

I proceeded to my dental appointment, where it was discovered that my pain was the result of an impacted portion of silver foil, from some confection or other, in an electrolytic reaction with the amalgam of an ancient filling. Fortunately the remedy for this was straightforward and the relief immediate.

As for Fullwood: I later discovered that he had been called away from his laboratory at short notice that day to attend a meeting at a government office across town. Furthermore, at the time of the incident his driver was, in fact, following a local diversion from his planned route, due to the rupture of a water main in the vicinity.

Later, by assessing the random variables involved, such as they were known, and by assigning values to them according to a system of my own devising, I made an attempt to calculate the statistical probability of this event, but it soon became obvious that the result would be so close to an infinitely negative value as to make any attempt at absolute quantification futile.

Quite suddenly the regular pattern of our arranged meetings was disrupted and I didn't see Fullwood for some time. At first, and in the absence of any word from him, I readily assumed some new development in his researches was distracting him. With keen anticipation I awaited news of some advance or other. Soon, however, this sense of anticipation was replaced with one of foreboding.

Although our regular meetings had lapsed, I still caught sight of him occasionally, in the random fashion that had now become almost commonplace. Now, however, a new element entered into these chance encounters. He would often refuse to acknowledge me, or if he did so it was in a peremptory fashion. If circumstances permitted he would frequently, it seemed, go so far as to take evasive action, deliberately turning aside rather than have our paths cross. In the park, for instance, he would strike off at a tangent into tangled shrubbery, often at the cost of some discomfort, rather than confront me. I confess that I was puzzled by his behaviour; at one point I thought he must have gone quite mad. He was a genius, of course, and the line between genius and insanity is often thinly drawn.

After a while my frustration became so intense that I resolved to waylay him at the next opportunity and demand an explanation. I waited for him in the park, concealing myself near the entrance. I was confident I would not have to wait long and, in fact, I had barely taken up my position when, almost as if on cue, he appeared. My belief that his reason had gone was reinforced by his appearance and behaviour. His normally tidy clothes were dishevelled and awry; he looked about him constantly, nervously, his eyes furtive. He looked, in short, haunted.

As he passed, I stepped out, calling his name and clutching at his sleeve. He gave a shocked cry and stared at me with a look approaching terror. Then, before I could consolidate my grasp, he turned and fled.

I returned to my residence, resigned now to continue my researches on my own, convinced that Fullwood would, before long, be lodged in an asylum.

That same evening, however, there was a loud and insistent drumming on my door and, opening it, I found Fullwood himself, haggard and distraught. There had been a heavy shower but he appeared to have taken no precaution to protect himself from it: his clothes were sodden.

I ushered him in and he tripped and nearly fell as he crossed the threshold. I noticed that his jacket was scuffed and even torn in one or two places.

I directed him to a chair, and as he settled his weight into it, there was a loud crack, and he hastily stood once more, shaking his head abjectly.

'We must stop,' he said. 'Do you realise what we have created?'

I pondered the question a moment. 'A field effect' I said then. 'If that is what you mean. That is certainly the object of our researches.'

Fullwood pulled a damp, scrumpled newspaper out of his pocket and held it out to me.

'Don't you know what's been happening?' he asked.

There was some lurid picture on the front page of people working amidst a pile of rubble. The headline was bold and black but had been torn across making it illegible. I paid it little attention. I never bother with newspapers, finding them full of mindless pap, for the most part. I was frankly surprised that Fullwood had time for their inanities, and I told him so.

Fullwood groaned. 'Come with me,' he said.

★

Fullwood took me to his laboratory.

On the way he saved my life. A car mounted the pavement and nearly struck me, but Fullwood was able to snatch me out of its path. I was surprised by the sharpness of his reactions; it was almost as if he had anticipated the mishap. The car veered back onto the road and I caught a glimpse of the driver's frightened face. He appeared unable to control his vehicle. I suspected he was under the influence of alcohol. A little further along the road he collided with another car turning from a side-street.

'What is a coincidence?' Fullwood asked me then, taking my arm almost protectively and leading me away.

'The discovery of a familiar object in unfamiliar surroundings,' I answered, after a moment's thought.

'And what is an accident?' Fullwood asked. Noting the rhetorical tone of his voice I waited for him to supply his own answer: 'The coincidence of objects or forces, mutually incompatible, familiar or unfamiliar. That's what our field effect does. It creates coincidences, accidents, disasters. The newspapers are full of them. I tell you, we must stop.'

Fullwood's machine was a splendid beast.

Toroidal in shape, it filled the cavern of his laboratory with its gleaming coils of burnished copper.

As I approached the machine, Fullwood rambled on inanely. My fears for his sanity may have been unfounded; he was obviously still rational. But there was no doubt the work had taken an emotional toll on him and he was no longer thinking as clearly and as logically as he should.

'The Web of the Norns,' he ranted. 'That's a good analogy for what we have here. Not just one web, though, but web after web, piled together, forming a matrix. The strands of fate and destiny entangle and intermesh under the distorting effect of our field-generator. The effect is probably localised to begin with but it spreads throughout the very matrix of existence everywhere, throughout the galaxy, the entire universe for all we know. It's a shunt-effect, in all probability, like wagons in a goods yard. Distort a few strands of the web-matrix and soon everything is irrevocably tangled.'

He caught my sleeve, suddenly. 'Take care,' he said. 'Don't go too close.'

He indicated a series of progressive chalk marks on the floor.

'As well as generating time-and-event-related coincidences over a wide area, there's a secondary effect. It's intensely local but it seems to be getting stronger daily.'

I took a step beyond the nearest chalk mark. How to describe it? I felt heavier, certainly, and correspondingly more lethargic in my movements. It was like walking through syrup, except that my feet seemed not so much to adhere, as to mesh with the smooth floor. There seemed to be a sense of tightness, of compression, on my skin. I rubbed my fingertips together but could not dislodge the sensation of something clinging and cloying adhering to them.

'I call it "amassing",' Fullwood said, as I slowly retreated from the machine. 'There's no other way to describe it. It's coincidence on an atomic and sub-atomic scale, the coincidence of the very particles of existence, binding together, each unable to escape the other's proximity. I'll show you its ultimate outcome.'

He took me up onto a gantry, overlooking the enormous central well of the toroid. He took from his pocket a cigar, not a cheroot but a substantial corona, and tossed it down into the dark centre of the copper coils. As the cigar entered the central field its rate of descent slowed. It seemed to fall through the air in slow motion. At the same time it appeared to get shorter, squatter. It turned as it slowly drifted down, its hue changing gradually to the densest obsidian black. Then, quite suddenly, it imploded, contracting into a dense black core no more than a centimetre across that hung, in stasis, at the very heart of the flux field.

'Imagine,' said Fullwood, 'an infinitely small core of impacted matter, incredibly dense. The gravitational force at the heart of the field must also be exponential, approaching infinity. It sucks everything in: matter, light. What we "see"

103

is merely an illusory wavefront. And its outer limit is expanding daily. What will happen? It will consume us all.'

'This is certainly inconsistent with our desired aims,' I said. 'If that is what is happening there is certainly an error in our calculations, or at least an oversight.'

For the next few hours I pored over the figures, searching for the error, the oversight. I found it eventually in the form of a harmless quadratic. Incorrectly transcribed, quite early in our investigations, it had entangled our subsequent calculations. Just like Fullwood's blessed Web.

I left Fullwood to re-work the calculus and apply it to his machine. I returned to my residence, heartened by the way things had gone. There is a satisfaction one feels when predicted effects follow specified causes.

I had no doubt that my theorems, when applied, would work as anticipated. They would untangle Fullwood's web-matrix and render all the strands in perfect alignment. In Fullwood's fanciful terms, there would then be no question of happenstance, coincidence or accident within such a matrix. For the first time we would have an area of local space subject to null-distortion.

There was no question that the effect *would* be localised, of course, within the coils of Fullwood's toroid. Fullwood's ideas of shunt-propagation in respect of this or any other field-effect were half-baked. He never was good on theory.

That was a week ago.

I may have been wrong. I admit it.

I have visited Fullwood's laboratory on several occasions, hoping to discover how he has progressed with his work, but we always seem to miss one another, if only by minutes. (Several times I have found a still-warm cigar butt, one of those same West Indian cheroots, stubbed out in an ashtray.) Once he left a note for me. It simply said: 'What's happening?'

In so far as I can bring myself to be interested in such questions, I have lately been asking myself: What would be the ultimate effect of space subject to null-distortion? What sort of universe could exist without some degree of coincidence?

The prospect of developing the mathematical theorems to embrace such a concept, a concept directly the converse of Fullwood's poetic 'amassing', might once have excited me, but I confess that more practical considerations weigh on me at the moment.

Where I once happened upon Fullwood frequently by chance, now the man eludes me.

And it's not just Fullwood. It's things, objects. My tooth-brush seems to be developing an aversion for my teeth. I find it increasingly hard to bring a match to the tip of my cigar. I tap my foot and there is no answering click on the boards. A numbness pervades my extremities. There is a certain insubstantiality about my finger-tips.

Any bearing on matter?

Write no more

Difficulty

                    gripping

          pen

ROBERT HOLDSTOCK

Scarrowfell

1

In the darkness, in the world of nightmares, she sang a little
song. In her small room, behind the drawn curtains, her
voice was tiny, frightened, murmuring in her sleep:

> Oh dear mother what a fool I've been . . .
> Three young fellows . . . came courting me . . .
> Two were blind . . . the other couldn't see . . .
> Oh dear mother what a fool I've been . . .

Tuneless, timeless, endlessly repeated through the night,
soon the nightmare grew worse and she tossed below the
bedclothes, and called out for her mother, louder and louder,
Mother! Mother! until she sat up, gasping for breath and
screaming.

'Hush child. I'm here. I'm beside you. Quiet now. Go
back to sleep.'

'I'm frightened, I'm frightened. I had a terrible dream
. . .'

Her mother hugged her, sitting on the bed, rocking back
and forward, wiping the sweat and the fear from her face.
'Hush . . . hush, now. It was just a dream . . .'

'The blind man,' she whispered, and shook as she thought
of it so that her mother's grip grew firmer, more reassuring.
'The blind man. He's coming again . . .'

'Just a dream, child. There's nothing to be frightened of.

107

Close your eyes and go back to sleep, now. Sleep, child . . .
sleep. There. That's better.'

Still she sang, her voice very small, very faint as she drifted
into sleep again. '*Three young fellows . . . came courting me
. . . one was blind . . . one was grim . . . one had creatures
following him . . .*'

'Hush, child . . .'

Waking with a scream: 'Don't let him take me!'

2

None of the children in the village really knew one festival
day from another. They were *told* what to wear, and *told* what
to do, and *told* what to eat, and when the formalities were
over they would rush away to their secret camp, in the
shadow of the old church.

Lord's Eve was different, however. Lord's Eve was the
best of the festivals. Even if you didn't know that a particular
day would be Lord's Eve day, the signs of it were in the
village.

Ginny knew the signs by heart. Mr Box, at the Red Hart,
would spend a day cursing as he tried to erect a tarpaulin in
the beer garden of his public house. Here, the ox would be
slaughtered and roasted, and the dancers would rest. At the
other end of the village Mr Ellis, who ran the Bush and Briar,
would put empty firkins outside his premises for use as seats.
The village always filled with strangers during the dancing
festivals, and those strangers drank a lot of beer.

The church was made ready too. Mr and Mrs Morton,
usually never to be seen out of their Sunday best, would dress
in overalls and invade the cold church with brooms, brushes
and buckets. Mr Ashcroft, the priest, would garner late
summer flowers, and mow and trim the graveyard. This was
a dangerous time for the children, since he would come
perilously close to their camp, which lay just beyond the iron
gate that led from the churchyard. Here, between the church
and the earth walls of the old Saxon fort – in whose ring the

108

village had been built – was a tree-filled ditch, and the children's camp had been made there. The small clearing was close to the path which led from the church, through the earth wall and out onto the farmland beyond.

There were other signs of the coming festival day, however, signs from outside the small community. First, the village always seemed to be in shadow. Yet distantly, beyond the cloud cover, the land seemed to glow with eerie light. Ginny would stand on the high wall by the church, looking through the crowded trees that covered the ring of earthworks, staring to where the late summer sun was setting its fire on Whitley Nook and Middleburn. Movement on the high valley walls above these villages was just the movement of clouds, and the fields seemed to flow with brightness.

The wind always blew from Whitley Nook towards Ginny's own village, Scarrowfell. And on that wind, the day before the festival of Lord's Eve, you could always hear the music of the dancers as they wended their way along the riverside, through and round the underwood, stopping at each village to collect more dancers, more musicians (more hangovers) ready for the final triumph at Scarrowfell itself.

The music drifted in and out of hearing, a hint of a violin, the distant clatter of sticks, the faint jingle of the small bells with which the dancers decked out their clothes. When the wind gusted, whole phrases of the jaunty music could be heard, a rhythmic sound, with the voices of the dancers clearly audible as they sang the words of the folk songs.

Ginny, precariously balanced on the top of the wall, would jig with those brief rhythms, hair blowing in the wind, one hand holding on to the dry bark of an ash branch.

The dancers were coming; all the Oozers and the Pikers and the Thackers, coming to join the village's Scarrowmen; and it was therefore the day of Lord's Eve: the birds would flock and wheel in the skies, and flee along the valley too. And sure enough, as she looked up into the dark sky over Scarrowfell, the birds were there, thousands of them, making streaming, spiral patterns in the gloom. Their calling was inaudible. But after a while they streaked north, away from

109

the bells, away from the sticks, away from the calling of the Oozers.

Kevin Symonds came racing round the grey-walled church, glanced up and saw Ginny and made frantic beckoning motions. 'Gargoyle!' he hissed, and Ginny almost shouted as she lost her balance before jumping down from the wall. 'Gargoyle' was their name for Mr Ashcroft, the priest. A second after they had squeezed beyond the iron gate and into the cover of the scrub the old man appeared. But he was busy placing rillygills – knots of flowers and wheat stalks – on each gravestone and didn't notice the panting children just beyond the cleared ground, where the thorn and ash thicket was so dense.

Ginny led the way in to the clear space among the trees in the ditch. She stepped up the shallow earth slope to peer away into the field beyond, and the circle of tall elms that grew at its centre. A scruffy brown mare – probably one of Mr Box's drays – was kicking and stamping across the field, a white foal stumbling behind it. She was so intent on watching the foal that she didn't notice Mr Box himself, emerging from the ring of trees. He was dressed in his filthy blue apron but walked briskly across the field towards the church, his gaze fixed on the ground. Every few paces he stopped and fiddled with something on the grass. He never looked up, walked through the gap in the earthworks – the old gateway – and passed, by doing so, within arm's reach of where Ginny and Kevin breathlessly crouched. He walked straight ahead, stopped at the iron gate, inspected it, then moved off around the perimeter of the church, out of sight and out of mind.

'They've got the ox on the spit already.' Kevin said, his eyes bright, his lips wet with anticipation. 'It's the biggest ever. There's going to be at least two slices each.'

'Yuck!' said Ginny, feeling sick at the thought of the grey, greasy meat.

'And they've started the bonfire. You've got to come and see it. It's going to be huge! My mother said it's going to be the biggest yet.'

'I usually scrub potatoes for fire-baking,' Ginny said. 'But I haven't been asked this year.'

'Sounds as if you've been lucky,' Kevin said. 'It's going to be a really big day. The biggest ever. It's *very* special.'

Ginny whispered, 'My mother's been behaving strangely. And I've had a nightmare . . .'

Kevin watched her, but when no further information or explanation seemed to be forthcoming he said, '*My* mother says this is the most special Lord's Eve of them all. An old man's coming back to the village.'

'What old man?'

'His name's Cyric, or something. He left a long time ago, but he's coming back and everybody's very excited. They've been trying to get him to come back for ages, but he's only just agreed. That's what Mum says, anyway.'

'What's so special about him?'

Kevin wasn't sure. 'She said he's a war hero, or something.'

'Ugh!' Ginny wrinkled her nose in distaste. 'He's probably going to be all scarred.'

'Or blind!' Kevin agreed, and Ginny's face turned white.

A third child wriggled through the iron gate and skidded into the depression between the earth walls, dabbing at his face where he had scratched himself on a thorn.

'The tower!' Mick Ferguson whispered excitedly, ignoring his graze. 'While old Gargoyle is busy placing the rillygills.'

They moved cautiously back to the churchyard, then crawled towards the porch on their bellies, screened from the priest by the high earth mounds over each grave. Ducking behind the memorial stones – but not touching them – they at last found sanctuary in the freshly polished, gloomy interior. Despite the cloud-cover, light was bright from the stained-glass windows. The altar, with its flowers, looked somehow different from normal. The Mortons were cleaning the font, over in the side chapel; a bucket of well-water stood by ready to fill the bowl. They were talking as they worked and didn't hear the furtive movement of the three children.

111

Kevin led the way up the spiralling, footworn steps and out onto the cone-shaped roof of the church's tower. They averted their eyes from the grotesque stone figure that guarded the doorway, although Kevin reached out and touched its muzzle as he always did.

'For luck,' he said. 'My mother says the stone likes affection as much as the rest of us. If it doesn't get attention it'll prowl the village at night and choose someone to kill.'

'Shut *up*', Ginny said emphatically, watching the monster from the corner of her eye.

Michael laughed. 'Don't be such a scaredy-hare,' he said and reached out to jingle the small bell that hung around her neck. Her ghost bell.

'It's a small bell and that's a big stone demon,' Ginny pointed out nervously. Why was she so apprehensive this time, she wondered? She had often been up here and had never doubted that the stone creature, like all demons, could not attack the faithful, and that bells, books and candles were protection enough from the devil's minions.

The nightmare had upset her. She remembered Mary Whitelock's nightmare a few years before – almost the same dream, confided in the gang as they had feasted on stolen pie in their camp. She had not really liked Mary. All the same, when she had suddenly disappeared, after the festival, Ginny had felt very confused . . .

No! Put the thought from your mind, she told herself sternly. And brazenly she turned and stared at the medieval monstrosity that sat watching the door to the church below. And she laughed, because it was only frightening when you *imagined* how awful it was. In fact, it looked faintly ludicrous, with its gaping V-shaped mouth and lolling tongue, and its pointed ears, and skull cheeks, and its one great staring eye . . . and one gouged socket . . .

Below them, the village was a bustle of activity. In the small square in front of the church the bonfire was rising to truly monumental heights. Other children were helping to heap the faggots and broken furniture onto the pile. A large

112

stake in its centre was being used to hold the bulk of wood in place.

Away from where this fire would blaze, a large area was being roped off for the dancing. The gate from the church had already been decked with wild roses and lilies. The Gargoyle himself always led the congregation from the Lord's Eve service out to the festivities in the village. Ginny giggled at the remembered sight of him, dark cassock held up to his knees, white boney legs kicking and hopping along with the Oozers and the local Scarrowmen, a single bell on each ankle making him look as silly as she always thought he was.

At the far end of the village, the road from Whitley Nook cut through the south wall of the old earth fort and snaked between the cluster of tiled cottages where Ginny herself lived. Here, two small fires had been set alight, one on each side of the old track. The smoke was shattered by the wind from the valley. On the church tower the three children enjoyed the smell of the burning wood.

And as they listened they heard the music of the dancers, even now winding their way between Middleburn and Whitley Nook.

They would be here tomorrow. Sunlight picked out the white of their costumes, miles distant; and the flash of swords flung high in the air.

The Oozers were coming. The Thackers were coming. The wild dance was coming.

3

She awoke with a shock, screaming out, then becoming instantly silent as she stared at the empty room and the bright daylight creeping in above the heavy curtains of her room.

What time was it? Her head was full of music, the jangle of bells, the beating of the skin drums, the clash and thud of the wooden hobby poles. But now, outside, all was silent.

She swung her legs from the bed, then began to shiver as

113

unpleasant echoes of that haunting song, the nightmare song, came back to her.

She found that she could not resist muttering the words that stalked her sleeping hours. It was as if she had to repeat the sinister refrain before her body would allow her to move again, to become a child again . . .

'Oh dear mother . . . three young men . . . two were blind . . . the third couldn't see . . . oh mother, oh mother . . . grim-eyed courtiers . . . blind men dancing . . . creatures followed him, creatures dancing . . .'

The church bell rang out, a low repeated toll, five strikes and then a sixth strike, a moment delayed from the rest.

Five strikes for the Lords, and one for the fire! It couldn't be that time. It couldn't! Why hadn't mother come in to wake her?

Ginny ran to the curtains and pulled them back, staring out into the deserted street, crawling up onto the window ledge so that she could lean through the top window and stare up towards the square.

It was full of motionless figures. And distantly she could hear the chanting of the congregation. The Lord's Eve service had already started. Started! The procession had already passed the house, and she had been aware of it only in her half sleep!

She screeched with indignation, fleeing from her bedroom into the small sitting room. By the clock on the mantlepiece she learned that it was after midday. She had slept . . . she had slept fifteen hours!

She grabbed her clothes, pulled them on, not bothering with her hair but making a token effort to polish her shoes. It was Lord's Eve. She *had* to be smart today. She couldn't find her bell necklace. She had on a flowered dress and red shoes. She pulled a pink woollen cardigan over her shoulders, grabbed at her frilly hat, stared at it, then tossed it behind the hat rack . . . and fled from the house.

She ran up the road to the church square, following the path that, earlier, the column of dancers must have taken. She felt tears in her eyes, tears of dismay, and anger, and

114

irritation. Every year she watched the procession from her garden. *Every year*! Why hadn't mother *woken* her?

She loved the procession, the ranks of dancers in their white coats and black hats, the ribbons, the flowers, the bells tied to ankle, knee and elbow, the men on the hobby horses, the fools with their pigs' bladders on sticks, the women in their swirling skirts, the Thackers, the Pikermen, the Oozers, the black-faced Scarrowmen . . . all of them came through the smouldering fires at the south gate, each turning and making the sign of peace before jigging and hopping on along the road, keeping time to the beat of the drum, the melancholy whine of the violin, the sad chords of the accordion, the trill of the whistles.

And she had missed it! She had slept! She had remained in the world of nightmares, where the shadowy blind pursued her . . .

As she ran she *screamed* her frustration!

She stopped at the edge of the square, catching her breath, looking for Kevin, or Mick, or any others of the small gang that had their camp in the earthen walls of the old fort. She couldn't see them. She cast her gaze over the ranks of silent dancers. They were spread out across the square, lines of men and women facing the lych-gate and the open door of the church. They stood in absolute silence. They hardly seemed to breathe. Sometimes, as she brushed past one of them, working her way towards the church where Gargoyle's voice was an irritating drone in the distance, sometimes a tambourine would rattle, or an accordion would sigh a weary note. The man holding it would glance and smile at her, but she knew better than to disturb the Scarrowmen when the voice was speaking from the church.

She passed under the rose and lily gate, ducked her head and made the sign of peace, then scampered into the porch and edged towards the gloomy, crowded interior.

The priest was at the end of his sermon, the usual boring sermon for the feast day.

'We have made a pledge,' Mr Ashcroft was intoning. 'A

115

pledge of belief in a life after death, a pledge of belief in a God which is greater than humankind itself . . .'

She could see Kevin, standing and fidgeting between his parents, four pews forward in the church. Of Michael there was no sign. And where was mother? At the front, almost certainly . . .

'We believe in the resurrection of the Dead, and in a time of atonement. We have made a pledge with those who have died before us, a pledge that we will be re-united with them in the greater Glory of our Lord.'

'*Kevin!*' Ginny hissed. Kevin fidgeted. The priest droned on.

'We have pledged all of this, and we believe all of this. Our time in the physical realm is a time of trial, a time of testing, a testing of our honour and our belief, a belief that those who have gone are not gone at all, but merely waiting to be rejoined with us . . . '

'*Kevin!*' she called again. '*Kevin!*'

Her voice carried too loudly. Kevin glanced round and went white. His mother glanced round too, then jerked his attention back to the service, using a lock of his curly hair as her means. His cry was audible to the Gargoyle himself, who hesitated before concluding,

'This is the brightness behind the feast of the Lord's Eve. Think not of the Death, but of the Life our Lord will bring us.'

Where was her mother?

Before she could think further someone's hand tugged at her shoulder, pulling her back towards the porch of the church. She protested and glanced up, and the solemn face of Mr Box stared down at her. 'Go outside, Ginny,' he said. 'Go outside, now.'

Inside, the congregation had begun to recite the Lord's Prayer.

He pushed her towards the rose gate, beyond which the Oozers and Scarrowmen waited for the service to end. She walked forlornly towards them, and as she passed the man

116

who stood closest to her she struck at his tambourine. The tambours jangled loudly in the still, summer square.

The man didn't move. She stood and stared defiantly at him, then struck his tambourine again.

'Why don't you *dance*?' she shrieked at him. When he ignored her, she shouted again. 'Why don't you make *music*? Make *music*! Dance in the square! Dance!' Her voice was a shrill cry.

4

There was no twilight. Late afternoon became dark night in a few minutes and a torch was put to the fire, which flared dramatically and silenced all activity. Glowing embers streamed into a starless sky and the village square became choking with the sweet smell of burning wood. The last smells of the roasted ox were banished and in the grounds of the Red Lion the skeleton of the beast was hacked apart. A few pence each for the bones with their meaty fragments. In front of the Bush and Briar Mr Ellis swept up a hundred-weight of broken glass. Mick Ferguson led a gang of children, chasing an empty barrel down the street, towards the south gate where the fires still smouldered.

For a while the dancing had ceased. People thronged about the fire. Voices were raised in the public houses as dancers and tourist alike struggled to get in fresh orders for ale. A sort of controlled chaos ruled the day, and in the centre of it: the fire, its light picking out stark details on the grey church and the muddy green in the square. Beyond the sheer rise of the church tower, all was darkness, although men in white shirts and black hats walked through the lych-gate and rounded the church, talking quietly, dispersing as they re-emerged into the square. Here, they again picked up sticks, or tambourines, or other instruments of music and mock war.

Ginny wandered among them.

She could not find her mother.

And she knew that something was wrong, very wrong indeed.

It came as scant reassurance when a bearded youth called to the Morrismen again, and twelve sturdy men, all of them strangers to Scarrowfell, jangled their way from the Bush and Briar to the dancing square. There was laughter, tomfoolery with the cudgels they carried, and the whining practice notes of the accordion. Then they filed into a formation, jiggled and rang their legs, laughed once more and began to hop to the rhythm of a dance called the *Cuckoo's Nest*. A man in a baggy, flowery dress and with a big frilly bonnet on his head sang the rude words. The singer was a source of great amusement since he sported a bushy, ginger beard. He wore an apron over the frock and every so often lifted the pinny to expose a long red balloon strapped between his legs. It had eyes and eyelashes painted on its tip. The audience roared each time he did this.

As Ginny moved through the crowds towards the new focus of activity, Mick Ferguson approached her, grinned, and went into his Hunchback of Notre Dame routine, stooping forward, limping in an exaggerated fashion and crying, 'The bells. The bells. The jingling bells . . . '

'Mick . . .' Ginny began, but he had already flashed her a nervous grin and bolted off into the confusing movement of the crowds, running towards the fire and finally disappearing into the gloom beyond.

Ginny watched him go. Mick, she thought . . . Mick . . . why?

What was going on?

She walked towards the dancers and the bearded singer and Kevin turned round nervously and nodded to her. The man sang:

'Some like a girl who is pretty in the face
And some like a girl who is slender in the waist . . .'

'I missed the procession,' Ginny said. 'I wasn't woken up.'

Kevin stared at her, looking unhappy. He said, 'My mother told me not to talk to you . . .'

118

She waited, but Kevin had decided that discretion was the better part of cowardice.

'Why not?' she asked, disturbed by the statement.

'You're being denied,' the boy murmured.

Ginny was shocked. 'Why am I being denied? Why me?'

Kevin shrugged. Then a strange look came into his eyes, a horrible look, a man's look, arrogant, sneering.

The man in the hideous dress sang:

'But give me a girl who will wriggle and will twist
Each time I slap my hand upon her cuckoo's nest . . .'

Kevin backed away from Ginny making 'cuckoo' sounds.

'It's a *rude* song,' Ginny said.

Kevin taunted, '*You're* a cuckoo. *You're* a cuckoo . . .'

'I don't know what it means,' Ginny said, bewildered.

'Cuckoo, cuckoo, cuckoo,' Kevin mocked, then jabbed her in the groin. He cackled horribly then raced away towards the blazing bonfire. Ginny had tears in her eyes, but her anger was so intense that the tears dried. She glared at the singer, still not completely aware of what was going on except that she knew the song was rude because of the guffaws of the adult men in the watching circle. After a moment she slipped away towards the church.

She stood within the lych-gate watching the flickering of the fire, the highlit faces of the watching crowds, the restless movement, the jigging and hopping . . . hearing the laughter, and the music, and the distant wind that was fanning the fire and making the flames bend violently and dangerously towards the south. And she wondered where, in all this chaos, her mother might have been.

Mother had been so supportive to her, so gentle, so kind. During the nights when the nightmare had been a terrible presence in the house by the old road, where Ginny had lived since her real parents had died in the fire, during those terrible nights the Mother had been so comforting. Ginny had come to think of her as her own mother, and all grief, all sadness had faded fast.

Where *was* the Mother? Where *was* she?

She saw Mr Box, walking slowly through the crowds, a

baked potato in one hand and a glass of beer in the other. She ran to him and tugged at his jacket. He nearly choked on his potato and glanced round urgently, but soon her voice reached him and, although he frowned, he stooped down towards her. He threw the remnants of his potato away and placed his glass upon the ground.

'Hello Ginny . . .' He sounded anxious.

'Mr Box. Have you seen mother?'

Again he looked uncomfortable. His kindly face was a mask of worry. His moustache twitched. 'You see . . . she's getting the reception ready.'

'What reception?' Ginny asked.

'Why, for Cyric, of course. The war hero. The man who's coming back to us. He's finally agreed to return to the village. He was supposed to have come three years ago, but he couldn't make it.'

'I don't care about him' she said. 'Where's mother?'

Mr Box placed a comforting hand on her shoulder and shook his head. 'Can't you just play, child? It's what you're supposed to do. I'm just a pub landlord. I'm not part of the Organisers. You shouldn't even . . . you shouldn't even be *talking* to me.'

'I'm being denied,' she whispered.

'Yes,' he said sadly.

'Where's mother?' Ginny demanded.

'An important man is coming back to the village,' Mr Box said. 'A great hero. It's a great honour for us . . . and . . .' he hesitated before adding, in a quiet voice, 'And what he's bringing with him is going to make this village more secure . . .'

'What *is* he bringing?' Ginny asked.

'A certain knowledge,' Mr Box said, then shrugged. 'It's all I know. Like all the villages around here, we've had to fight to keep out the invader, and it's a hard fight. We've all been waiting a long time for this night, Ginny. A very long time. We made a pledge to this man. A long time ago, when he fought to save the village. Tonight we're honouring that pledge. All of us have a part to play . . .'

120

Ginny frowned. 'Me too?' she asked, and was astonished to see large tears roll down each of Mr Box's cheeks.

'Of course you too, Ginny,' he whispered, and seemed to choke on the words. 'I'm surprised that you don't know. I always thought the children knew. But the way these things work . . . the rules . . .' he shook his head again. 'I'm not privileged to know.'

'But why is everybody being so horrible to me?' Ginny said.

'Who's everybody?'

'Mick,' she said. 'And Kevin. He called me a cuckoo . . .'

Mr Box smiled. 'They're just teasing you. They've been told something of what will happen this evening and they're jealous.'

He straightened up and took a deep breath. Ginny watched him, his words sinking in slowly. She said, 'Do you mean what will happen to *me* this evening?'

He nodded. 'You've been *chosen*,' he whispered to her. 'When your parents were killed, the Mother was sent to you to prepare you. Your role tonight is a very special one. Ginny, that's all I know. Now go and play, child. Please . . .'

He looked suddenly away from her, towards the dancers. Ginny followed his gaze. Five men, two of whom she recognised, were watching them. One of them shook his head slightly and Mr Box's touch on Ginny's shoulder went away. A woman walked towards them, her dress covered with real flowers, her face like stone. Mr Box pushed Ginny away roughly. As she scampered for safety she could hear the sound of the woman's blows to Mr Box's cheek.

5

The fire burned. Long after it should have been a glowing pile of embers, it was still burning. Long after they should have been exhausted, the Scarrowmen danced. The night air was chill, heavy with smoke, bright with drifting sparks. It echoed to the jingle of bells and the clatter of cudgels. Voices

121

drifted on the wind; there was laughter; and round and round the Morrismen danced.

Soon they had formed into a great circle, stretched around the fire and jigging fast and furious to the strident, endless rhythm of drums and violin. All the village danced, and the strangers too, men and women in anoraks and sweaters, and children in woolly hats, and teenagers in jeans and leather jackets, all of them mixed up with the white-and-black clothed Oozers, Pikers, Thackers and the rest.

Round the burning fire, stumbling and tottering, shrieking with mirth as a whole segment of the ring tumbled in the mud. Round and round.

The bells, the hammering of sticks, the whine of the violin, the Jack Tar sound of the accordion.

And at ten o'clock the whole wild dance stopped.

Silence.

The men reached down and took the bells from their legs, cast them into the fire. The cudgels, too, were thrown onto the flames. The violins were shattered on the ground, the fragments tossed into the conflagration.

The accordions wept music as they were slung onto the pyre.

Flowers out of hair. Bonnets from heads. Rose and lily were stripped off the lych-gate. The air filled suddenly with a sharp, aromatic scent . . . of herbs, woodland herbs.

In the silence Ginny walked towards the church, darted through the gate into the darkness of the graveyard . . . Round between the long mounds to the iron gate . . .

Kevin was there. He ran towards her, his eyes wide, wild. 'He's coming!' he hissed, breathlessly.

'What's going on?' she whispered.

'Where are you going?' he said.

'To the camp. I'm frightened. They've stopped dancing. They're burning their instruments. This happened three years ago when Mary . . . when . . . you know . . .'

'Why are you so frightened?' Kevin asked. His eyes were bright from the distant glow of the bonfire. 'What are you running from, Ginny? Tell me. Tell me. We're friends . . .'

122

'Something is wrong,' she sobbed. She found herself clutching at the boy's arms. 'Everybody is being so horrible to me. *You* were horrible to me. What have I done? What have I done?'

He shook his head. The flames made his dark eyes gleam. She had her back to the square. Suddenly he looked beyond her. Then he smiled. He looked at her.

'Goodbye, Ginny,' he whispered.

She turned. Kevin darted past her and into the great mob of masked men who stood around her. They had come upon her so quietly that she had not heard a thing. Their faces were like black pigs. Eyes gleamed, mouths grinned. They wore white and black . . . the Scarrows.

Unexpectedly, Kevin began to whine. Ginny thought he was being punished for being out of bounds. She listened, and then for one second . . . just one second . . . all was stillness, all was silence, anticipation. Then she reacted as any sensible child would react in the situation.

She opened her mouth and screamed. The sound had barely echoed in the night air when a hand clamped firmly across her face, a great hand, strong, stifling her cry. She struggled and pulled away, turned and kicked until she realised it was the Mother that she fought against. She was no longer wearing her rowan beads, or her iron charm. She seemed naked without them. Her dress was green and she held Ginny firmly still. 'Hold quiet, child. Your time is soon.'

The iron gate was open. Ginny peered through it, into the darkness, through the grassy walls of the old fort and towards the circle of great elms.

There was a light there, and the light was coming closer. And ahead of that light there was a wind, a breeze, ice cold, tinged with a smell that was part sweat, part rot, and unpleasant in the extreme. She grimaced and tried to back away, but the Mother's hands held her fast. She glanced over her shoulder, towards the square, and felt her body tremble as the Scarrows stared beyond her, into the void of night.

Two of the Scarrows held tall, hazel poles, each wrapped

123

round with strands of ivy and mistletoe. They stepped forward and held the poles to form a gateway between them. Ginny watched all of this and shivered. And she felt sick when she saw Kevin held by others of the Scarrows. The boy was terrified. He seemed to be pleading with Ginny, but what could she do? His own mother stood close to him, weeping silently.

The wind gusted suddenly and the first of the shadows passed over so quickly that she was hardly aware of its transit. It appeared out of nowhere, part darkness, part chill, a tall shape that didn't so much walk as *flow* through the iron gate. Looking at that shadow was like looking into a depthless world of dark; it shimmered, it hazed, it flickered, it moved, an uncertain balance between that world and the real world. Only as it passed between the hazel poles held by the Scarrows, and then into the world beyond, did it take on a form that could be called . . . ghostly.

Distantly the priest's voice intoned a greeting. Ginny heard him say, 'Welcome back to *Scarugfell*. Our pledge is fulfilled. Your life begins again.'

A second shadow followed the first, this one smaller, and with its darkness and its chill came the sound of keening, like a child's crying. It was distant, though, and uncertain. As Ginny watched, it took its shadowy form beyond the Scarrows and into the village.

As each of them had passed over, so the Scarrowmen closed ranks again, but distantly, close to the fire in the square, an unearthly howling, a nightmare wind, seemed to greet each new arrival. What happened to the spirits then, Ginny couldn't tell, or care.

Her mother's hand touched her face, then her shoulder, forced her round again to watch the iron gate. The Mother whispered, 'Those two were his kin. They too died for our village a long time ago. But Cyric is coming now . . .'

The shadow that moved beyond the gate was like nothing Ginny could ever have imagined. She couldn't tell whether it was animal or man. It was immense. It swayed as it moved,

124

and it seemed to approach through the darkness in a ponderous, dragging way. Its outlines were blurred, shadow against darkness, void against the glimmering light among the trees. It seemed to have branches and tendrils reaching from its head. It made a sound that was like the rumble of water in a hidden well.

It seemed to fill her vision. It occupied all of space. Its breath stank. Its single eye gleamed with firelight.

One was blind . . . one was grim . . .

It seemed to be laughing at her as it peered down from beyond the trees and the earth walls that surrounded the church.

It pushed something forward, a shadow, a man, nudged it through the iron gate. Ginny wanted to scream as she caught glimpses, within that shadow, of the dislocated jaw, the empty sockets, the crawling flesh. The ragged thing limped toward her, hands raised, bony fingers stretched out, skull face open and inviting . . . inviting the kiss that Ginny knew, now, would end her life.

'No!' she shouted, and struggled frantically in the Mother's grip. The Mother seemed angry. 'Even now it mocks us!' she said, then shouted, 'Give the Life for the Death. Give it now!'

Behind Ginny, Kevin suddenly screamed. Then he was running towards the iron gate, sobbing and shouting, drawn by invisible hands.

'Don't let him take me! Don't let him take me!' he cried.

He passed the hideous figure and entered the world beyond the gate. He was snatched into the air, blown into darkness like a leaf whipped by a storm wind. He had vanished in an instant.

The great shadow turned away into the night and began to seep back towards the circle of elms. The Mother's hands on Ginny's shoulders pushed her forwards, towards the ghastly embrace.

The shadow corpse stopped moving. Its arms dropped. The gaping eyes watched nothing and nowhere. A sound issued from its bones. 'Is she the one? Is she my kin?'

Mother's voice answered loudly that she was indeed the one. She was indeed Cyric's kin.

The shadow seemed to turn its head to watch Ginny. It looked down at her, then reached up and pulled the tatters of a hood about its head. The hood hid the features. The whole creature seemed to melt, to descend, to shrink. Ginny heard the Mother say, 'Fifteen hundred years in the dark. Your life saved our village. Our pledge to bring you back is honoured. Welcome, Cyric.'

Something wriggled below the tatters of the hood. The Mother said, 'Go forward, child. Take the hare. *Take him!*'

Ginny hesitated. She glanced round. The Scarrows seemed to be smiling behind their masks. Two other children, both girls, stood there. Each was holding a struggling hare. Her Mother made frantic motions to her. 'Come on, Ginny. The fear is ended, now. The day of denial is over. Only you can touch the hare. You're the kin. Cyric has chosen you. Take it quickly. Bring him over. Bring him back.'

Ginny stumbled forward, reached below the stinking rags and found the terrified animal. As she raised the brown hare to her breast she felt the flow of the past, the voice, the wisdom, the spirit of the man who had passed back over, the promise to him kept, fifteen hundred years after he had lain down his life for the safety of *Scarugfell*, also known as the *Place of the Mother*.

Cyric was home. The great hunter was home. Ginny had him, now, and *he* had her, and she would become great and wise, and Cyric would speak the wisdom of the Dark through her lips. The hare would die in time, but Cyric and Ginny would share a human life until the human body itself passed away.

And Ginny felt a great glow of joy as the images of that ancient land, its forts, its hills, its tracks, its forest shrines, flooded into her mind. She heard the hounds, the horses, the larks, she felt the cold wind, smelled the great woods.

Yes. Yes. She had been born for this. Her parents had been sacrificed to free her and the Mother had kept her ready

126

for the moment. The nightmare had been Cyric making contact as the Father had brought him to the edge of the dark world.

The Father! The Father had watched over her, as all in the village had often said he would. It had been the Father she had seen, a rare glimpse of the Lord who always brought the returning Dead to the place of the Lord's Eve.

Cyric had come a long, long way home. It had taken time to make the Lord release him and allow Cyric's knowledge of the dark world back to the village, to help Scarrowfell, and the villages like it keep the eyes and minds of the invader muddled and confused. And then Cyric, too, had waited . . . until Ginny was of age. His kin. His chosen vehicle.

Ginny, his new protector, cradled the animal. The hare twitched in her grasp. Its eyes were full of rejoicing.

She felt a moment's sadness, then, for poor, betrayed Kevin, but it passed. And as she left the place of the gate she joined willingly in reciting the Lord's prayer, her voice high, enthusiastic among the rumble of the crowd.

Our Father, who art in the Forest
Horned One is Thy name.
Thy Kingdom is the Wood, Thy Will is the Blood
In the Glade, as it is in the Village.
Give us this day our Kiss of Earth
And forgive us our Malefactions.
Destroy those who Malefact against us
And lead us to the Otherworld.
For Thine is the Kingdom of the Shadow, Thine is the Power
and the Glory. Thou art the Stag which ruts with us, and We
are the Earth beneath thy feet.
Drocha Nemeton

MICHAEL MOORCOCK

The Frozen Cardinal

Moldavia. S. Pole. 1/7/17

Dear Gerry,

I got your last, finally. Hope this reaches you in less than a year. The supply planes are all robots now and are supposed to give a faster service. Did I tell you we were being sent to look over the southern pole? Well, we're here. Below zero temperatures, of course, and at present we're gaining altitude all the time. At least we don't have to wear breathing equipment yet. The Moldavian poles have about twice the volume of ice as those of Earth, but they're melting. As we thought, we found the planet at the end of its ice-age. I know how you hate statistics and you know what a bore I can be, so I won't go into the details. To tell you the truth, it's a relief not to be logging and measuring.

It's when I write to you that I find it almost impossible to believe how far away Earth is. I frequently have a peculiar sense of closeness to the home planet, even though we are light years from it. Sometimes I think Earth will appear in the sky at 'dawn' and a rocket will come to take me to you. Are you lying to me, Gerry? Are you really still waiting? I love you so much. Yet my reason cautions me. I can't believe in your fidelity. I don't mean to make you impatient but I miss you desperately sometimes and I'm sure you know how strange people get in these conditions. I joined the expedition, after all, to give you time by yourself, to reconsider our relationship. But when I got your letter I was overjoyed. And, of course, I wish I'd never signed up for Moldavia.

129

Still, only another six months to go now, and another six months home. I'm glad your mother recovered from her accident. This time next year we'll be spending all my ill-gotten gains in the Seychelles. It's what keeps me going.

We're perfectly safe in our icesuits, of course, but we get terribly tired. We're ascending a series of gigantic ice terraces which seem to go on forever. It takes a day to cross from one terrace to the wall of the next, then another day or so to climb the wall and move the equipment up. The small sun is visible throughout an entire cycle of the planet at this time of year, but the 'day', when both suns are visible, is only about three hours. Then everything's very bright, of course, unless it's snowing or there's a thick cloud-cover, and we have to protect our eyes. We use the brightest hours for sleeping. It's almost impossible to do anything else. The vehicles are reliable, but slow. If we make any real speed we have to wait a consequently longer interval until they can be re-charged. Obviously, we re-charge during the bright hours, so it all works out reasonably well. It's a strangely orderly planet, Gerry: everything in its place. Those creatures I told you about were not as intelligent as we had hoped. Their resemblance to spiders is remarkable, though, even to spinning enormous webs around their nests; chiefly, it seemed to us, for decoration. They ate the rations we offered and suffered no apparent ill-effects, which means that the planet could probably be opat-gen in a matter of years. That would be a laugh on Galtman. Were you serious, by the way, in your letter? You couldn't leave your USSA even to go to Canada when we were together! You wouldn't care for this ice. The plains and jungles we explored last year feel almost deserted, as if they were once inhabited by a race which left no mark whatsoever. We found no evidence of intelligent inhabitants, no large animals, though we detected some weirdly-shaped skeletons in caves below the surface. We were told not to excavate, to leave that to the follow-up team. This is routine official work; there's no romance in it for me. I didn't expect there would be, but I hadn't really allowed for the boredom, for the irritation one begins to feel with one's colleagues. I'm so glad you wrote to say you still love me. I joined to find myself, to let you get on with your life. I hope we both will be more stable when we meet again.

The gennard is warmed up and I'm being signalled, so I'll close this for the time being. We're about to ascend another wall, and that means only one of us can skit to see to the hoist, while the others go up the hard way on the lines. Helander's the leader on this particular op. I must say he's considerably easier going than old I.P. whom you'll probably have seen on the news by now, showing off his eggs. But the river itself is astonishing, completely encircling the planet; fresh water and Moldavia's only equivalent to our oceans, at least until this ice age is really over!

8/7/17 'Dawn'

A few lines before I fall asleep. It's been a hard one today. Trouble with the hoists. Routine stuff, but it doesn't help morale when it's this cold. I was dangling about nine hundred metres up, with about another thousand to go, for a good hour, with nothing to do but listen to Fisch's curses in my helmet, interspersed with the occasional reassurance. You're helpless in a situation like that! And then, when we did all get to the top and started off again across the terrace (the ninth!) we came almost immediately to an enormous crevasse which must be half-a-kilometre across! So here we are on the edge. We can go round or we can do a horizontal skit. We'll decide that in the 'evening'. I have the irrational feeling that this whole section could split off suddenly and engulf us in the biggest landslide a human being ever witnessed. It's silly to think like that. In relationship to this astonishing staircase we are lighter than midges. Until I got your last letter I wouldn't have cared. I'd have been excited by the idea. But now, of course, I've got something to live for. It's peculiar, isn't it, how that makes cowards of the best of us?

9/7/17

Partridge is down in the crevasse at this moment. He

131

thinks we can bridge, but wants to make sure. Also our instruments have picked up something odd, so we're duty-bound to investigate. The rest of us are hanging around, quite glad of the chance to do nothing. Fedin is playing his music and Simons and Russell are fooling about on the edge, kicking a ration-pack about, with the crevasse as the goal. You can hardly make out the other side. Partridge just said he's come across something odd imbedded in the north wall. He says the colours of the ice are beautiful, all dark greens and blues, but this, he says, is red. 'There shouldn't be anything red down here!' He says it's probably rock but it resembles an artefact. Maybe there have been explorers here before us, or even inhabitants. If so, they must have been here relatively recently, because these ice-steps are not all that old, especially at the depth Partridge has reached. Mind you, it wouldn't be the first practical-joke he's played since we arrived.

Later

Partridge is up. When he pushed back his visor he looked pale and said he thought he was crazy. Fedin gave him a check-up immediately. There are no extraordinary signs of fatigue. Partridge says the outline he saw in the ice seemed to be a human figure. The instruments all suggest it is animal matter, though of course there are no life-functions. 'Even if it's an artefact,' said Partridge, 'it hasn't got any business being there.' He shuddered. 'It seemed to be looking at me. A direct, searching stare. I got frightened.' Partridge isn't very imaginative, so we were all impressed. 'Are we going to get it out of there?' asked Russell. 'Or do we just record it for the follow-up team, as we did with those skeletons?' Helander was uncertain. He's as curious as the rest of us. 'I'll take a look for myself,' he said. He went down, said something under his breath which none of us could catch in our helmets, then gave the order to be hoisted up again. 'It's a Roman Catholic cardinal,' he said. 'The hat, the robes, everything. Making a benediction!' He frowned. 'We're going to have to send back on this and await instructions.'

132

Fedin laughed. 'We'll be recalled immediately. Everyone's warned of the hallucinations. We'll be hospitalised back at base for months while the bureaucrats try to work out why we went mad.'

'You'd better have a look,' said Helander. 'I want you to go down one by one and tell me what you see.'

Partridge was squatting on his haunches, drinking something hot. He was trembling all over. He seemed to be sweating. 'This is ridiculous,' he said, more than once.

Three others are ahead of me, then it's my turn. I feel perfectly sane, Gerry. Everything else seems normal – as normal as it can be. And if this team has a failing it is that it isn't very prone to speculation or visual hallucinations. I've never been with a duller bunch of fact-gatherers. Maybe that's why we're all more scared than we should be. No expedition from Earth could ever have been to Moldavia before. Certainly nobody would have buried a Roman Catholic cardinal in the ice. There is no explanation, however wild, which fits. We're all great rationalists on this team. Not a hint of mysticism or even poetry among us. The drugs see to that if our temperaments don't!

Russell's coming up. He's swearing, too. Chang goes down. Then it's my turn. Then Simons'. Then Fisch. I wish you were here, Gerry. With your intelligence you could probably think of something. We certainly can't. I'd better start kitting up. More when I come up. To tell you the absolute truth I'm none too happy about going down!

Later

Well, I've been down. It's dark. The blues and greens glow as if they give off an energy of their own, although it's only reflections. The wall is smooth and opaque. About four metres down and about half a metre back into the ice of the face you can see him. He's tall, about fifty-five, very handsome, clean-shaven and he's looking directly out at you. His eyes seem sad but not at all malevolent. Indeed, I'd say he seemed kind. There's something noble about him. His clothes are scarlet and fall in folds which suggest he became frozen while standing naturally in the spot he stands in now. He couldn't, therefore, have been dropped, or the clothing would be disturbed. There's no logic to it, Gerry. His right hand is raised and he's making some sort of Christian sign. You know I'm not too hot on anthropology. Helander's the expert.

His expression seems to be one of forgiveness. It's quite overwhelming. You almost find your heart going out to him while at the same time you can't help thinking you're somehow responsible for his being there! Six light years from Earth on a planet which was only catalogued three years ago and which we are supposedly the first human beings to explore. Nowhere we have been has anyone discovered a shred of evidence that man or anything resembling man ever explored other planets. You know as well as I do that the only signs of intelligent life anyone has found have been negligible and certainly we have never had a hint that any other creature is capable of space-travel. Yet here is a man dressed in a costume which, at its latest possible date, is from the twentieth century.

I tried to stare him down. I don't know why. Eventually I told them to lift me up. While Simons went down, I waited on the edge, sipping ade and trying to stop shaking. I don't know why all of us were so badly affected. We've been in danger often enough (I wrote to you about the lavender swamps) and there isn't anyone on the team who hasn't got a sense of humour. Nobody's been able to raise a laugh yet. Helander tried, but it was so forced that we felt sorry for him. When Simons came up he was in exactly the same state as me. I handed him the rest of my ade and then returned to my biv to write this. We're to have a conference in about ten minutes. We haven't decided whether to send back information yet or not. Our curiosity will probably get the better of us. We have no specific orders on the question, but we're pretty sure we'll get a hands off if we report now. The big skeletons were one thing. This is quite another. And yet we know in our hearts that we should leave well alone.

The conference is over. It went on for hours. Now we've all decided to sleep on it. Helander and Partridge have been down for another look and have set up a carver in case we decide to go ahead. It will be easy enough to do. Feeling very tired. Have the notion that if we disturb the cardinal we'll do something cataclysmic. Maybe the whole planet will dissolve around us. Maybe this enormous mountain will crumble to nothing. Helander says that what he would like to do is send back on the cardinal but say that he is already carving, since our instruments suggest the crevasse is unstable and could close. There's no way it could close in the next week! But it would be a good enough excuse. You might never get this letter, Gerry. For all we're told personal mail is uninspected I don't trust them entirely. Do you think I should? Or if someone else is reading this, do they think I should have trusted to the law? His face is in my mind's eye as I write. So tranquil. So sad. I'm taking a couple of deegs, so will write more tomorrow.

10/7/17

Helander has carved. The whole damned thing is standing in the centre of the camp now, like a memorial. A big square block of ice with the cardinal peering out of it. We've all walked round and round the thing. There's no question that the figure is human. Helander wanted to begin thawing right away, but bowed to Simons, who doesn't want to risk the thing deteriorating. Soon he's going to vacuum-cocoon it. Simons is cursing himself for not bringing more of his archaeological gear along with him. He expected nothing like this, and our experience up to now has shown that Moldavia doesn't *have* any archaeology worth mentioning. We're all convinced it was a living creature. I even feel he may still be alive, the way he looks at me. We're all very jittery, but our sense of humour has come back and we make bad jokes about the cardinal really being Jesus Christ or Mahomet or somebody. Helander accuses us of religious illiteracy. He's the only one with any real knowledge of all that stuff. He is behaving oddly. He snapped at Russell a little while ago, telling him he wasn't showing proper reverence.

Russell apologised. He said he hadn't realised Helander was superstitious. Helander has sent back, saying what he's done and telling them he's about to thaw. A *fait accompli*. Fisch is unhappy. He and Partridge feel we should replace the cardinal and get on with 'our original business'. The rest of us argue that this *is* our original business. We are an exploration team. 'It's follow-up work,' said Fisch. 'I'm anxious to see what's at the top of this bloody great staircase.' Partridge replied: 'A bloody great Vatican, if you reason it through on the evidence we have.' That's the trouble with the kind of logic we go in for, Gerry. Well, we'll all be heroes when we get back to Earth, I suppose. Or we'll be disgraced, depending on what happens next. There's not a lot that can happen to me. This isn't my career, the way it is for the others. I'll be only too happy to be fired, since I intend to resign as soon as I'm home. Then it's the Seychelles for us, my dear. I hope you haven't changed your mind. I wish you were here. I feel the need to share what's going on – and I can think of nobody better to share it than you. Oh, God, I love you so much, Gerry. More, I know, than you'll ever love me; but I can bear anything except separation. I was reconciled to that separation until you wrote your last letter. I hope the company is giving you the yellow route now. You deserve it. With a clean run through to Maracaibo there will be no stopping the old gaucho, eh? But those experiments are risky, I'm told. So don't go too far. I think I know you well enough to be pretty certain you won't take unnecessary risks. I wish I could reach out now and touch your lovely, soft skin, your fine fair hair. I must stop this. It's doing things to me which even the blunn can't control! I'm going out for another walk around our frozen friend.

Later

Well, he's thawed. And it is human. Flesh and blood, Gerry, and no sign of deterioration. A man even taller than Helander. His clothes are all authentic, according to the

136

expert. He's even wearing a pair of old-fashioned cotton underpants. No protective clothing. No sign of having had food with him. No sign of transport. And our instruments have been scouring a wider and wider area. We have the little beeps on automatic, using far more energy than they should. The probes go everywhere. Helander says that this is important. If we can find a vehicle or a trace of habitation, then at least we'll have the beginnings of an answer. He wants something to send back now, of course. We've had an acknowledgement and a hold-off signal. There's not much to hold-off from, currently. The cardinal stands in the middle of the camp, his right arm raised in benediction, his eyes as calm and sad and resigned as ever. He continues to make us jumpy. But there are no more jokes, really, except that we sometimes call him 'padre'. Helander says all expeditions had one in the old days: a kind of psych-medic, like Fedin. Fedin says he thinks the uniform a bit unsuitable for the conditions. It's astonishing how we grow used to something as unbelievable as this. We look up at the monstrous ice-steps ahead of us, the vast gulf behind us, at an alien sky with two suns in it; we know that we are millions upon millions of miles from Earth, across the vacuum of interstellar space, and realise we are sharing our camp with a corpse dressed in the costume of the sixteenth century and we're beginning to take it all for granted . . . I suppose it says something for human resilience. But we're all still uncomfortable. Maybe there's only so much our brains can take. I wish I was sitting on a stool beside you at the Amset having a beer. But things are so strange to me now that *that* idea is hard to accept. This has become normality. The probes bring in nothing. We're using every instrument we've got. Nothing. We're going to have to ask for the reserve stuff at base and get them to send something to the top. I'd like to be pulled back, I think, and yet I remain fascinated. Maybe you'll be able to tell me if I sound mad. I don't feel mad. Nobody is behaving badly. We're all under control, I think. Only Helander seems profoundly affected. He spends most of his time staring into the cardinal's face, touching it.

Later

Helander says the skin feels warm. He asked me to tell him if I agreed. I stripped of a glove and touched the fingers. They certainly feel warm, but that could just be the effect of the sun. Nevertheless, the arm hasn't moved, neither have the eyes. There's no breathing. He stares at us tenderly, blessing us, forgiving us. I'm beginning to resent him. What have I done that he should forgive me? I now agree with those who want to put him back. I suppose we can't. We've been told to sit tight and wait for base to send someone up. It will take a while before they come.

11/7/17

Russell woke me up. I kitted up fast and went out. Helander was kneeling in front of the cardinal and seemed to be mumbling to himself. He refused to move when we tried to get him to stand up. 'He's weeping,' he said. 'He's weeping.'

There did seem to be moisture on the skin. Then, even as we watched, blood began to trickle out of both eyes and run down the cheeks. The cardinal was weeping tears of blood, Gerry!

'Evidently the action of the atmosphere,' said Fedin, when we raised him. 'We might have to refreeze him, I think.'

The cardinal's expression hadn't changed. Helander became impatient and told us to go away. He said he was communicating with the cardinal. Fedin sedated him and got him back to his biv. We heard his voice, even in sleep, mumbling and groaning. Once, he screamed. Fedin pumped some more stuff into him, then. He's quiet now.

Later

We've had word that base is on its way. About time, too, for me. I'm feeling increasingly scared.

'Dusk'

I crawled out of my biv thinking that Helander was crying again or that Fedin was playing his music. The little, pale sun

138

was high in the sky, the big one was setting. There was a reddish glow on the ice. Everything seemed red, in fact. I couldn't see too clearly, but the cardinal was still standing there, a dark silhouette. And the sounds were coming from him. He was singing, Gerry. There was no one else up. I stood in front of the cardinal. His lips were moving. Some sort of chant. His eyes weren't looking at me any longer. They were raised. Someone came to stand beside me. It was Helander. He was a bit woozy, but his face was ecstatic. He began to join in the song. Their singing seemed to fill the sky, the planet, the whole damned universe. The music made me cry, Gerry. I have never heard a more beautiful voice. Helander turned to me once. 'Join in,' he said. 'Join in.' But I couldn't because I didn't know the words. 'It's Latin,' said Helander. It was like a bloody choir. I found myself lifting my head like a dog. There were resonances in my throat. I began to howl. But it wasn't howling. It was chanting, the same as the cardinal. No words. Just music. It was the most exquisite music I have ever heard in my life. I became aware that the others were with me, standing in a semi-circle, and they were singing too. And we were so full of joy, Gerry. We were all weeping. It was incredible. Then the sun had set and the music gradually faded and we stood looking at one another, totally exhausted, grinning like coyotes, feeling complete fools. And the cardinal was looking at us again, with that same sweet tolerance. Helander was kneeling in front of him and mumbling, but we couldn't hear the words. Eventually, after he'd been on the ice for an hour, Fedin decided to sedate him. 'He'll be dead at this rate, if I don't.'

Later

We've just finished putting the cardinal back in the cre-vasse, Gerry. I can still hear that music in my head. I wish there was some way I could play you the recordings we've made, but doubtless you'll hear them in time, around when you get this letter. Base hasn't arrived yet. Helander said he was going to let it be their responsibility. I'm hoping we'll be relieved for those medical tests we were afraid of at first. I want to get away from here. I'm terrified, Gerry. I keep wanting to climb into the crevasse and ask the cardinal to sing for me again. I have never known such absolute release, such total happiness, as when I sang in harmony with him. What do you think it is? Maybe it's all hallucination. Someone will know. Twice I've stood on the edge, peering down. You can't see him from here, of course. And you can't see the bottom. I haven't the courage to descend the lines.

I want to jump. I would jump, I think, if I could get the chance just once more to sing with him. I keep thinking of eternity. For the first time in my life I have a glimmering of what it means.

Oh, Gerry, I hope it isn't an illusion. I hope you'll be able to hear that voice on the tapes and know what I felt when the frozen cardinal sang. I love you Gerry. I want to give you so much. I wish I could give you what I have been given. I wish I could sing for you the way the cardinal sang. There isn't one of us who hasn't been weeping. Fedin keeps trying to be rational. He says we are more exhausted than we know, that the drugs we take have side-effects which couldn't be predicted. We look up into the sky from time to time, waiting for base to reach us. I wish you were here, Gerry. But I can't possibly regret now that I made the decision I made. I love you, Gerry. I love you all.

GARRY KILWORTH

Triptych

The Black Wedding

He was looking out of the window at the fragile day. It seemed too still, too delicate to be real. At any second it might shatter before his eyes into crisp, thin flakes of mirror glass and he would turn from the window to exclaim to Celia, only to find that the day was behind him, hiding at the back of the room, and what he had been studying was a reflection, a looking-glass image of the morning.

A bird flew past as he watched, appearing out of nowhere. A unique spectacle. Where had it learned to do that? Fly? It had to be an omen, but whether good or bad, he was unsure. It would be unwise to mention it to Celia. Her superstition was invariably negative in its bias. War, famine, pestilence. That would be her response. He felt utterly depressed by the whole business.

Guthrie moved from the window to the table where the wedding presents were displayed. An array of trivia. He picked up an object like two knives riveted together. The blades opened and closed when he worked the handles.

'What's this?' he asked.

Celia glanced across and then continued with her make-up. 'It's a pair of secateurs – yes, I'm sure that's what Alec called them. They're for cutting the heads off flowers or something.'

Guthrie held the instrument with its little curved blades gingerly between two fingers. Horror and disgust fought for

141

control of his feelings. A device for murdering flowers? God, that was really ugly. What sort of warped mind would stoop to such an evil invention?

'You're not going to keep them, are you?'

'What? Oh, I see what you mean. No, not permanently. We'll get rid of them after the wedding.'

'Amazing, the way some minds work. Who sent them?'

'One of Alec's aunts.'

Guthrie was impressed. 'Aunts? He has more than one?'

'Two in fact.' She began to clamber into her wedding dress.

'Hmm. Nice to be wealthy. Most people are satisfied with just the one.'

Celia gave him a superior smile.

'You're just envious, Guthrie. No, really, he does have two. One lives in Brighton – the other in Bath.'

'Well, I still think it's decadent. I can't think why you want to marry such a man.'

Celia gave a patient sigh. 'Because he needs a wife. Now help me on with my track suit, or I'll never be ready in time.' She began pulling on the black silk wedding outfit, trying not to crush the folds. Reluctantly, he went to give her assistance. He really couldn't forgive her for ruining his Thursday. Why did she have to marry *every* man she met? That, in itself, seemed decadent.

He made sure his hand did not touch her skin and she looked at him pointedly, her voice taking on a prim tone.

'I can't think why you always have to be so obscene, Guthrie. It's only *me*, after all.'

'Just put it down to my low upbringing,' he said, angrily. Hell, their relationship was uncomplicated enough without all this sort of thing.

'Why can't we just have a quiet evening indoors,' he grumbled.

She was tempted. He could tell by her silence. Then just as he thought he had won, the clock lurched heavily and she shook her head.

142

'No. I promised him. This is the only Thursday he has free for a month. I don't want to disappoint him.'

Guthrie bit his lip. Well, it had been worth a try. She might just have fallen for the idea. He strolled over to the wedding presents again, scanning them in a desultory fashion. Suddenly, something caught his interest.

'Who sent the ash-tray?'

'No idea. Why?'

'Why? Because it's going to be bloody useful. Don't forget we're going to Cyprus for our holidays.'

Celia paused in the act of pulling on her running shoes.

'I must admit it had slipped my mind. How thoughtful. It can't be someone who knows us very well.'

'We'll work it out later. I do hope it is a stranger.' He couldn't keep the acid out of his tone, though he could have bitten his tongue off afterwards.

'It's bound to be. God, don't you trust me after all this time? How long have we been together?'

Guthrie decided it was time for them to thrash it out.

'Yes, only . . .'

'Only *what*?'

'Only I haven't seen you with anyone I don't know lately, that's all.' There, it was said.

She rounded on him, her face suffused with anger.

'Look, just because you're too idle to follow me when I go out in the evenings, doesn't mean I'm being faithful. Sometimes I wonder about you, Guthrie. Sometimes I wonder if you're paranoid at all.'

He was incensed by this accusation.

'Of course I'm paranoid. What on earth do you take me for? An insensitive brute? Why do you torture me like this? You want to get me to stay with you, don't you?'

They stood there, glaring at one another for a long while. He knew he was being unfair. She wanted his suicide as much as he did himself, but they both had a touch of the sadist in them. Neither would give in.

Celia turned away from him.

'Guthrie, I'm sorry. I suppose I'm just bored that's all. It is my wedding day, after all.'

He was still a little stiff and formal. He was damned if he was going to please her.

'No, no, it's my fault,' he said, claiming the victory. He consulted his watch. 'Good Lord. It's five past already. You'd better start running – they'll all be at the church.'

She took her mark by the door.

'Stopwatch?' She reminded him.

'Yep. Ready. Ste-ady. *Go!*'

And she was off, out of the room, the house, and running up the hill towards the little church. A few minutes later he heard the cheer and he knew she had broken the tape. Spitefully, he let the watch run on for a few more seconds. He had still not completely forgiven her for being alive this morning.

Then he himself made his way slowly towards the church, knowing they could not start without him. Impatience makes the heart grow fonder, he thought.   *How trite*. At the edge of the highway a badger was sleeping. The event was causing a traffic jam with a two mile tailback, as motorists leaned out of their windows to look. Some people have all the luck, thought Guthrie bitterly. Only it wasn't people. It was an animal. Still, he was jealous.

At the gate to the church he paused. A shudder went through him. One more night. Perhaps one more night. Oh, please . . .

Inside the church the organ was in full flood. Strangers smiled at him as he walked to the front pew and took his place. Twenty minutes. It wasn't a record, but it was a respectable delay. He wasn't out to impress, he told himself. A quiet, simple life – that's all he wanted. Just then, right on cue, two penguins entered the church and began to waddle down the aisle. Perfect. He hadn't guessed. New twists, new turns. That was the way things were meant to be.

The vicar nodded at the pair, before calling, 'Is the bride present?' His voice was muffled from inside his suit of armour.

'Here,' shouted Celia, from the back row of pews.

'And the groom?'

'Yes. Er, here.'

This must be Alec, standing right next to him. On his left. On his left? Guthrie broke out into a cold sweat. This wasn't right. Both men looked at each other and knew instantly. Hastily, they changed places before the horror built up to a pitch in one of them and the screaming started. Nameless terror. Things not being *right*, when right was not known, only *felt*. They gave each other a nervous smile. The panic began subsiding. It seemed okay now. They both avoided physical contact of any kind, though Guthrie was itching to hold somebody's hand, just for a shred of comfort.

Finally the vicar said, 'Do you, penguin female, take the other to be your lawfully wedded husband?'

'I do,' cried Celia from the back of the church.

The process was repeated with the other penguin and Alec answered, 'I do.'

Then, said the vicar, smiling, 'I pronounce you – man and wife.'

Someone moved forward and put a paper cup on each of the hallowed penguin's heads.

'It's supposed to hypnotise them,' the person whispered to Guthrie.

'Good.'

It seemed good. It *was* good. He turned to Alec, who hadn't disappeared.

'Congratulations old man.'

Alec blushed, shyly. 'Thanks.'

Then the other man had to leave. The penguins had been hired for the event from the local zoo. But Guthrie was pleased he had made the gesture. It had made Alec light-headed enough to tear off his watch and throw it in the font on his way out.

Guthrie was feeling aroused when he raced Celia back to the house, but nothing could spoil the fact that the wedding had gone well. They both undressed and lay between the sheets, waiting. Nothing happened of course.

'Why don't you go and do it, Guthrie. I won't mind.'

She was sweet, but he just couldn't. It wasn't fair of her to ask him to. She should be the one. What a pity it was that they loved each other so much. Other couples they knew had gone long ago. *You first. No, after you.*

'We could do it together,' he suggested.

But that wasn't the answer. One of them would be bound to go first, if only by a split second. They just had to wait, and hope. There would have been five murders already in the city. The night was well advanced. Surely there was a possibility, however remote, that their turn would come soon?

By two o'clock he was as wide awake as ever. Celia was snoring loudly, but he knew she was faking it. There was only one way they would ever get any sleep and that was permanent: the big one. He looked forward to that.

In the meantime, dawn was a thousand years away.

Murderers Walk

Place

There is a city-state, lying between two large countries, where killers take refuge from the law, but not from justice. Justice finds its own way.

A long street, not much wider than an alley, cuts through the middle of the city. The street is called Murderers Walk and over its cobbles, slick even on dry days, tread the malefactors who have run to its shadows to escape the rope.

The houses are old and overhang the walk, keeping it permanently in the shade. Along its cobbles it is not unusual to see a man or woman being dragged, or driven, or forcibly carried. Sometimes they are screaming; sometimes they are stiff with fear.

146

Rope

There are many reminders of rope in Murderers Walk. The limbs of those lounging in apathy against crumbling windowsills are knotted and sinuous; the washing over the street is crowded onto short lines and consequently hangs narrow and long; the shadows that ripple in the poorly-fashioned windows tend to be thin and twisted due to the warping of the glass. A walk along the street on any day will bring you into contact with men and women who know death first-hand: they have dealt with it directly; they stand on the brink of death themselves. You see them waiting in shop doorways, wearing hollows in the wood with restless shoulders. No one knows what or who they are waiting for – not even those who wait. There is no expectancy in the air.

The Game

They play a game in the inns along Murderers Walk, which newcomers shun when they first arrive. Newcomers are detached and need nothing but themselves. They are either elated or relieved at having escaped the law in their own countries, and for a time this is sufficient to sustain them. The game is played in groups of nine, called 'scaffolds'.

The Rules

Each player draws cards from the pack containing two jokers, until none remain. The players look at their hands and the one holding the ace of spades must commit suicide, by hanging, twenty-four hours later, on the stroke of 8 a.m. It is a simple game, with simple rules, but the winning players recharge those feelings of elation and relief that they felt on first arriving in Murderers Walk. They have beaten death yet again.

The Victim

The players keep all their cards secret until the time arrives to take account. They gather at the inn where the game took place. One of the players will be missing and he or she will hold the ace of spades. The other players then go to the victim's rooms to witness the self-inflicted execution. Victims who are not ready at the appointed time are hunted down by the scaffold and the deed is done for them.

Alternative

There is an alternative to suicide. The victims can leave the city-state and the sanctuary of Murderers Walk to take their chances with the law on the outside. Not many do. It is not fear of death that is responsible but terror of dying in the hands of strangers: a ritual death conceived by a morality since rejected. It is a repulsion stronger than the fear of suicide.

Reprieve

There is however another possibility of escaping death. If a player, other than the victim, holds both jokers – those wild cards of Fortune – in one hand, these may be displayed at the last moment before the hanging. The game is then declared void and the victim is reprieved.

Murderers

Only confessed murderers are admitted to a scaffold. Membership is permanent and quarterly games mandatory for all members. As a new murderer in the walk, you survey the faces of the established population with scorn. 'I shall never become like them,' you tell yourself, as you stroll down the street, studying the apathy, the suppressed desperation. Yet, gradually, over the course of time your contempt dissolves into that same desperation. Inside you, the ghost of your victim begins its slow, insidious possession of your soul. You may relive, time and time again, those moments when you killed, especially if your victim was a former loved one. If you are without guilt, there is the bitterness of discovery and consequent flight. Eventually you sink into the same morass as your fellow malefactors and are drawn into the game out of despair.

Play

You begin the walk along the narrow street to your first game. Eventually you arrive at the inn where you are to play for your life. The faces of the other players register vague anticipation. The cards are dealt. The faces turn to stone.

You play the game perhaps once a quarter at first – then more frequently as the drug takes holds. As one of the eight winners, you feel the exhilaration of defeating the spectre of death. The group changes as new members are taken on in place of those who have drawn the death card. The more you win, the more you come to believe in a charmed existence, a superior destiny fashioned partly from luck and partly from the essential ingredient of a special *self*. You are not like the others. You move on a higher plane, god-like in your ability to thwart the noose.

Time

But eventually there comes a time when you draw the death card. At first the ace fails to register. It is tucked partly behind an innocent card. Then, suddenly, you see it. Inside you a silent scream begins. All the moisture leaves your mouth and your brain ferments with terror. You are sure all the other members know already, for how can such inner turmoil not show on your face? You put your own cards in your pocket, managing a smile, and call for a round of drinks. Then you slip away, after the first sip of ale, which tastes like vinegar, out into the night air. You begin running. You run north along the street, pausing only to puke. You run to the edge of the city-state, where the border guards of the neighbouring country stand ready. You turn and run in the opposite direction, to find them waiting there too. Then east. Then west. Finally, you trudge back to your lodgings in order to think, to formulate plans.

Twenty-four hours

There is only one thing worse than not knowing when you are going to die - that is, *knowing*. You sit on the edge of your bed and stare around your room. You envy the cockroach that moves across the floor: you envy its lack of imagination. One minute your hands are dry, the next, damp. The weight of guilt has gone. You are about to atone. You try to tell yourself that what you feel is remorse, but you know that it is only regret for the deed that cannot be undone, the act that placed you in this uncompromising position. Your head turns over a thousand thoughts, but none of them lead to escape. Suddenly you understand why this sanctuary exists. It is a prison as secure as any with high walls and guards. In Murderers Walk, the prisoners try each other, and sentence each other to death.

Death

You wonder what the feel of the rope will be like against your neck. You touch your throat with your fingers. Will the spine break or will you expire slowly? Perhaps your lungs will burst? You try to imagine the pallor of your distended face: purple perhaps? Your eyes, huge balls easing out of their sockets? Your tongue hanging long between blue lips? You weep. Your mind goes numb. Your eyes are dry. Your head is full of a thousand active thoughts, each one a nightmare.

Void game

There is of course the possibility of a void game. It is not so unusual. But the closer the time comes, the surer you are that you will not be granted a reprieve. You have taken life and deserve no mercy. The hours pass quickly, and slowly; time races and stands still, depending on whether it is the pain of

150

life, or death, that occupies you. One thing you are sure of: you cannot hope.

Absence

It is three minutes to the appointed hour. The other players will gather together with their cards. They will know, of course, by your absence, that you are the victim. They will be feeling high, victorious, excited. They will be talking in quick voices. Their eyes will be bright.

Eight a.m.

You drag the chair beneath the beam as the others arrive. You hear their feet on the wooden stairs. These are sounds to treasure: every creak, every hollow footfall. They open the door and enter. Their faces are as ashen as yours had been on witnessing other deaths. The elation has been put aside for the moment. But it has to be done, for without a death there is no game, and without the game there is no life. This is as much an ordeal for them as it is for you – only the standpoint is different.

One of them hands you the rope. You stand on the chair hoping your legs will support you for just a few moments longer. You tie the rope to the beam. Your hands are unsteady. *Then – suddenly – you are ready to die.* In that moment all the terror has gone. You may still tremble, or wince, or blanch, but you are *ready*. It is not the moment of death that is so terrible, it is the preparation leading up to that moment. You are ready. You are ready. Just a moment longer . . .

End

One of the party steps forward and waves two jokers in your face. 'Void game,' he cries. 'You live to play again.' They pull you from the chair and jostle you towards the door, down the stairs and out into the street. Inside you the fear erupts again, and that precious moment, the moment when you were ready to die, has gone. They have stolen your death from you and you know you cannot retrieve that state of mind again, without reliving another twenty-four hours of terror.

That is when you dig your heels into the unyielding cobbles and grip a passing windowsill with fingers that would squeeze a rock to powder. That is when your mind flies open like a sprung trapdoor. That is when they drag you along the street, kicking and screaming, like a man being led to his execution.

Hogfoot Right and Bird-hands

There lived, high above the empty streets in a tall building, an old woman whose pet cat had recently died. In those days cats were rare and the old woman had not the means to purchase another. So she called for the machine whose duty it was to look after the welfare of lost and lonely people.

The welfare machine came to her apartment in the middle of the night, and when she explained her plight it suggested that the old woman replace her cat with a pet fashioned from a part of her body. It said it could remove and modify one of her feet to resemble a piglet, and the old woman agreed to this scheme. Since she spent all her time in the mobile bed-chair that saw to all her needs, she did not require the use of her feet, nor any other part of her body for that matter, apart from her brain, to which the bed-chair and other appliances were connected. The old woman was not sick, unless apathy and idleness be looked upon as an illness, but she had no desire to take part in any physical activity of any sort. She merely went from one grey day to the next, sleeping, eating, and watching a device called wallscreen, on which she could witness the lives of others, long since dead, over and over again.

Thus, her right foot was removed and roughly shaped and given a life of its own. This appendage she called Hogfoot Right, and it gave her much pleasure to see the creature scuttling around the floor and nosing in the corners of the rooms the way such creations did. However, Hogfoot Right was not one of those pets that liked to be stroked and fussed over, the way the old woman's cat had been when it was alive, and eventually she grew tired of its company, wanting something more. Watching the creature grub around the carpet was interesting enough at first, but when she had seen it done once or twice the novelty began to pall. So she called her welfare machine again and had her other foot removed. This one she called Basil, in the hope that giving it a proper name would make it more affectionate towards its mistress.

Basil turned out to be such a sweet creature. He would sit on the old woman's lap and let her stroke him for hours, his little hog nose twitching in ecstasy as she ran her hands over his dozing form.

Hogfoot Right, however, was moody and irritable and would skulk around in the darker corners of the house and cower away from the old woman when she approached him. He did not actually hiss or spit at her, but his bad temper was evident in the expression on his blunted face and in the sour line of his crudely-fashioned mouth.

However, Hogfoot Right was Basil's good companion and in that respect the old woman had no complaint. He served his brother well, snuggling up with him at night and making sure he did not get too excited when something happened to amuse him. Sometimes even Hogfoot Right would join in with his brother's antics, and the two of them would butt each other's rumps and roll around the carpet like six-month-old piglets. Then suddenly, Hogfoot Right would become resentful of something and would sidle away to frequent the edges of the room, glowering at both his brother and the old woman if they tried to entice him to play again. The old woman despaired of this temperamental pet and eventually gave up on the beast.

It was because of her great success with Basil that she

decided to increase her menagerie. The welfare machine called one day to see how she was faring and she asked for more surgery. She told it she wanted to lose her hands and her ears. Her bed-chair responded to brain impulses, and she said she could not see what use both these sets of her appendages were to her any more.

The welfare machine was all in favour of the idea. The ears were fused together to make a moth, and the hands became a beautiful pale bird-like creature that soared gracefully around the room and was really the most delicate, delightful pet the old woman had ever set eyes on. She loved it from the first moment she saw it. It would perch on the back of the bed-chair and flutter its fingerfeathers with more dignity than a fantailed dove, and though it remained aloof from the other creatures in the room it would often sit and watch their games from a suitable place above their heads.

Moth-ears was a bit of a disappointment. She fluttered here and there occasionally and was best seen floating past the window with the light shining through her transluscent form, but mostly she hung from the old woman's collar with her wings closed. It was almost as if she were trying to get back to her original positions on the old woman's head. She was nervous and shy and tended to start at sudden, loud noises and was really quite useless as a pet. Yet the old woman was happy to keep her, seeing in her an aspect of her own personality.

Bird-hands liked to perch on the light fittings or sit on the windowsill with folded wings, looking out at the sky. She would watch the house martins – the way they swooped before alighting on the outer sill, and she would copy their flight patterns. Since the old woman could not fondle her pets any more, Bird-hands would stroke her instead, running her fingerwings along the old woman's shoulders and down her neck. At night she nestled in her warm lap while the others slept. The old woman loved her dearly.

Bird-hands seemed the most contented of the group of creatures. There was a musical instrument in the apartment which could be played manually if required, and this the

154

creature would do, running her fingerwings over the keys and producing the most delightful melodies. Occasionally she would switch the instrument to automatic and fly to the rhythm of the tune, adding that extra dimension to the unfolding of the notes with her graceful motion.

The group prospered. Even when Snake-arm came along the harmony remained, though at times the sinuous movements alarmed the old woman when she caught sight of it suddenly out of the corner of her eye.

Thus, they all lived together in a harmonious group, apart from the unsociable Hogfoot Right. The old woman could not thank the welfare machine enough, pouring praises on its mechanical parts whenever it came to see how she was getting along. Sometimes the machine would sit with Bird-hands and squeak at it in its high-pitched language, always ending in a rattling laugh. Once, it brought a pair of satin gloves, white, with lace around the cuffs, which Bird-hands wore to fly around the room while the old woman exclaimed upon the beauty of the creature.

Another time, the welfare machine brought an old leather boot, and forced Hogfoot Right to wear it, making the foot clump around the room while the old woman sniggered at such a humorous sight. The welfare machine carefully watched her heartbeat monitor at times like these, intently observant for any variation in its pace and strength.

It was a very happy time for the old woman.

Until, one night, it all went wrong.

A terrible noise woke the old woman. It was the sound of crashing furniture and struggling bodies. A glass ornament smashed against a wall, spraying her legs with fragments. There was a life-and-death struggle going on somewhere in the room. A standard lamp fell across a table and shattered the ceramic stem. The old woman was too frightened even to turn on the light. She was sure that an android had entered her apartment: a rogue machine whose brain had suffered a malfunction and was on the rampage. All she could do was

155

quietly guide her bed-chair to the corner of the room and stay there until the ruckus was over.

The fighting, she was sure, was between her pets and the intruder, and since there was little she could do she had to await the outcome without interfering.

Finally, after a long while, there was silence, and she ordered the light switch on. The scene that met her eyes was horrific.

In the centre of the room were Bird-hands and Hogfoot Right, obviously squaring up to one another. Around them, bleeding, broken and bruised, were the other pets. Moth-ears had been torn and crushed and was obviously dead. Snake-arm had been pierced by a long ceramic splinter which protruded from its head. It, too, was deathly still. Basil was black with bruises, having been beaten, fatally it seemed.

The old woman had not the slightest doubt that Hogfoot Right had gone berserk. There was no sign of any android intruder, and Hogfoot Right looked as though he were now about to attack Bird-hands.

The two combatants fell upon one another. There was a frenzied scrambling and clawing. The old woman began yelling like crazy for Bird-hands, telling her to dig her claws in, while the seemingly mad hog was butting her round and round the walls with its heel-hard head.

It was a vicious battle.

Furniture was scattered this way and that, and twice the old woman had to move her bed-chair to get out of their path as they rolled across the floor, locked in a tight ball. Once, she thought Hogfoot had had enough, as he backed away into a corner, but again he went forward, just when Bird-hands was trying to recover.

Finally, Bird-hands picked him up by the hindquarters and flung him at the exposed end of the standard lamp. It was bristling with live contacts. With a bouncing arc of his body he twisted in agony as the shock went through him. He lay broken and still, across the sputtering wires.

Bird-hands fluttered to the middle of the room.

'Well done,' cried the old woman. 'Well fought.'

156

Bird-hands just sat there, her thumb-head turned towards the window, through which the dawn was just beginning to emerge. Then suddenly the creature launched herself into the air and began throwing her body at the glass panes in a seemingly desperate attempt to smash her way through, like a wild bird that is trapped in a closed room.

Then the old woman understood. It had not been Hogfoot Right, but Bird-hands. She had seen the martins cutting through the blue sky outside and she wanted to be free too. She wanted to be out amongst those of her own kind. Maybe she had run amok amongst the others because they refused or were unable to understand her desire for escape? Perhaps she had tried to get them to open the window – something only the old woman could do with a brain command – only to find they could not help her? Anyway, she had killed them all. Even little Moth-ears. And Hogfoot Right, the bad-tempered one, had given her the toughest opposition of all.

Poor Hogfoot, misjudged right to the end.

Now Bird-hands sat on the ledge, her nails dripping with blood. She seemed to be waiting for the old woman to open the window, which could only be done by direct order. There came, in the silence, the sound of real birds chirruping outside, and Bird-hands displayed restlessness. The old woman, still in a state of shock, refused to respond.

Bird-hands carefully wiped the gore from her fingerwings on one of the curtains. By this time the old woman had recovered a little but she had much of the stubbornness of her erstwhile right foot and she made it obvious that she was not going to comply.

Finally, Bird-hands flew from the ledge and settled on the old woman's neck. The creature began to stroke the withered throat sensuously, hoping perhaps to persuade her mistress to do what she wished. The woman sat rigidly still, grim-faced. Gradually the stroking became firmer. At the last, the fingerwings tightened and squeezed, slowly but effectively. There were a few minutes during which the old woman convulsed. Then the body went slack.

Bird-hands, after a long while, released her grip and fluttered down to the floor. She crabbed her way amongst the dead creatures, inspecting them for signs of life. Then she came to Hogfoot Right, lying across the electrified strands of the light socket. Bird-hands observed her victim with seeming dispassion. She inched forward, close to the hog's head, looking down.

Suddenly there was a jerk from Hogfoot Right, as his head flashed out and his jaws clamped on a little finger. A brilliant shower of blue-white sparks rained around the pair, and then the stillness in the room was complete.

Later, the welfare machine came to call and surveyed the scene with mechanical surprise. It made a careful note of all the damage and recorded a verdict of suicide. Just as it was about to leave, it sensed some vibrations coming from somewhere in the room. One of the creatures had stirred. Suddenly something snapped at its metal leg and then went careering through the open doorway and along the corridor . . .

(For Lisa)

R.M. LAMMING

Sanctity

'You sure this won't involve us with the . . .?'

Another of his irritating habits, he paused before any reference to authority. He went through a sort of mental cowering, as if law-enforcers were made of finer stuff than other men.

My luck! thought Lewis, disgusted to see the politeness and fright at war in Hoskin's face: an ass in the family! How his sister could go with such a man . . . He began to give elaborate reassurance, something he did only when he felt contempt.

'Don't worry,' he said. 'It's quite safe. No one bothers any more. When there were still things to steal – and before there were Shelters – they had patrols then. But not any more. There's no need. The only dangers now are rotten floors, old beams.'

Hoskin was not comforted. Soon his voice rose again, and although it was diffident, there was a sharpness to it, an edge of anxiety.

'It's just that, as the Veto was never rescinded . . .'

'They simply never got round to it.'

'And you . . .' a cautious glance, 'visit these places frequently?'

'Why not?'

There was no answer to that: for a time, the two men walked in silence, Lewis with his fists clenched. 'Frequently' – a clerical, bookish word. Hoskin did not even speak like a human being. Oh, he was terrible, almost stomach-turningly

159

terrible, this fool who thought he was good enough for Cath. On his lapel glinted a Social Rectitude badge, a tin moon pretending at moonlight, while as he walked, he seemed to be dangled from somewhere overhead – a puppet made of soft stuff, without a spine, stirring the air with involuntary movements of his loose hanging hands, and splaying out his feet. Lewis kept at a distance to avoid any accidental contact, and in the silence his contempt blossomed. It was easy to see that Hoskin was a sedentary man: the fool really seemed not to know how to walk. The use of his limbs was novel to him; and his expression clearly said that he was not enjoying the experience. Rather, it was an ordeal, to be survived without loss of face if possible, but at all costs to be survived.

Lewis had chosen a route through the narrower streets where, by main road standards, the lighting was dim, but a quaintly bright moon shone, silvering Hoskin's hair, and, presumably, his own. They met no one, although at the second junction, far down the street they were about to take, they saw a figure in State Employ overalls, walking away from them.

'Look,' began Hoskin, coming to a halt, 'I don't think we
. . .'

'Scared?' Lewis laughed. 'There's no need. What would Cath say?'

If I went back without you. The implication hovered between them with all the power of a threat, and Lewis was glad of that. Oh, he'd take the ass back all right, but still, it was a pleasant thought. Cath saved from her – what was it? a temporary perversion? a bid to throw herself away? – in any case, from her mistake. No more Hoskin at the apartment, planting wet kisses on her neck, kisses that left shining rings of saliva.

'It simply isn't a question of being scared . . .' A coward, Hoskin reacted at once to the taunt, giving himself away. Stupid. As he spoke, his head jerked, small sharp stabs of indignation. 'It's just that, if there did happen to be a patrol . . . I have my position to consider. One can't be too careful
. . .'

160

His 'position'. Sweet life. A data clerk. A miserable clerk in a soap factory. Hoskin's grandiose words fell limply to the pavement, and perhaps embarrassed by them himself, he added, '. . . anything on my record, you know, just as your sister and I . . .'

This fool and Cath. Lewis tried not to imagine it, could not keep from imagining it, and he stepped up the pace so that he'd have the satisfaction of Hoskin's puffing and scuffling, possibly even an ignominious request to slow down . . .

But somehow the other man kept up, along the deserted street (whoever else was out, he was no longer in sight), past the high walls of Approved Residences, their windows glowing with fashionably dark purple and mauve blinds, past a school, its mural an impersonal chequerboard of yellow and black, and so to the next corner.

Here Lewis slowed down. He disliked rushing the final approach. And Hoskin managed to pant out, 'Does your sister know about these . . . escapades?'

'Ah.' Lewis smiled. He knew she would not have approved. But then, she enjoyed a brother of whom she could not approve. No support for the clerk there. And this attempt by Hoskin to enlist Cath's aid made him the more contemptible.

'An *escapade*, you call it? Don't you have any sense of occasion? We're on a Voyage Back – our mysterious past, our Dark Ages – aren't you curious? Haven't you ever wondered what it *was* we Vetoed?'

No, said the silence eloquently, no.

'There aren't so many of these places left,' went on Lewis, rubbing it in. 'I really thought you'd be interested. Cath says you're a bit of a poet.'

'Only sometimes . . .'

Hoskin was not joking. He said it as he might have said that he remembered his dreams, or liked beer with his meat. Only sometimes.

Lewis spat into the gutter. Then he swung out into the road for a better view of the spire that rose over the roofs, a grey elongated spindle turned white along one edge by the

161

moon. If Hoskin was anything like the others, he would not have seen the spire yet: he had probably never seen one.

'There it is!'

'What?'

The clerk jumped, not his whole body, but his flesh inside his skin, a peculiar nervous jolt that was communicable to the air, and so to Lewis who detected it with pleasure.

'There it is!' he repeated, 'the Chur -'

'Vetoed Edifice . . .' gasped Hoskin, staring, 'where?'

And then, his eyes, trained to ignore these things, admitted what they saw; and very faintly he said, '. . . yes . . .'

They walked on slowly, the closer they came to the building, the more slowly, while Hoskin's fear mounted. His eyes swivelled; his face grew yellowish.

'If a patrol comes, just as we're breaking in . . .'

'I told you. There aren't any.'

At any moment, Lewis saw, the fool might panic. But not too soon, he hoped, not before they were inside. For the night-time walk through the streets, so far outside the Recommended Hours, and the appearance of the spire dominating (if one cared to notice) the silhouettes of the sky-line – these were such a small part of the whole thing.

They came opposite the building and crossed to it. As they did so, the spindle on the roof seemed to stretch even higher, then squat suddenly, becoming a fraction of its former height – an effect which Lewis had seen often enough, but it never failed to impress him. Why, he could not have said.

There were stone steps leading to where the main doors had been, and where now there was bricked wall.

'There'll be no way in . . .'

'There is,' said Lewis, 'there always is.'

Because, when the Authorities had bricked up the doors, they had left the windows, and by the time the Public had sanctioned a shattering of those, along with other defacements, there were no longer the funds for such expensive barricades, so the windows had been merely boarded up, and the boards rotted. Simple. Hoskin, like most, would never have thought about that, never have asked himself how the homeless had got in to the Vetoed places before there were Shelters built for them.

At the foot of the steps, they stood still.

'It's the only one for miles,' said Lewis.

Hoskin shuddered – a real shudder this time, that made him look round guiltily, as if his movement must have been the work of someone else; but there was no one in the street except themselves.

He whined, 'You should be sent for treatment, Lewis . . . It's sheer madness . . .'

Lewis took hold of his arm.

'Come on. We can get in round the side.' – and he led his shrinking companion along a concrete alley that stank of damp walls never touched by the sun.

Near the back of the building, they came to a small boarded window at ground level. Hoskin watched, his face a blend of horror and disbelief, while Lewis skilfully worked the board loose, and pushed aside the rusty wiring behind it. The glass had been smashed in, of course, generations before.

'In we go!'

Crouched beside his handiwork, Lewis spoke in a whisper. It came naturally to do that: he was excited. Always, just before entering these places, he was gripped by excitement. He smiled fiercely at Hoskin, who had not turned tail and run – they hardly ever did – but stood pressed up against the far wall of the alley, shaking his head from side to side.

'No.'

'Yes.'

Then Lewis sprang, fastened on the clerk, and bundled him towards the window. Hoskin did not resist. Maybe some vestigial concern for his dignity prevented him. The only protest he made was a kind of whimper when, as he pushed his legs through the hole, he felt his trousers catch on the wiring. Then he had disappeared, into the darkness.

Lewis followed quickly, without a word, pulling the board back into place behind him. The result was a temporary blindness filled with the stench of mould. He could not see

163

Hoskin, but he could hear him panting somewhere close to his right shoulder.

The clerk was so terrified that he retreated into politeness, and when he spoke, it was in a mild, almost conversational tone: 'Do you think there might be rats?'

'Plenty.'

Not many. The Shelters offered richer pickings. But why enlighten the idiot?

Lewis switched on his torch, knowing that this sudden splash of light would be a shock to the other man. He could sense the stutter in Hoskin's heart: the clerk took a step back, his hands fluttering, his mouth open.

'What's the matter?' asked Lewis softly.

The torch beam travelled across the walls: they were brown-stained and sweating, pocked with dark recesses where cupboards had been. All the wood - shelves and doors – had been stripped out. A wire hung from the ceiling.

'Is this it?' asked Hoskin, after what he must have hoped was long enough. 'Is this all?'

'No.'

To hope that a building the size of this one could be contained in a space no bigger than a dressing room . . . For a moment Lewis forgot that Hoskin, like the others, would never have taken a hard look at the dimensions of such a building, and he wondered if the man was going mad. But then he remembered. People had no idea.

'Come on.' He shone the torch towards a black tunnel in the wall. 'I'll show you.'

Out, along a passage, through a second doorway, round an evil-smelling, spongey curtain, and they stood in the vast interior. Unashamedly, Hoskin was now holding on tightly to Lewis's sleeve – not to any part of his flesh, only to his sleeve. And his eyes were fixed on the torch Lewis held. The light thinned as it fell across the floor.

There was no furniture, but down the centre of the floor ran a line of white mosaic paving, like a vein, on either side of which there might once have been a seating arrangement of some sort. Now there was only concrete - and litter: heaps of

164

mouldering cloth, paper and food containers from those years when the homeless had defied the laws by camping here.

And between the white paving and the walls, presumably where the chairs had ended, there rose lines of pillars, marking side-walks. Huge pillars, As the torchlight shone across them, they surged out of the gloom so dramatically that Hoskin suppressed a cry.

'A rat,' said Lewis. 'Did you hear it?'

Along the far wall moved the torchlight, up to the blind socket of a window, then down again and along to the next window, a white taper of light feeling its way across irregular shapes that adhered to the wall like scabs.

Hoskin's hand remained tight on his sleeve.

'Like it?'

'It's . . . it's empty!' Hoskin whispered.

'What did you expect? Treasures? Anyway, it's not empty. What you mean is, you don't see anything. Look again.'

'I can't see . . .'

'Let yourself.'

And in a few seconds, Lewis knew by Hoskin's wide-eyed silence that he had seen.

'They're memorial tablets.' Obligingly, Lewis played the torch over the broken edge of one, and across the deep scorings made in its surface. 'If you look closely,' he said, 'you can still make out the odd word. Windows erected in memory of so and so, and to the glory of . . .'

'Don't!'

In the shadows, Lewis smirked. He had not intended to say the word. In fact, he did not know the word. But it gave him a feeling close to pride to think that Hoskin had feared he might know it and would even dare to say it.

He stared at the tablets. Grey plaques of marble riveted to the wall. All defaced. Stone on stone. Simple. And yet here was Hoskin, shaking – Lewis could feel how the clerk shook through the hand that gripped his sleeve.

'I don't see them,' said Hoskin. 'I don't.'

'In that case, if you can't see anyway . . .' Lewis shrugged, 'you won't mind if I-' He switched off the torch.

Side by side they stood, listening. Something – possibly this really was a rat – was scrabbling through the litter behind one of the pillars. Otherwise it was so quiet that with a small effort of the imagination it was possible to pretend the silence might be meaningful – although the meaning was lost.

'What do you think,' said Lewis suddenly, 'do you think they sang, or maybe chanted?'

He had often wondered. What had it sounded like, worship? What was it? As it had been a collective activity, he thought there might have been sound, and for reasons he could not understand any more than he knew where he'd heard such Vetoed words as 'church', 'spire' and 'worship', he felt this activity might have had to do with music. Very sober and grand, he imagined, or else a kind of communal bleating, he could not decide which. Sometimes when Cath played her guitar, he wondered if that was not closer.

'Light . . .' begged Hoskin, '*please!*'

'We don't need it. Stop panicking. There are gaps in the ceiling. You'll get used to it in a minute.'

Lewis himself could already see. He was pleased and fascinated by Hoskin's tortured face, his cheeks drawn, his lips quivering.

'What's the matter with you? I told you, there's no patrol.'

Not the patrol. It was not the thought of patrols that frightened Hoskin now. Lewis could tell the difference: he could read those signs that showed a fear had changed from the explicable into – something else, and he let out a barely audible sigh. He bathed in the other man's fear. Such strangely redirected fear. It didn't always happen, but it was what he waited for, even when the other man was not this particular fool who thought he had a right to Cath. Being unafraid himself Lewis enjoyed his sense of advantage. But that was only part of it, and regardless of the fact that he despised Hoskin, tonight it was just the same: his advantage was there, yes, only with it came a contradiction: bewilderment.

What was it people felt? What, beyond the thought of

166

patrols, made the men he brought here sweat and shiver? It was extraordinary to watch, their panic. It provoked in him a curiosity that was almost physical pain, strangely seductive, and in the last analysis it was this which drew him back with another man and another, over and over again.

Hoskin began to pluck at the sleeve he held, his breath coming in short snatches.

'Why?' he whispered. 'Why did you bring me here?' He thrust his neck forward; he was perspiring. 'Aren't you afraid too? You need treatment . . .'

'Come on. I'll show you the rest of it.'

'No, no.'

All the same, Hoskin followed, along the white flooring with the pillars rising blue and massive on either side. Shadows collected around these giants, as if organised and watchful. Then there were two long rifts in the ceiling, where slates and timbers had been wrenched out, presumably for some patching up job in the district, and through these gaps came moonlight, that gave the unpatterned mosaic an icy luminescence and made the boarded windows look matt black against the walls.

As they went, for some reason Hoskin gave up his hold on Lewis, and fell in behind him, shuffling along close to his heels, as if to walk anywhere but on the mosaic would be to perish.

'There won't be any . . . Vetoed Art?' he called. 'Will there?'

'See for yourself.'

Up three low, widely spaced steps, past where a partition or half-screen must once have stood – stumps of it still jutted out of the concrete – and along to several more broad steps, Lewis led the way. He had given a lot of thought to these steps: he saw in them the idea of progression through stages of a ceremony – or even through stages of understanding? But a progression towards what? That was it. All it amounted to, when you summed it up, was stone, and damp, and darkness. Nothing to make the voice crack or the body tremble, the way he'd seen in some of these others – not in all but in most, and definitely in Hoskin . . . Where was that fool?

Lewis turned back to find that the clerk had stopped, rigid, in front of the first steps, and was gaping stupidly at a piece of rubble near his foot.

'It's only a bird's head,' said Lewis, 'something like an eagle. Come and look at this.'

He had reached the most intriguing object, and, in any case, he could go no further: behind it there was only blank wall.

Hoskin raised his eyes.

'I don't see anything.'

'Yes you do. Come and look. What's the matter with you?' *What's the matter with you?* Always the same question.

Lewis stared. For a moment, Hoskin, the gangling splay-footed puppet, acquired a feline sharpness; he twisted his head this way and that, now craning his neck at the ceiling, now darting a look back across his shoulder down the building's long, central vein. He was tensed, ready to run. It was as though he expected to see something grow out of the place, just because he stood in it.

'It's . . . it's the Veto,' said Hoskin lamely. 'I can feel it.' And he rubbed at his Social Rectitude badge for comfort.

Lewis spat on to the concrete. He had hoped . . . Well, trust a fool to say nothing worth hearing. He reached forward and rubbed the top of the thing that stood before him.

'It could be a container,' he said, 'or else a platform. Or a kind of desk . . .'

'No, no. They wouldn't have left anything like that . . . I can't see anything,' protested Hoskin, staring straight at it.

'My guess is, they forgot to take it away.'

Smooth black marble, cold beneath Lewis's hand.

Hoskin came up the first steps, took a couple more paces forward, then stopped again just a few feet from the second flight of steps, a narrow figure with an astonishingly narrow and anguished face that appeared to flicker with an unusual sensitivity. Lewis had seen that flickering before, too, in others – it was part of the fascination – but to see it in this

168

spineless groper who was stealing Cath . . . it filled him with such an envious loathing that he wanted to rush at the data clerk and knock him to the ground.

'Come on up, Hoskin,' he mocked. 'It won't bite.'

To control himself, he turned back to the object, crouching to run his hand down the front of it. He had never thought to do that before: there was no point. Every side of the thing was defaced, with wide cracks and extensive rough, unpolished areas where features of the original design had been chiselled off. He only started to explore it thoroughly this time to keep himself from hitting Hoskin, and also, of course, to aggravate the man, who rewarded him with a groan.

'You're a coward, Hoskin, you know that?' Lewis smiled round, down the steps. 'I hate to say it, but you're a . . .'

Then he touched – or rather it touched him . . . not an irregularity where the marble had splintered: this was a purposeful, sculptured shape, raised an inch or so above the rest; and it had taken hold of his index finger. Lewis snatched back his arm. He switched on the torch, flashing it across the ravaged surface to the left, high up, beneath the overhanging slab -

And found what it was. A human hand, miniature but perfectly formed as far as the wrist. So incongruous, straining from the stone like that, it was indisputably a hand, slanting towards the top left corner, the palm faced outwards. Its thin fingers curled in at a sharp angle like the limbs of a stricken crab, and it must have been those he had felt, seeming to close round his own finger. Peering hard, he could just make out a blemish, an inexplicable knob-like thing at the centre of the hand's palm; he could remember having felt that.

Vetoed Art.

'Hoskin . . . Hoskin . . . look at this!'

Lewis forgot about Cath. He forgot that he hated the clerk. His discovery – it was nothing; even as he called out, he told himself it was nothing – sent a shiver of emotion through him that was alien and indescribable.

'Hoskin!' Fingernails, tiny, exact; and the beginnings of tendons in the wrist . . .

But the data clerk did not move. Instead, he let out a curiously soft piping sound. It was so unexpected that, despite his find, Lewis twisted to look back: Hoskin stood with his mouth open, his hands rising slowly to his ears . . . then abruptly he fell forward on to his knees, and his lips began to move.

The worst of it was that contradicting this movement of Hoskin's lips, the piping sound continued.

And then there came other, faint scuffling noises from behind the curtain that concealed the passage to the ante-room.

A patrol.

Impossible. They'd been scrapped years ago. Lewis could not move. He was paralysed not by fear but by amazement. Patrols did not exist.

He lost seconds recovering, and so, when he rose to his feet, several blue-white search-lights had already burst round the edge of the curtain, such brilliant lights that not one corner of the building escaped them: the stains and graffiti on the walls, the boards lashed to the windows, the litter and defaced tablets, the mildewed pillars – every part of the dereliction was clinically exposed. Not one shadow was left to contrive a nuance. The place was a wreck.

There was no hunt. Both offenders were immediately obvious – and where was there to run to? They stayed where they were; and the patrol men, evidently following a set procedure, did not surge forward to seize them, but came to a halt there by the curtain, waiting civilly. Only one of them called out – a reasonable voice, inviting Hoskin and Lewis to 'come down': no threat, just an appeal to sanity. Four men in a white and blue uniform that Lewis had never seen before – but he'd heard about it: he recognised it from descriptions that were scarcely more than legend.

What now?

The patrol men were humane. They held their search-lights pointed away or at the ceiling, so as not to dazzle their

170

quarry, and Lewis could see wry half-smiles on their faces. Yes, they were smiling, they were mildly amused; and that decided him. For him, their smiles were more persuasive than any guns could have been – although these men certainly did have guns – and he began to walk down towards them.

But Hoskin did not get up. He was still kneeling, and after a quick, panicky turn towards the intruders, he was facing up the building again, towards the marble, desk-like object. When he reached him, Lewis stopped and gave the clerk a kick on the thigh, but Hoskin seemed not to feel it. 'Oh, please . . .' he was whispering, 'please . . .' His eyes were fixed on the lump of marble. 'Please . . .'

The idiot wouldn't get up. He swayed and jabbered, 'Oh, please . . .' his hands clenched. At the sight of him, Lewis fell into a fury of revulsion, and he kicked him again, harder. No effect.

'Hoskin!'

Should he pull him to his feet? But the thought of touching him was horrible. Exasperated, Lewis hovered by the kneeling man.

Then one of the patrol men came quickly along the white mosaic. He wore felt-soled shoes, and the silence of his approach made a bizarre contrast to the briskness of his movements. He came up the first flight of steps to Hoskin's side, and stooped to speak in the clerk's ear. His face wore the composure of efficiency and right thinking. His slender, beautiful gun touched Hoskin's cheek, as if in reassurance, and Hoskin rose like a dreamer, and went with him.

Lewis was left to follow. There was no gun trained on *him*, he noticed. In fact, the other patrol men were already turning back to the curtain. They apparently took it for granted that he would follow, that *he* had sense, and the strangeness of his arrest pained him. He felt a need to mark what was happening with some form of contact, if not with the shock of a grasp on his arm like that vouchsafed to Hoskins, then at least with words. The loss of one's liberty, after all, is of some importance.

171

So he spoke to the uniform that moved ahead of him, guiding Hoskin down the steps. 'I didn't know . . .' he began, 'I didn't know you people still existed.'

The man smiled back across his shoulder.

'No one does,' he said.

DAVID S. GARNETT

Moonlighter

There was nothing Alan could do except watch as the side of
the car scraped against the corner of the concrete pillar. He
spun the steering wheel as far as it would go, and the vehicle
finally pulled clear. Reversing until he was well away from
the parking place, he wound up the window, then drove
towards the exit ramp.

It was a company car, so it didn't really matter and he
shouldn't have cared. But he was annoyed, and he only had
himself to blame. If he hadn't been late this morning, he
wouldn't have tried squeezing into such a small space; and if
he'd gone forward as far as he could before reversing, he
wouldn't have hit the pillar.

It was wet and gloomy outside, and he had to switch on his
lights as well as the windscreen wipers. Winter was just
beginning to establish its miserable grip. It was so depress-
ing. His birthday was next week, maybe that had something
to do with the way he felt about this time of year. He was
about to clock up another figure on his lifedial. As if ageing
wasn't a day to day process, but instead, once every twelve
months, he was suddenly a year older.

Sometimes he could hardly remember what had happened
the previous day – perhaps because it was so much like the
one before, and the one before that – while the events of two
or three years ago remained vivid. Only it wouldn't be two or
three years, but five or six. The intervening years seemed to
have slipped past without him noticing, each successive one
speeding by even faster.

Parking outside the block of flats where he lived, Alan crossed the road to the off-licence. As he returned with two bottles of German wine, he looked for the long scratch just above the rear wheel arch, but there was nothing. He ran his fingers across the metal. There wasn't even the slightest mark on the paintwork.

He couldn't understand it. He'd seen the impact, watched the concrete scrape the side of the car, but there was no sign of any damage at all.

He walked around the car. And there, above the back wheel, was a strip where most of the paint had been gouged away. He touched the abrasion with his hand, refusing to believe the evidence of his eyes.

It was in the right place and approximately the size he'd guessed it would be – but on the wrong side, on the passenger side. He'd had his head out of the driver's window, and the graze had occurred on that side. He knew it, he'd have staked anything on it. But the evidence of the collision was on the nearside.

As he entered the flat, he heard Ruth humming tunelessly in the shower. He took a can of beer from the fridge, ripped it open and swallowed almost half of it in one thirsty gulp. Then he glanced down out of the window.

Even from six floors up, Alan could see that the scratch was still on the wrong side. Perhaps there hadn't been any damage caused by the pillar; the car had taken a knock on the other side, and he hadn't noticed before. Someone could have grazed it while it was parked. Except that there'd been traces of cement dust mixed with the scraped paint.

He went into the bedroom and undressed, wondering how long Ruth had been in the bathroom, and whether she'd be out soon. It was Friday and they were having visitors tonight. Caroline and Jeff. No, not Jeff – Jeffrey. He didn't like to be called Jeff.

The bathroom door was locked. Ruth always locked the door when she was alone; and locking it when she wasn't alone was even more annoying. He kicked the door a couple

174

of times with the side of his foot, to make himself heard above the noise of both Ruth and the shower.

'Who's that?'

Who did she think it was?

'It's the milkman,' said Alan.

'Just a mo.'

He heard the latch, but before he stepped inside Ruth was already back behind the shower curtain.

Still holding his beer, Alan climbed into the bath and stood behind her, bending to kiss her neck, just below the shower cap where she was least soapy.

'Two pints please, ' said Ruth, then she glanced around. 'Oh, it's only you. Hello.'

She turned away again, reaching for the sponge, and Alan put his hand on her left buttock; the hand which had held his ice cold beer.

'Bastard!' Ruth screamed, jumping forward. She turned to face him, all shiny and wet and smooth, pulling her head away when he tried to kiss her.

Alan raised the can over her breasts and started to tilt it. 'Want a beer?'

She grabbed his wrist, and he took her around the waist, drawing her close. He kissed her for a few seconds, until Ruth pulled free and began sponging herself, but Alan pushed her arm down.

'Let me finish, will you?' said Ruth.

'We haven't had a shower together for ages. Remember when we always used to?'

'Yes, but in those days it wasn't because we needed to get clean. Go on, Alan. Out. Now.'

Reluctantly, Alan climbed out.

'Did you buy the wine?'

'Yes. What time are they coming?'

'I told Caroline eight.'

'You'd better hurry up. You've only got two more hours.'

It was over an hour before Ruth finally emerged, and Alan followed her into the bedroom. All she was wearing was a

175

towel – around her head. She was standing on one leg in front of the dressing table, her other foot resting on the table top as she trimmed her toenails. She seemed to be deliberately teasing him: her breasts swaying as she leaned forward; the inviting curve of her bottom, so pale within the bikini line of her suntan; the way she straightened up, then raised the other leg, opening it slightly before the mirror as she scratched the inside of her knee. Yet she was completely oblivious of him.

He waited. When she opened the drawer where she kept her underwear, he took a few steps towards her and put his hand on her shoulder.

She shuddered. 'Don't, you're making me cold.' She turned her back to him, pulling on her pants.

Alan slid his left hand down the front of her briefs, while his right cupped her right breast, feeling the hardness of the nipple against his palm.

'Get into bed, I'll warm you up.'

'There isn't time.'

'Plenty of time.'

'Stop,' she said, lifting his hand out, 'it.'

'Plenty of time,' he repeated, and began chewing her left ear.

'There isn't.' Ruth twisted away. 'I've got to get the meal ready.'

'We never used to bother about the time. Or anything else. Remember when you worked in that clothes shop? That time I met you in the stockroom during your tea break?'

'Yes, yes, yes. You always mention that, Alan. But stop living in the past. Let me finish getting dressed. This isn't the right time.'

'It never is, is it?'

Alan went back into the living room. He supposed Ruth was right to some degree; he did spend a lot of time remembering the ways things used to be. They had been married six years, and they'd lived together for two years before that. Those first two years had been the best. Now they were drawing apart, had less in common with every passing year.

176

Maybe it had been a mistake to get married, or possibly they'd just known each other too long and had grown bored.

How long was it since they'd last made love? Two weeks? Three?

Half an hour later, Ruth was still only wearing her pants and the towel around her wet hair, although a lot of clothes were scattered on the bed.

'What's the time?'

'About half-seven,' Alan said, his eyes following her accusingly as she went to the wardrobe to select something else. Even when her outfit was decided, there'd still be her hair, her make-up, and then the meal.

Time had absolutely no meaning for Ruth. She was totally reliable in this one respect: she'd always be late.

He returned to the living room. To his surprise, Ruth appeared within a few minutes, pirouetting to demonstrate that she was ready.

Alan watched – and wondered who the hell she was. She wasn't the girl he'd met in a pub nine years ago, not the one he'd married, not even the one in the shower.

The stranger smiled at him, sitting down on the sofa by his side, running her fingers through her damp hair.

'I forgot my brush. Get it for us, will you?'

There was absolutely no reason why she couldn't go for it herself, but Alan stood up and went into the bedroom. The hairbrush was on the dressing table, and he took it back to Ruth.

In the few seconds he'd been gone, she'd found a paperback and was reading it. She reached for the brush, not even looking up, and he handed it to her. Alan slowly and purposefully studied his watch; but she missed the gesture.

'Good book?' he asked.

She nodded.

'Not a cook book, is it?'

'No. It's the one you gave me last Christmas.' Ruth showed him the cover.

It was a book on reincarnation – and Alan had never seen it before.

'Sorry we're a bit late,' said Caroline, when Alan let them in, 'but I knew Ruth wouldn't be ready.'

'Yeah', Alan agreed, and they both smiled.

The meal was ready as soon as they'd finished their first drink. It was as if Ruth had planned it to happen that way. She'd done everything wrong, but it all worked out perfectly – as usual. Whenever Alan complained about her lateness, she'd shrug it off. She believed that time wasn't important, that the world would pause, waiting for her to catch up. And mostly it did.

But if Alan was ever late, it always meant the worst – whether it was a parking ticket, missing a train, or not getting a drink a few seconds after time had been called.

Jeffrey didn't have much to say during the meal, which came as no surprise. He'd never said very much before. He was the silent type, or as Ruth put it: the weak, silent type. Caroline had been going out with the creep for a few months. Alan had always disliked Caroline's friends and lovers. Most of all he'd hated Simon, her ex-husband.

He had known Caroline exactly as long as Ruth. He and Pete had met them both in a pub, getting them pissed on vodka. If things had worked out only slightly differently, he might have been married to Caroline, and Ruth would be here for dinner.

He watched the two of them eating. They were very much alike, in character if not physically. Caroline had shared their flat before they were married, then later had stayed with them when her own marriage was crumbling. In some respects, he was closer to her than Ruth. He'd helped her over the traumatic split with Simon, but there had been no such emotional crisis which bound him to Ruth. All three of them played the role of psychoanalyst to each other: Alan and Caroline; Caroline and Ruth. But never Alan and Ruth.

'What are you staring at?' Caroline asked suddenly, feigning aggression.

Alan became aware that he was absently gazing at her and he said: 'Your bra strap's showing.'

Instinctively, she looked down – but she was wearing a low-cut dress, and Alan had noticed as soon as she arrived that she didn't have a bra.

'You!' Caroline smiled as she playfully kicked him under the table.

They frequently flirted with one another, but only when Ruth was there and for her benefit. It had never been serious; but now, it seemed, Caroline was there for the asking. How many times had she said: 'If only it had been you and me who went off together that first night . . .' Although it was always a joke, there was more than an underlying hint of total seriousness. But he'd never kissed her, not even on her wedding day. Especially not on her wedding day.

He glanced at Ruth, expecting to see a trace of disapproval in her green eyes. Green? Ruth's eyes were grey; it was Caroline's that were green.

'Remember that time when we went rowing?' Caroline said. 'You fell in the lake when you tried to get into the boat. Whenever I feel like a laugh, I just think of that.'

'I didn't fall in the lake,' Alan told her. 'My foot slipped off the bank and my leg went into the water, that's all.'

'Come on, Alan,' said Ruth. 'You tripped and went head-long into the lake. Drunk, as usual – which is probably why you don't remember.'

'We had to drag you out,' said Caroline. 'You were soaked through.' She nodded to Ruth, confirming her story, but she winked theatrically at Alan. 'I wanted to help you out of your wet things, but Ruth wouldn't let me.'

He wondered if they were both kidding. It didn't seem so. He remembered the incident fairly well, although it was of minor importance and none of them had ever mentioned it again. It was a Sunday, and they'd been to the pub at lunchtime before going to the park; but he certainly hadn't fallen into the lake, merely got one leg wet up to the knee. He couldn't be mistaken about something like that – and neither should they have been.

179

'Maybe it was someone else,' said Ruth, and she and Caroline both laughed.

Alan looked at them both. 'Odd thing happened today,' he said, to change the subject. He related the story about his car and the scrape on the wrong side. 'Explain that,' he concluded.

'Simple,' said Ruth. 'You're a rotten driver.'

'Or you were pissed again,' said Caroline.

'You couldn't have been looking in the nearside mirror?' said Jeffrey, unexpectedly.

'Haven't got one.'

'It's as though it happened in reverse, as if seen through a mirror.' Jeffrey sipped his wine, frowning thoughtfully. 'No, that wouldn't work, because even if your car was left-hand drive – er, if you see what I mean.'

'Talking of cars,' said Caroline, 'we heard on the radio as we came over that Greg Hunter was just killed in a smash-up on the M1. Remember him? He used to be in that band. You know. What were they called?'

'He died of an overdose last year,' said Alan. 'You must remember – they played all the group's old records on the radio the next day.'

Ruth shrugged. 'Don't ask me.' She'd never had much interest in rock music.

'No, he wasn't dead,' said Caroline. 'But he is now, isn't he?'

Jeffrey nodded.

Alan wasn't convinced. 'I'd have sworn he died last year.' He handed his empty plate to Ruth. 'I must have dreamed it,' he said – and instantly wished he hadn't.

'I've had prophetic dreams, too,' said Caroline, and when Ruth brought in the dessert they were off on one of their favourite topics.

They both believed in everything irrational, anything involving astrology or telepathy, palmistry or tarot cards, ouija boards or UFOs, mysticism or ghosts. They'd discuss dreams endlessly, what they meant, what they predicted, and

180

they even claimed to have shared the same dream on more than one occasion.

So far as Alan was concerned, there was nothing more boring than other people's dreams, but Ruth always went into long involved detail, wasting words on something which had never even happened.

He remembered few of his own dreams, although he knew he'd never had serialised dreams, or flying dreams, or any of the other varieties which Ruth and Caroline endlessly compared. And the nearest he ever came to a nightmare was a recurring dream in which he was about to take an exam but hadn't done any revision. Then, still asleep, he'd realise that he had left school years ago. Which proved what a dull, safe life he'd led if that was the only phantom his subconscious could summon up to terrify him.

'I've often thought,' said Caroline, 'that it's as though our minds lead a different existence while we sleep, slipping through into a much more interesting world. When we sleep, our minds go -' she shrugged, searching for an appropriate word '- moonlighting.'

'Moonlighting,' Ruth echoed. 'Yes, I like that. We travel to a place which is less boring, more exciting, where fact and fantasy are all mixed up.'

Ruth and Caroline both nodded and smiled; they'd finally solved the ultimate riddle of the universe.

While they continued talking, Alan suddenly had a flash of déjà vu: Time seemed to slow to a crawl, colour drained from the room, and he could only faintly hear what was being said. The whole scene was so familiar – Ruth and Caroline chattering away, with him watching them, thinking of something else. The room, the table, the glasses and dishes, these were the usual props.

But the experience was more than merely similar. It was exactly the same – including Jeffrey sitting across from Alan, idly fingering his empty glass and looking bored. Their eyes met for a split second, and that broke the spell.

Volume and colour abruptly returned. Ruth and Caroline kept talking; Jeffrey continued twisting the glass in his hand;

181

Alan looked on, his voyage through life resuming as though never temporarily halted.

He pushed the wine bottle towards Jeffrey. 'Help yourself, Jeff.'

Odder than déjà vu were the occasions when he'd relive a trivial incident from his past. For no reason, when nothing could have provoked the reminiscence, his memory would produce the image of a forgotten scene. On his way to buy the newspaper, perhaps, for an instant he would picture the inside of a pub he'd visited once several years ago. Or watching television, he'd be thrown back to a time he had been in his car, waiting for a set of traffic lights to change, and he'd be able to recall exactly where and when it had been. It didn't happen very often, but it always struck him as so odd that such moments stayed in his mind, while those of déjà vu faded away. Neither was it a deliberate process, because they weren't things he'd ever have chosen to remember.

As Caroline stood up and began to clear the dishes, Alan selected a particular memory of her: the time he'd seen her naked on the roof, sunbathing, when she thought she was alone in the flat. He'd only been at the attic window for a couple of seconds until she sensed his eyes on her. She'd looked towards him briefly, then returned her attention to her magazine, ignoring him. Feeling guilty, Alan had retreated. But now the memory was becoming faded and less clear through too much replaying, like an old film print.

Alan watched her taking the things through into the kitchen, admiring her legs, the sway of her hips. Out in the hall, she started to sing a song which he half-recognised but couldn't place. When she came back, he made a deliberate effort not to stare at her breasts, instead spinning around in his seat and switching on the stereo.

'Shall I make the coffee?' she said. 'Where's the percolator?'

'In the cupboard next to the sink,' said Ruth.

Alan pressed the FM button, and Greg Hunter's voice came from the speakers. It was the track Caroline had begun singing a few seconds earlier.

She paused, then nodded to Alan. 'Listen. I told you he was dead. That must be why they're playing this.'

She was probably right, he decided, although it was something of a coincidence that she'd been singing the same number. Had she picked up the radio waves in her head? He had frequently wondered the same thing about himself. He'd be thinking of a tune, then hear it immediately he turned on the radio.

'No coffee for me,' Alan said. 'There's some duty-free brandy left. Anyone else want some?'

Caroline did; and Ruth ended up making the coffee for herself and Jeffrey. Caroline sat on the sofa next to Alan. She crossed her legs, her skirt riding up her thighs, and leaned against him.

He tried not to be too obvious as he finally gave up resisting and stared down her cleavage, wondering again if he'd have been better off with her rather than Ruth.

Ruth filled the sink, pulled on her rubber gloves, and began washing up.

'Why don't you leave it?' said Alan. 'It's late. Let's go to bed.'

'I'll only have to do it tomorrow if I leave it now.'

'No, you won't; I'll do it tomorrow.'

'Ha!'

She swept the pile of plates into the sink, sending a tidal wave of suds and water all down her dress and onto the floor.

Now look what you've made me do, said Alan to himself.

'Now look what you've made me do!' said Ruth.

And I'm a mind reader as well, he thought.

'My dress! It's ruined!'

He didn't believe that it could have been ruined by soapy water, but he said: 'I'll buy you another.'

As he spoke, he slid his hands up her bare legs, slipped his thumbs into the elastic of her pants and started tugging down.

'Alan! What do you think you're doing?'

It was obvious what he was doing, and he didn't reply. He

183

pulled her briefs down to her knees, and as Ruth spun around they fell to her ankles. Alan grabbed her wrists, raising them together above her head, then grasped them both in his right hand. Her expressionless face was only a few inches from his; she wasn't sure whether to be angry or amused. Trying to match her lack of expression, with his free hand he slowly lifted the hem of her dress, higher and higher.

'Alan, stop it!'

She could easily have wriggled loose, but she didn't even try.

'Stop what?' Alan asked innocently.

Ruth sighed, making it clear that she was simply tolerating his whims.

He pulled down his zip. 'Ever been fucked against a sink?'

She almost smiled. 'Let go, you idiot.'

'All I want is me conjugals.'

'Not here!' she hissed, as though she might be overheard.

He lowered her arms, then led her out of the kitchen. Ruth hobbled behind him, along the hall and into the bedroom. When they reached the bed, he pushed her down and swung her legs up onto the duvet, not even bothering to remove her shoes. She lay without moving as he stripped, making no attempt to escape. Alan climbed onto the bed, spread her legs and bunched her dress up around her waist.

Ruth kept completely still, her eyes open and staring at the ceiling. It didn't take long.

'Now can I finish washing up?' She slid free and left the room.

After a few minutes, he went to look for her. Her clothes and shoes lay discarded on the hall floor, a trail leading to the kitchen. She really had gone back to continue washing up, and all she wore was the pair of rubber gloves.

'Should have thought of this years ago,' she said, aware of him in the doorway. 'Don't get my clothes wet like this.'

'And I'd never let you finish the washing up, either. Come back to bed.'

'What? For another thirty seconds of unbridled passion? No thanks.'

184

'Yeah. Well. You know.'

'Enjoy yourself tonight, did you?'

'What? Just then, you mean?'

'With Caroline.'

Alan said nothing.

'She was all over you, wasn't she?'

Ruth glanced around, flicking her hair over her shoulder.

'Not that I blame her,' she added, then she laughed. 'Don't look so solemn. I've known you long enough. I know what you're like – both of you.'

'Yeah,' said Alan, which seemed safe enough.

The difference in Ruth was amazing. She was like – he hesitated before the inevitable cliché – like a different woman. He felt much more affection towards her, and surely not because of a brief fuck: that was all it had been, it couldn't be called making love.

They still had a hell of a lot going for them, he realised, far more pluses than minuses. Had he been seriously preferring Caroline only an hour before? He must have been mad.

And if not for a chance conjunction of time and space, they'd never have met. He and Pete had no reason to go to that pub, it wasn't one of their regular haunts; Ruth and Caroline were only there because they'd made a mistake about the time of a cinema programme and decided to have a drink first. It was just coincidence – or fate. But wasn't life simply one long series of coincidences? He might very easily have wound up with Caroline. And what if there'd been no Ruth, no Caroline? If they'd decided to go to a café instead, or if he and Pete had arrived fifteen minutes later or not persuaded them to give the movie a miss . . . ?

It couldn't be that Ruth was the only woman in the world for him, because the odds against them ever having met were too astronomical to consider. If he'd married someone else, maybe his life would have been even better. After all, the Ruth standing naked in front of the sink was infinitely preferable to the Ruth he'd lived with for the past few days.

He watched her, his desire returning.

'Doing anything special tomorrow?' she asked.

'Why?'

'Because I've a real treat for you. You can come shopping with me. A new dress, remember?'

Alan walked over, and they kissed.

'Let's go to bed,' he said.

'I want to get this finished first; I won't be long.'

He'd heard that before, and he didn't believe her.

Alan reached over to Ruth's side of the bed for the lamp, but he couldn't find it. He sat up, then noticed that the lamp was on the table next to him. What was it doing over there? It was always on the other side, by the electric point. He pressed the button, and then he saw the flex. The lamp was plugged into the socket just above the skirting board – on his side of the bed.

He tried to make his mind go blank, not to think of scrapes against concrete pillars, and paperbacks he'd never bought, and dead rock stars, and power points that moved, and falling into lakes – or not falling into lakes.

He heard Ruth go into the bathroom. She seemed to spend at least an hour in there every night. He'd no idea what she could possibly find to do for so long. By the time she came out, he was usually asleep. In the mornings, the situation was reversed; he was always up while she remained sleeping.

But after only five minutes in the bathroom, Ruth joined him in bed. One thing led to another, and when he rolled above her she reached for the lamp so that the light wasn't in her eyes. She found the switch at once, as if it was always on that side of the bed.

'I've been thinking about what Caroline mentioned last night,' said Ruth, sipping her cup of tea. 'About moonlighting. Maybe we all have two bodies, one for the day, one for the night. While we sleep, our minds leave our daytime bodies and enter our other selves on a different world. Another planet. An alternate dimension.'

'So that's where all my odd socks come from,' said Alan. 'They've migrated.'

186

'The time scale can't be the same,' Ruth continued, 'because we spend more time awake than sleeping.'

'Not in your case.'

'While we're sleeping, our minds tune in to what our doppelgängers are doing.' She nodded, as though there could be no possible doubt.

'You mean,' said Alan, 'that when I'm asleep, my head is a television set, picking up whatever my alter ego is doing? The poor sod must have a hell of a life. Always taking exams. Teeth dropping out all the time. Falling from great heights. Not all bad though – he's a randy bastard.'

Ruth stretched to put her cup on the floor by the bed, then looked towards the window.

'Seems a nice day,' she said. 'It's warm, isn't it, with the sun shining in? Completely different from yesterday.'

So were a lot of things, thought Alan – but now he knew why.

The key was the damage to his car. For the first time he had proof – concrete proof! At some time while driving home, between backing into the pillar and discovering that the damage had shifted to the other side of the car, it had happened.

He'd gone moonlighting.

Thanks to Ruth's and Caroline's theories of dreams, he had a word which fitted perfectly.

And now that he knew what was going on, what was always going on, all he had to do was get used to it.

'Hey, you,' he said softly.

She looked around at him. Then she smiled and lay back against the pillow, and they kissed.

Alan realised he'd have to make the most of her while they were both here together. After all, the next Ruth might be one of the less compatible ones.

DAVID LANGFORD

In a Land of Sand and Ruin and Gold

By now all the legends had been written, and rewritten, until long polishing had worn them smooth. It was the same with the continents. In the sky, a dragon which older myths called entropy was nibbling at the last of the stars. Except on the rare frosty nights, the sky was hidden in an ancient haze. Nobody cared.

Meckis thought he did, though only for himself and the hope that something could be different. Over a dozen centuries he'd put together a personal philosophy which in the great tradition of personal philosophies revealed him as singular and special. His touchstone was boredom: he'd convinced himself that of all the complaisant thousands on the dull Earth, Meckis was one of a very few still capable of finding this cosy eternity a bore.

He prowled through caressing haze, looking for a different liaison which he knew would be the same. Underfoot lay threadbare grass with desert patches peeping through, concrete gone to sand. At intervals the old world's permanent machines lay canted or half-buried, eager to serve him food, drink, drugs, visions. Meckis grudgingly ate and drank, but no more. He wanted 'something real.'

The aspect of the machines he liked best was their tiny element of chance. Clocks were running down, here as in the faded sky. Even electrons seemed to tire; ancient logical

pathways grew clogged and furred with age, until, sometimes
. . .

Not many decades before, an insane machine coloured green and gold had fed him tainted meat. The experience was new, delirious, a finger-touch of the Real. Fog roared in his brain, fire and acid scoured his gullet, black stars danced: in a world of grey it was a volcano of fresh sensation. Before the relic could shut itself down for repair, Meckis had vomited out his desires and the insane machine had given him an insane gift. He carried the blue cones now, with a sly smile. They helped him know he was special, wielder of a drug both forbidden and forgotten.

So he walked through light and dark and light again, and again he found her . . . but then he was always finding her, the special partner who would add meaning to endless twilight. He saw her, crosslegged in thin grass, and almost sighed. *Time, swift to fasten and swift to sever*: even at first meeting the favourite melancholy verse sang through his head.

She eyed him with a bird's bright incuriosity, bending again over a bit of the old world: a creamy, glassy whorl. Twisted in her hands, it sprayed rainbow patterns into the mist. Every encounter was a special intimacy, Meckis thought, two people in a mist-walled cell of air.

The light-sculpture exploded into a hot crawl of after-images while he was still straining to distinguish the colour of her pale hair, to find some mark of difference. Today's people were too alike in body (the old mixture had levelled itself, flat as the former hills) and in mind. Her hands evoked a new, glowing shape which Meckis admired and she regarded with neither pride nor disappointment. The plangent reds and greens assaulted one another in a display of frozen fireworks.

'A good piece of work,' Meckis said.

The woman cancelled the image, and looked at him as she had looked at it. Afterimages chequered her body and made it . . . different.

190

'Perhaps we might copulate,' he said politely, a fine trembling already spreading over neck and torso in anticipation of what he'd ask afterwards. She smiled; they exchanged names, Meckis and Rhee; the light-machine fell and rolled sluggishly, pulsing with dying colours at the edge of violet.

Their liaison was skilled and passionless, a gentle touching and sliding, a discreet hiccup of orgasm. Rhee smiled coolly up at him as he gently ran the comb of his fingers through her hair. 'I think you've been a woman once,' she said. 'You know just how it should be. Well: many thanks . . .'

(It had been centuries ago: he'd submitted to a major bodychange machine and drifted through decades as woman-Meckis. She'd smiled at partners with hope and longing, and they'd smiled back and walked away. As man-Meckis he smiled at partners of any sex, and they too went away. When you have forever you know there's no permanence. The custom of brief encounter hardens into law. Unless . . .)

'Many thanks. And goodbye.'

His hands twitched. 'I'd like to stay with you a while.'

'What? What do you mean? I don't understand.'

'Listen. I'm different from other people. I can show you things, tell you things, give you things. We can do whatever we like. Why not together? Why wander all alone?'

'I don't want together. Goodbye.'

They rolled apart and rose with practised grace. That might have been the end of it, as in so many other encounters – King's Gambit Declined – had Rhee not turned her back so sharply. In a swirl of pale-gold hair, Meckis saw what had been hidden at the nape of her neck. Still flushed, he stepped forward and parted the strands with damp fingers. She stood rigid: 'Goodbye. Please. Goodbye.'

'It's a mole. You have a mole.'

There lived a singer in France of old
By the tideless dolorous midland sea;
In a land of sand and ruin and gold
There shone one woman, and none but she –

'I don't talk about it. Let go of me, leave me *alone*.'

'I tried it once,' he said. 'I had a machine change my skin,

191

stripe me and swirl me black and white. There's a beast like that in the legends. I thought I'd shout out how I was different. But no one came near me at all . . . This is what I *should* have done. A secret mark.'

'No! It's not meant to be there. I hide it, it's shameful. I have it erased but it grows again. You're not supposed to notice it.'

'It makes you different like me. I'll have a mole too, just that honey brown, you won't be alone. If -'

'Go away. Go away. *Now.*' She turned again, fingers touching the turquoise band on her right wrist. A privacy weapon, of course. It was then that Meckis went mad, leapt from the inner precipice where so often before he'd halted. There was a wild joy in sitting far back in his own skull, watching this *different* person move unrestrained.

Meckis grasped his own left hand. He bent back the middle finger, straining the joint the wrong way until with a tiny *click* the fingernail flipped up like a lid. In the implanted cavity were the three blue cones. Rhee watched, uncertain, as he fumbled one free and held it securely between finger and thumb. Meckis stepped forward.

'Let me explain,' he said to fill the foggy silence. Then he dived awkwardly, arm outstretched with the blue stinger towards her. The sandy grass came up to slap him in the belly; pain and an orange sunburst flared as his elbow found the forgotten light-machine where it lay; his fanged hand struck at her shin.

Thrust into flesh, the cone dissolved, its deep blue stain seeping through olive skin like ink dropped into water. Meckis gasped in triumph, horror, pain, all lost in the sudden high whine from Rhee's wrist, a sound which curdled thought. She'd turned the turquoise band on him at last. *Too late*, he thought before all thought went into eclipse.

He swam through dreams of light and faces, hunting a small insistent pain and eventually running it to ground at the side of his own neck. With a sudden pulling of curtains he was awake, head throbbing (how long since he'd rested without a sleepmaker?) and neck locked in angular cramp. It

192

was twisted because his head didn't lie naturally but was raised up, cradled in warm flesh. A thigh. Rhee's thigh. How long since he, since anyone, slept touching?

Meckis jerked and stared up into her face. The hard-edged, conventional smile had lost focus and taken on the softness of dream. She stroked his hair.

'Stay with me,' he whispered, still not daring to believe.

'Yes.' She groped for unfamiliar words. 'Yes. . . my love.'

Once when more lights were in the sky and there were still children, there'd been a war where loyalties wavered and were changed by subtle tools. One such was the cone, outlawed and locked – since nothing could ever be wholly lost – behind triple walls of programming. Even in the legendary days when stone walls were reckoned equally impregnable, people would have had no trouble in putting a name to the nameless weapon, the blue cone of fixation. They would have called it a love potion.

That night the thin grass stiffened with frost: a buried machine hummed and cast a field of warmth over Rhee and Meckis, a field of softness beneath. As they went through the motions of love, the sky cleared and old light from long-dead stars fell on them. Meckis, still tight with exultation, found himself repeating the same inanities.

'Stay with me, stay with me forever . . .'

'Meckis. Stay with *me*.'

He studied her face and eyes, phosphorescent white and unfathomable black in the meagre light, and at last looked beyond the horizon of his old hopes and fears. What happens after triumph? He had no idea; he never had. But this second instalment of forever must be different from, and therefore better than, the first.

Rhee clung to him even in sleep. Accustomed to solitude, he found this disconcerting but didn't like to thrust her away. So Meckis slept uneasily, perspiring in an embrace which was just too warm.

Sleeping, Rhee smiled.

In the morning they moved on, Meckis sore-eyed and stiff.

New mists swathed the path ahead. They didn't walk in any special direction: all directions were the same unless you reached the tideless sea.

'What did you do before we got together?' he said.

'Oh, I hunted for toys in the ground. You lift the grass and there's nearly always something there. Like the lightmaker . . . that was a good find.'

'You left it there. We could go back.'

'It doesn't matter; not any more.' She squeezed his arm, the arm she hadn't released since they began walking. Her stride was longer than his, which made for another tiny discomfort: but never mind! Changing step once again, Meckis smiled to himself. Grubbing for fragments of old technology was the favourite pastime of the despised Others. Now he'd made Rhee different, one of his own kind. Her mole, that merely accidental difference, was forgotten.

They found an eating place, a thicket of pastel tubes extruding spicy doughs or squirts of beverage. They passed a windowed hulk of blue-grey metal, still manufacturing coloured dodecahedra even while being dismantled by buzzing steel mice. One wide tract of ground roiled and churned with subterranean motion, but politely held still in the zone where they walked. They saw, and pointed out to each other, an occasional tree or swaying flower. Once, a bird flew overhead.

'I love you,' she said late in the afternoon.

'Love you too. You don't need to keep saying it.'

'Words don't get used up: you can say them again and again, and they stay true. Say it again, Meckis. Please.'

'Loveyou,' he said rapidly. Her mouth clamped on his, and they both swayed. Rhee giggled.

'This is ridiculous,' he muttered, remembering to smile.

'Let's stop here . . . you look tired.'

'No. We'll go on a while yet.'

'Of course, if you want to.'

A shadow wavered in the fog, and resolved itself into a dark plump man making water against a puzzle machine. He turned and politely offered intercourse. Meckis was nodding mechanically when Rhee spoke in a clear, firm voice: 'Thanks, but no. Meckis and I are together.'

'Yes . . .?'

'Permanently together,' she said without flinching. The plump one blinked, twice; his mouth opened and closed. He did not speak, but walked rapidly away.

'He doesn't understand,' she murmured.

'Triples can be, well, good fun.'

'Oh . . . If that's what you *wanted*, love . . .'

'Never mind.'

Next came a playground where gravity was partly annulled: they chased each other in vast slow leaps, and Meckis felt silly. Here the evening mist glowed ultramarine. They coupled in illusory fathoms of water. Rhee said insistently, 'I love you, I love you.'

'Me too,' he replied automatically.

On the second night as on the first, Meckis didn't sleep well.

The pearly morning found him in a vile humour. His groin ached from excess, his head from sleeplessness, and Rhee was so eager to kiss him anew that she failed to freshen her mouth first.

'It's so marvellous the way I feel,' she told him.

He gnawed his lip, struggled upright and spat. 'Look. This is no good. It's not real.'

'The realest thing in the world.'

'None of it's real! You're changed, drugged, you don't know what you're talking about. Fucking perfect love all day and all night -' The observer in the back of Meckis's skull was surprised to find he was shouting. 'All out of a drug machine! See – see this cone? That's your perfect love in there. I raped your *brain* with a blue stinger, don't you remember?'

Rhee was briefly silent. 'I love you,' she said with radiant calm. 'I'm so grateful, you don't know how grateful, that you gave me the medicine. I wasn't real before.'

'No. *This* is the dream. This is the nightmare. *That* was the real thing back then, don't you under*stand*?' His voice was breaking with the intensity of feelings never before felt. There were always new internal cliffs and precipices.

'I know I'm not good enough for you . . .' she began.

It was then that he hit her in the face.

Rhee lay momentarily stunned while Meckis's feelings surged in standing waves, from guilt to a sort of savage triumph. His fist throbbed, each knuckle a separate point of pain. Over the edge of the new cliffs, new depths. This was the end of all things.

Then she was back, on her knees, dizzily swaying like a shape seen through blowing fog. 'Do what you like. I know I deserve whatever you do. I'd rather be hit by you than loved by anyone else. Go on.'

Meckis couldn't go on. Instead he succumbed to hardening physical desire; he thrust her down and entered too quickly. They made a kind of love more violently than ever before, while all the time Rhee looked appallingly, frighteningly happy. Afterwards, he could hardly walk.

Fog trembled as they wandered on, wavering in shapes of guilt and fear at the borders of Meckis's vision. He stole sidelong glances at the dark bruises which made Rhee even more different and exciting. *She wants me to do whatever I want. So no matter what I do, it must be all right. So why should I feel bad about it? After all, she wants me to . . .*

'Love you,' she whispered through swollen lips as they moved among a forest of gleaming rods between which random lightnings played. (When a bolt caught them, as occasionally happened, a shattering pulse of pleasure would make them stumble or fall.) The words of the endearments might be perennially fresh and new, but mere repetition had eroded them to meaningless noise.

Presently, half reluctant and half curious, he struck her again. She stood passively, even ecstatically, as he experimented with forehand and backhand slaps. Her nose bled. She whispered: 'Don't stop.'

So then, sweating and panting from the exertion, Meckis found it good to exert his own free will by not hitting her.

New feelings were churning in his mind, with hints that Rhee's unreal devotion was an admirable thing. How marvellous to look at the world through that roseate haze.

They must both have been drooping a little: soft chairs unfolded from the bare ground, and a table of multicoloured sweetmeats thrust itself up like a mushroom. Meckis glowered, persuading himself that he'd enjoyed the faint hunger-pangs. They sat down anyway.

'I'm sorry I hurt you.'

'You must have *needed* to do it. That's what I'm here for. To give you everything I can.'

'Suppose I didn't want to take it? Suppose I told you to go away and leave me alone.' He hid his face behind a mug of frothing chocolate, and looked at her over the top.

'Please don't.' Her eyes were wet; she was ugly with bruises and caked blood. There was no reason at all that now, for the first time, Meckis should feel almost fond of her.

'I don't love you, Rhee. Nobody loves anybody any more. We've grown out of that . . .'

'I can keep trying,' she mumbled, and put a soft hand on his thigh. Meckis suddenly identified a further component of his churning emotional stew. She was happy. Simply being with him, she could be happy: and he was bitterly envious.

'Let's walk some more before we sleep,' he said lamely.

As one always did, they came to the sea. Sandy grass gave way to grassy sand, sloping to a grey-green stagnation swayed only by the distant sun. The salt-heavy air moved sluggishly over them. It looked easy to wade out into choking fluid and escape the tedium of forever; but of course smooth inhuman arms would prevent such a major mishap.

Meckis patted the drooping woman's shoulder. 'I wish I felt like you. You must be the happiest person alive, since I cheated you. I envy you, you know?'

'Then be happy with me.'

He sighed. But she was looking at him earnestly, her head a little on one side, as though he were failing to grasp an essential truth. To be happy.

'Oh. No,' Meckis said. 'That . . . hadn't occurred to me. Not that.'

He unlocked the modified finger, shook a tiny blue cone into his right palm. His lips moved soundlessly as he stared at it.

'Yes,' she said.

The second instalment of forever, he thought.

Changing other people will never help, he thought.

You have to change yourself.

'I think it might be . . . better if you did it,' said Meckis, holding out the cone. Rhee's face glowed with a brief beauty, shining through the bruises and negating them, as she took the thing from him. With a slow creamy smile of fulfilment, she pushed it into his arm. The instant's pinprick pain gave way to icy cold as the blue tint spread and faded. Without motion, Meckis was falling. The chill embraced his whole body, leaving a numbness like hoarfrost on the flesh. Vision became remote, as though he saw the world through intricacies of mirrors.

After a long silence he stared into the face of the same woman like so many other women, a face disfigured and swollen-lipped. It held no more attraction than before.

'I don't think it's working,' he wanted to say. 'I don't think it's working,' he, the inner Meckis who sat somewhere at the back of his own skull, tried to say. But now a new and alien program was in charge, primed with its own imperatives, armed with Meckis's memories:

'I do love you, Rhee,' was the meaningless noise which came from his lips. And from hers: 'Oh, I'm so glad,' as the bodies put their arms about each other.

The inner Meckis thought about being bored and being different. Forever. He wanted to send some message to that other intelligence which must lie trapped in a forever loving body, snared until the sun broke down: *I'm sorry, Rhee, I'm sorry*. He remembered again those old verses about the triumph of time . . .

For this could never have been, and never
Though the gods and the years relent, shall be.

And so, he thought as the kiss prolonged itself on his lips, we live happily ever after.

KEITH ROBERTS

Piper's Wait

There is a forest in England. It is an ancient place; there are
mile on mile of trees, villages and towns that huddle to this
day behind walls of living green. There are roads to serve
those towns, modern roads that thrust their tarmac spears
through what is still in parts a wilderness; and vehicles travel
these roads, cars and lorries and the yellow vans of com-
merce. Down and down, pushing always to the coast; across
the heath, through the blazing rhododendrons, into the
proud towns where the cranes work in pairs and the ships
come in from the salt sea.

Close to that forest's heart lies a village that to this day has
no name. A little distance off there is a glade, the trees that
ring it gnarled and dark. A road runs by it, dropping through
a little hollow before rising again to meet the endless woods.
The road, and the clearing it skirts, share a name. That name
is Piper's Wait.

For some years now the place has been a campsite. There
the trailers come and the motor caravans, to set their brakes,
erect their privies and their little striped awnings. There the
dreadful batwinged women set about their suppers, bored
children play dutifully with their frisbees and pingpong bats
and wait to be called in. As night falls the windows glow, one
after another, with their endless patternings of floral cloth,
and all is peace. Or seemingly so; for occasionally a family
will couple up their rig, make all secure and slip quietly
away. Because for some folk when night falls the character of
the glade appears to change. So they creep away, and their

199

plastic cups and saucers do not rattle; for it is not good camping practice to allow such things to happen.

In the morning the ponies and cattle edge cautiously back to bully the tourists for their scraps; for they too, at night, seem to avoid the place. Why is unclear; though the old folk who live round about have been heard to mutter in their cups that beasts alone understand the whisperings of leaves.

The name of the glade has caused debate among the idly curious. Letters have been written, to the cheerful magazines that guard the interests of such people as caravanners; but to my knowledge no certain answer has been made. I know that answer; it was given me on a day lightless and flaring as the Piper himself knew. Once it was his secret, then it was mine; now, by your leave, I offer it to you. For secrets, like curses, are meant for handing on.

Once, long ago when men wore cowls and jerkins and sowed grain broadcast from baskets on their hips, there was a man they called the Piper. A very strange man he was too. None understood him; yet folk comprehended his every mood. Never had he been known to utter human words; and yet he spoke from dawn to sunset, on his flute. And when he played, folk somehow felt the meaning. Shrill sometimes was his music, shrill as the pain of knives: it spoke of death and separation, the pain of loss and love. Sometimes it was soft, soft as the murmurs of a dreaming child; and then the hearers thought of times of plenty, of fulfilment and peace. All who heard the Piper marvelled; but all privately shook their heads. For these things, sweet though they might be to the ear, were nonetheless spells; spells conjured from a tube of fretted wood. And no good comes of dabbling with the dark.

The Piper was a tall man for his times; tall and slender, with deepset eyes of a curious dark blue. Some said there was unfriendliness in their gaze; others that there was much sadness and compassion – which latter view seemed the more likely, for surely no man who sees the world and its folk as they truly are can for ever hold his spirit aloof. Whatever the truth, it is certain that the Piper never spoke. Some claimed he was incapable of speech; but that was not the case. His flute spoke for him so clearly he had never found a use for human words.

Sometimes he would play at harvests home, and then the dancing went the brisker; folk looked at each other with new eyes and saw virtues they might otherwise have missed, and loved afresh. At other times, on heaths and barren moorlands, his flute spoke of darker things; then people would cringe and run, crouch closer to their cottage fires, glad of stout bolts and bars. They would wonder then, with knuckles to their mouths, how he could have acquired such skills; and of course with time the usual tales became current, the tales that are told of all such folk. He was under a curse; he had travelled to Fairyland to learn his piping from the Old Ones themselves; he had bartered his soul, his only gift from God. But the matter was never resolved. Sometimes, or so the rumours went, he played at the courts of kings; and they would laugh with joy, showering him with gold, or creep shivering away, according to the mood he had conjured. But such stories were never confirmed; it must suffice that he came again and again to the green glades of the forest. There he would play, and the children would gather round to listen and laugh, and he would seem content. In time their elders would come, to call him to their cottages; he would partake, smiling, of soup or gruel, and go his way.

Some claimed the Piper wasn't mortal; that he was a changeling, born of the Fairy Folk themselves. Some went further, speaking of him in hushed tones as they would speak of a god. He was mortal though; painfully so, as his tale will show. At one point only did the rumours near the truth; that was when they spoke of a curse. Cursed he certainly was, and with the oldest fate of all: that he was born, that he was flesh and blood, and that he was aware. That awareness grew on him, as of course it grows upon us all; and with it came responsibility. The responsibility he felt both to others and himself; for the things he saw so clearly had somehow to be given shape. And that was when his music had its birth, when he began to speak not with words but through his flute;

because the things he saw were not capable of normal utterance. He saw great kings, certainly: he saw women beautiful beyond dreams, he saw lovely girls in short white dresses, the like of which had surely never been. He saw machines that thundered along roads yet to be made. He saw the cargoes they carried, the foodstuffs and the wines; he saw the very lamps that lit their way, stretching out for ever, amber and silver fires that burned high and without heat. All this he saw, and more. He saw the hearts of his dream-folk, and knew that men can never change. This his flute sang; which is perhaps why his listeners sometimes crept away appalled.

He came one day, unannounced as was his wont, to that village which has no name. He walked slowly, with many a pause, brow furrowed as if in intense thought; for he was troubled in his mind. He had seen, more clearly than before, the strange low buildings of another age, each standing in its little plot of land. He had seen the trim-fenced gardens, the vehicles standing patient in their drives, the thin bright wands jutting talisman-fashion from the roof of every house. He shook his head as if to clear it; but the vision, rather than fading, intensified, till the cluster of wattle huts his human eye recorded seemed themselves mere ghosts, threatening to flicker and vanish. He shook his head again, exerted all his will. His eyes blazed, till a child who would have spoken ran scampering in fear, and at last the unwanted vision began to fade; though a part of his mind still wondered what it might portend.

He made his way to the house of Jack the Fletcher, for Jack had sheltered him times enough before – he was always sure of a welcome at his hearth. The food he was given, plain but nourishing, cheered him, so that the dull mood into which he had fallen lightened by degrees. He sat in firelight and candlelight – for in his honour they had even lit priceless tapers – and listened to the talk of Jack, his family and his guests and friends. Once he took the flute and gave them his new vision, or at least as much of it as seemed proper; but mostly he sat hands in lap, nodding and smiling as he heard their dreams. The dreams their lips spoke, the others that lay buried beneath the words. Mostly though, and as the evening wore on it was increasingly noted, he listened to one young girl. Lissom she was and slight, dressed all in white, with May blossoms twined in her hair. Her bearing was modest, her manner becomingly shy; but her hands made deft shapes in the flamelight, and her voice had the lisp and tinkle of a brook. This was why his flute was quiet; later it was said of him that he had never been known to pay so much attention to one person's speech. Jack Fletcher discussed it at length, in the tavern where they drank ale and mead and threw hand-arrows at a great wood board. But no conclusion was reached, save perhaps that voiced by Will the Tanner, a kindly, lonely man, who after much thought and considering his pot of ale said, 'Thou needst not have two flutes at once.' Jack and his friends shook their heads, uncomprehending; for they had already agreed among themselves that Will was a little touched in his wits. But the Tanner was right. For the first time, the Piper had heard a music sweeter than his own.

What happened next was surprising. At least the villagers who discussed the matter owned themselves puzzled; and since the affair formed the main topic of conversation for many weeks to come, that meant everybody save babes and the very sick. One would have thought that with such a new preoccupation the Piper would have stayed, if not within the village, at least in easy reach. Instead he vanished; from the forest, from the region, some said from all the haunts of men. Twice the crops were sown and gathered in; and still there was no word of him.

Meanwhile many things happened within the village; more in those two seasons, it seemed, than in the lives of many men. The girl, that slender stripling with her mane of brown and marvellous hair, became betrothed. The boy to whom she was promised was a sturdy lad, the son of a yeoman. Within the limitations of the times he seemed to have good prospects; for that class of person was then becoming discrete, aware of new strength. In the village the old ways still held sway: to marry, the girl needed permission of her feudal lord. So to his hall she went, her family and the family of her loved one in attendance, to seek his blessing.

Now the lord was not a bad man, though sometimes it was said of him he wore his duties heavy. Also it was clear enough to him the high old days were done: the sheep had eaten the men that tended them. So his blessing was given, and that handsomely; wine casks were broached, the whole village bidden to a feast in the great house that stood apart, grandly, on a rising swell of land. All rejoiced, looking to better times, not least the families of the betrothed. But there was a rub in the matter; for his lordship had a son.

What passed between the young man and the erstwhile bride none could tell; but from the very day of the betrothal, the rumours began, running like shadows, under the high bright sun. She was here, she was there; such a thing had taken place, such words had been said. The villagers put hands to their cheeks, widening their eyes with fear; for in those days all folk were strong for God. What is certain is that from that time on, the girl began to change. What had been graceful and proud began to sag, deteriorate, to shamble in drunkenness down the street, to frighten the goats and chickens once herded with such care, make them run in fear. Her family disowned her, driving her from the door with blows; she slept where best she could. She drained the tosspots in the village inn; for none dared give her nay. Those eyes that had been modest, downcast, shy, were fiery, dark and dead. None cared to meet them: folk stepped from her path, and held their peace as best they may.

So much, from wherever he might have been, the Piper heard. He returned to the village: the people were alarmed to see him one grey dawn, stalking the single street of the place as gaunt and ragged as a spectre. But none accosted him. He made his way to a small glade in the woods, a glade known only to him, and there he sat motionless a long while. It was evening before his decision was reached: he rose and made his way to the house of the old lord, standing alone and frowning on its hill. Once more he stared awhile; finally he looked up at the sky, filled now with a lowering, dusty light.

He placed the flute to his lips and began to play. He made a tune the like of which even he had never wrought; and fortunate it was that there were no folk near, because the melody he conjured was not for human ears. It called to old things, thought dead and certainly best forgotten, things from the start of Time itself. Nothing happened at first; but the tune crept higher by degrees, became a shrilling, an insistence. As it rose so the clouds massed, driving from the west. Finally the storm broke, with crash after ear-splitting crash. The lightning bolts struck the great house time and again, sending tiles spinning with the roof beams and ties that held them, singeing the Piper's clothes where still he stood and played. Flames leaped up, dancing, setting the last timbers ablaze, the last stick of wood from the meanest kitchen chair. Finally, when all was consumed, the rain came, in silver rods that seemed to stand up from the earth. At that, finally, the Piper lowered the flute; and he might or might not have smiled. He sat down on a stump of soaking wood and began, slowly and methodically, to pack the instrument away.

When he raised his eyes again a man was limping toward him, dimly visible against the banks of still-glowing ash. It was the old lord. His back was bowed, as if by the weight of years, and he carried a massive stick, on which he leaned continually for support. The Piper knew that now his home and treasures were burned he had little time to live; but his lip curled, because compassion was dead in him. The old man stared awhile; then he sat down on the drenched grass at his feet, and the Piper raised no hand to stay him. He fiddled with his stick; finally he said, 'Why have you done this thing?' There was no anger in his voice; merely a great weariness.

The Piper made no answer. But the old man read the reason in his eyes. 'It was for my son. It was revenge.' The Piper turned at that, and spoke the first word he had ever been known to utter. 'Yes,' he said.

The other shook his head at that, and passed a hand across

his face. He said gently, 'But my son is dead, Piper. He has been dead this many a month.'

The Piper looked at the ground between his feet. He was silent a long time; then he raised his head. It was full dark, so there was no reading the expression on his face. He touched his tongue to his lips, and used his second word. He said, 'Why?'

The old man shook his head again. 'I know your opinion of me,' he said. 'You artist, you Fairy, you rejector of normality, of pity; you shaper of patterns, you maker and unmaker of lives. But now you will hear me; and you will mark my words. Aye, even you; and that for the rest of Time.' He paused. 'Rear a child,' he said. 'Rear a daughter or a son. Then you will understand the pain of loss. You on your lofty pedestal, who can call the thunder and lightning to your bidding; become human if you dare. Be human for a day, an hour; then you can speak to me. Till then I spurn you, and all your kind; spurn you, and spit on your name.'

Now the Piper was human, with all the passions of a mortal man; so the words struck him to the core. The other had risen; he reached to grip his sleeve. 'How?' he cried, anguished. '*How* . . . ?' But the old man in his turn would not relent. 'This tale you contrived in your mind,' he continued, 'that you devised, to satisfy your pride. This saga of villains and excesses, so far from the truth. But you with your fine imagination, you the poet; you wouldn't be interested in that.' He shook his head once more. It seemed the only gesture left him. 'My son went with the girl,' he said. 'I make no bones of it, as he made no bones. She placed enchantment on him, and he yielded. From humanity; that humanity you laud in song, and counter by your acts. For payment, she destroyed him. She took his health, his life and his mind. She sucked him dry, left him a shell for which he had no further use. Now you, at your behest, have destroyed what used to be his home.' He drew a ragged breath. 'I am for death,' he said. 'We both know my time is short. But you will live; and for that life I pity you, Piper.' He turned then to the retainers who waited, sorrowing, by the still-glowing ash; they took his arms, bore him silently to the village.

The Piper sat a long, long while, staring at the flute he still gripped in his hands. His fists tensed time and again, as if he might break it to pieces; but the act could bring no relief, no act of destruction could truly bring relief. He had found this much already, to his cost and the cost of others. The fault lay square on him, not on a tube of harmless wood; so finally he rose. He stowed the flute carefully in his satchel and walked away.

He went to the house of the Fletcher, and Jack opened the door and regarded him. He was unsurprised, for the tale of the night's doings had been brought to him. He was a sturdy man, deep-chested and slow of speech; strong in the arm and weak in the head (they said), though that was far from the truth. What was true was that he had never found much use or need for thought. But thoughts came now, tumbling in baffling succession through his brain. He saw the man before him was much changed; and though he had scant notion of what had truly passed, his compassion was aroused. 'Who am I,' he thought in his slow way, 'to criticise another? Is it mine to blame? I fletch the arrows that are used in war. Is it mine to say whose heart they rest in, in Belgium or Normandy or France? No, that is for our lord the King; for his word it is, and his alone, that guides our host. If judgement is to be made in this, then it is a matter for God.' So he admitted the Piper, and gave him sanctuary for many days.

For his part, the Piper sat quiet and watched, in the Fletcher's tiny workshop at the back of the cottage. His mind, that had been so full, now seemed curiously empty; he relished, for a time, release from thought. He saw how fine goose quills were prepared, how they were trimmed and angled to the shaft to make that shaft rotate. None knew, in those days, why it was better for an arrow to spin, why it would fly more true; that secret had not been wrested from the Lord. But Jack knew it for a fact, and facts were all he dealt in. The Piper even helped him for a time, when and where he could, sorting the bundles of shafts, spinning each on his thumbnail to find the straightest; till he understood, by this small hint and that, his time was come. Jack was tiring of him; his patience had been extended to its limit.

So he moved out. He built himself a hut on the far edge of the village; a small and humble place, for he needed nothing grand. Cranky it was and leaning, but it would serve his purposes. For timbers he searched the forest round about. Fallen saplings he took, and branches dropped from trees; for he would assail no living thing. From Jack he borrowed a saw and adze; but some tasks remained beyond his power. At first no one would help him, till the day two sawyers arrived; grim, dour men as silent as he. They halved the dead trunks for the great crucks, shouldered their saw and walked away. Next morning others of the village arrived to load the timbers onto carts, and drag them to the appointed spot. Why they should do such a thing he could not understand. Perhaps through his music an answer could have been made; but his human mind was numbed.

He furnished the house in the same rough manner, took in the gifts left for him; the sacks of grain and meal on which he would live. He took to sitting at evening in his doorway, watching the green forest and playing his flute. The tunes he conjured were gentle; tunes of yearning and regret. No demands were in them; they raised no forces, either of the darkness or the light. Most of all he played the song of sorrow; sorrow for all humankind, that makes its hearers weep. Meanwhile the old lord died and was buried, as had been ordained. The site of the house he had lived in, the house he had shared with his broadfaced, curly-headed son, was shunned by sinners and righteous alike; no word was spoken, either of praise or blame, and it seemed the affair was at an end. Though that of course was not to be.

The girl continued her hectic course. Men saw her sometimes in the dusk, a white wraith flitting through the endless gloom of trees, poised brief against the harsh black boles of winter. God-fearing men would cross themselves then, turn shuddering away; but others, like as not, would follow. She walked unheeding through the summer rains, splashed knee deep, thigh deep if she chose, in the filthy mud of lanes. Always she called, though never with her voice; always men came, for few could resist her. The village grumbled, but to itself alone. In latter times perhaps she would have been brought to fire; but the folk of those days, for all their faults, were gentle. The people kept their counsel; for men, after all, are human, and their lives were harsh. Also, the best of wives grow fat with time.

The Piper watched and waited. Action, now, was foreign to him. He had made one grievous error: in the sight of God, he could not afford another. And of course the inevitable happened; finally, she came to him. A summer evening it was when she tapped upon his door, an evening warm with the scent of forest trees. She said in her tinkling voice, 'Can I come in?'

He considered carefully, for he must make no more hasty choices. Finally he said, 'Yes.' He stepped back from the entrance; there were tears on her face and throat, and he could not turn her away. He saw the young child she once had been, staring frightened from the backs of her almond-tilted eyes. She talked a great time that first night, sitting cross-legged on his bracken bed, her skirt modestly disposed. He saw the scars criss-crossing her calves and ankles, the wounds of careless brambles. The flesh that had been so sweet and perfect was marred for all time now; and once again his pity was aroused. She told how she'd been sleeping on Jack the Fletcher's floor, how she had no place now to call her own, nowhere to lay her head and be at peace. For men had used her for their purposes, then turned her out of doors.

Behind the little room he lived in lay another. Tiny, not more than a cubicle; but it too had a bracken bed, and to one side, on a little table, stood a pitcher of pure spring water. What purpose he'd had in building the place not even the Piper could have said; but he opened the door, and showed it her. 'This is yours,' he said in his harsh, rough voice, 'for as long as you desire.' She ran to him then, crying and kissing. 'I'll fetch my things,' she said. 'It won't take long, I haven't very much. All I want, now, is to be at rest. I've learned my

209

lesson; but nobody else believes.' So he gave her shelter, as shelter had once been given to him; and the village could talk and whisper as it chose. For his heart, at last, was radiant with joy.

He played for her later. He played the songs of peace and happiness, better, certainly, than even he had ever played them before; but to no avail. It seemed her mood had changed from the winsomeness of the afternoon, changed with the growing dusk; her eyes were opaque again and lifeless, it seemed she didn't even hear the notes. It was then, perhaps, that the first flickerings of doubt assailed him; he laid the flute aside, busied himself with a frugal supper. He sat and brooded after she had retired, sipping a little ale, staring at the single taper that was all he allowed himself. Once he looked in on her, quietly. She lay face down, her breathing steady and deep; the single coarsely-woven blanket had twitched aside, disclosing sweet nakedness. He brooded down at her awhile; then stepped forward gently to adjust the covering. She moaned a little in her sleep, but did not wake.

He resumed his vigil. The taper had burned down; he lit another from it, placed it in the holder on the table. His eyes in the tiny pool of light were dark, unfathomable. Finally he took up the flute again. He sat with it a moment in his hands, turning it to see the spindled gleams reflect from polished wood. Then he set it to his lips. The notes he made were soft, so as not to wake his charge; but they were nonetheless a summons. A summons, and a challenge; the first he had uttered for many weary months. Again and again, tirelessly, the call went out; but there was no response. The tree leaves whispered, round the little hut; a moth boomed and blundered, somewhere in the shadowed recesses of the roof. So he began again; for he had decided (and time alone would prove him right or wrong) that she was possessed, that a demon had snared her soul by some device, trapped it behind bars she could not break. That soul that once had been the world to him. Gently, beguilingly, using all his art, he called that demon to him. Nothing came of course; but he had hardly expected a result. Devils by all report are cunning; they'll not present themselves at the snapping of a pair of mortal fingers.

Nonetheless, the demon heard. The flush of dawn was showing above the trees before he flung himself down wearily to rest; but it seemed his head had scarcely touched the bracken before the hut shook to thunderous knockings. The door burst inward; instantly the room was filled with armed men. The King's own bodyguard, ridden hard from London. 'Where is the witch?' they shouted. 'Her fame has gone abroad through all the land. Deliver her to us, Piper; for she must stand her trial.' He cried out at that, would have intervened; but a blow from a mailed fist stretched him half-senseless on the floor. They straddled him contemptuously, standing on his hands; he could only rage and weep. They dragged her forth, her dress half ripped away, shrieking as if she was already damned. They sat her on a horse, bound her hands and feet. He called to her, desperate, and she gave one backward glance. His heart broke afresh at the contempt in it, the scorn for failure; then she was gone, cantering through the leafy glades to answer for her crimes.

Once again, his brain seemed numbed. He bathed his stiffening fingers, stared unseeing at the broken knuckles; sat beneath an oak and watched the sun rise, the forest breezes move the sprays of leaves. Once a hind came, stepping delicate and shy; but so still was he that she had no fear. She browsed awhile contentedly; then she too was gone.

The day wore on. Midges danced in the levelling beams of sunlight; finally the silence of the forest was broken. A troupe of dancers appeared, tumbling between the trees on their way to this village or that; the Moorish men, who in another life the Piper had loved with all his heart. They clustered round him, jabbering anxiously, touching his wounded hands; and he rose wearily to prepare a meal, for no stranger had ever left his hut unfed. They smiled, accepting; but when they came to dance their thanks, with their trews and napkins and bells, he silenced them with one note on his flute. They understood then; packed their things, and crept silently away.

211

Now that he was alone, the taunting began once more. He saw her at a thousand gentle moments; touching, kissing, patting others with her hands. She flung her head back, combed her lovely hair; tucked legs beneath her as she stared up at him, flamelight dancing on her solemn face. He heard her laughter, the tinkling of her voice; finally he fell into a species of trance. He saw a glade in the forest, a glade where few men came. She danced there for him, danced for him alone, swirled her skirt to show the perfection of her legs. He held his arms out, half started up; and on the instant the vision changed. He saw her pressed to grass, to earth; he saw her body jerk and tremble, heard her cry out. She locked her ankles above her partner's back; and the Piper's own shout woke him. He glared around him wildly, the demon's laughter still ringing in his ears; then comprehension came. It had been fantasy, all was fantasy; but he knew now where he must go.

He left the cottage with its door swinging free, for birds to roost in the rafters, dust to gather on the floor. He was done with housen, and the homes of men. He made his way to the glade that he had seen. By it ran a dipping, rutted track; and the trees about it were still. He chose his spot with care; a grassy hollow between the roots of an ancient, spreading beech. He played the song he had played before, the song of summoning. He listened, head cocked slightly to one side; and then he played again. Midnight, and the flute still sounded, echoing eerily between the unseen trees; dawn, and the notes still sounded firm and clear. Through the day that followed he went on untiring; and for many days to come. And this was the Piper's Wait.

Here too the legends began. Some said he sat ten years, some a hundred, some a thousand. But that was nonsense, for the Piper was still a mortal. Sometimes the notes seemed to falter, at others the sounds ceased altogether; then the villagers – those who had plucked the courage to creep within earshot – were sure the player had died, from hunger, exhaustion or cold. But always, somehow, the tune rose again, patient, indomitable. Because the Piper, now, was sustained by rage; a rage colder and more implacable than any he had known. His course lay clear enough. Wrongs were to be righted, more than the wrong to the girl. Blood was on the demon's hands, and on his own; his good name had been blighted in the sight of God. For that the fiend would answer, if it took the rest of Time. The shuddering villagers noted the strains of the flute had once more become raucous, harsh. Gone was the beguiling; the call was imperative now, not to be borne. Even they found themselves drawn closer by some force beyond their will; their nerve broke finally at that, they fled to their own huts, crouched in the dark to gabble hasty prayers, to thank their God, as in the old days, for padlocks and bars of oak.

As for the Piper, the visions burned now continuous and stark. He saw the blue-black roads slash into the forest, saw again the yellow vans that plied them. He saw the girl dance in a score of different garbs; while time and again the roaring in his ears became the noise of engines. The great trucks ground by night and day among the trees, up from the coast now, onward for ever to distant, boiling London. Other machines, greater and still more wonderful, sailed the very sky. All these things, he knew, would one day be; in a world cleansed of demons, cleansed of fear. Freed, perhaps, from the very shackles of death.

The demon came. What earthly form it took, no man could say. Nor did any dare to imagine. But one day, or one year, or one century, the Piper faced his enemy. The wait was over.

What passed between them again was never known. Perhaps they talked; though popular fancy quailed at the words they might have used. Perhaps the fiend was maddened finally by the one tune ringing in its ears; or perhaps the Piper's magic forced it from the fastnesses of Hell. The Piper played a song of rage against it; it laughed at that and grew larger, physically more powerful. It towered in the glade, triumphant; and the Piper understood, and turned the lay. He played the songs of contempt, indifference; finally he played the song of laughter, and at that the demon quailed.

213

So he played the songs of *her*, the songs of beauty; her hair and eyes, her legs, the lovely centre of her being. He played his love; and at that the demon cringed, covering its eyes and moaning. He capered toward it, triumphant in his joy; and it was shrinking, dwindling as he watched, reducing to a black thing smoking on the grass, a thing on which he could set his heel. He smashed his foot down and again, with all the force left in him; and the piping stopped at last. He stared round the glade, peaceful now and still, and knew that he had won.

His sight flickered. He sat down, passed a shaking hand across his face. In time, vision returned. His breathing steadied, and he looked about him once more, at the unmoving, gentle leaves, the grass, the green shades through which she would soon come walking. The demon's power was broken, after a weariness of time; so the power of his minions was broken too. This he knew infallibly, without question; all would be as it had been before. He smiled at the flute, the flute he would never need again, set it down gently at his side. Its purpose, at last, had been fulfilled.

He turned his head slowly, listening with all his being. The sound came again; the softest scuffing of a foot, faint snapping of a twig. Joy flooded him at that; the joy he had known before, but had never hoped to feel again. Joy at first sight of her, at her perfection, joy as she scraped his cabin door. For he could not mistake, he could never mistake; her lightest tread, soft whisper of her footfalls. He waited, breath stilled; and for him the birdsong faded, the roarings that had plagued him vanished quite away.

She stepped into the glade, and paused. He rose, slowly, from where he sat. He saw that once more she was perfection; her skin and hair, her dainty hands and feet. He held his arms out; and she came running. 'Thank you, Piper,' she whispered. 'Thank you . . .'

He held her, the warm slightness of her; and there were tears on his cheeks. He said, 'It is ended,' and she said, 'I know, I know . . .' He kissed her, and she returned his love; soft brushings of her lips, childlike as she clung with all her strength. He fondled her hair, smelling its sweetness; and she pushed away, gripped his hands to stare up into his face. 'All the course we ran is in the past,' she said. 'Now we begin again. It's a new world, Piper.' He swung her up at that, no longer able to restrain the happiness, waltzed her round while she laughed and struggled. 'Put me down,' she said. 'Put me down . . .' He set her on her feet; but she had not done. 'One more thing,' she said. 'One more thing, Piper. For me . . .' Her eyes had lighted on the flute, lying discarded on the grass. 'The joining,' she said. 'Play the song of joining. Then nothing will come between us, neither man nor demon. It will truly be for ever . . .'

He shook his head. 'We don't need it,' he said; but she grasped his hands again. 'Piper,' she said urgently, 'if you knew the fear I felt. The pain, the degradation . . . Do it for me,' she pleaded. 'Then we are safe twice over . . .'

Never had he refused her; he wouldn't begin now. He smiled, took up the flute. She sat at his feet, watching with troubled eyes; he thought he had never seen a thing more divine. He set the flute to his lips and began, softly, to play his final charm. And an ancient charm it was, the oldest in the world; something that reached back beyond the Celts, beyond the Flint Men with their great towns; back to a time before the hills were made, when there were naught but Gods. He saw the smile form round her lips, spread to her eyes. It was the greatest spell he cast; it joined her to him for ever.

His breath froze on the final note. An icy pang shot through him; for the smile, that had been so innocent and sweet, was broadening, becoming fixed. Turning to a rictus, the preparation for a scream.

The flute fell from his hands. He saw the eyes fixed on his face were dead once more; dead, but lethal. She raised her skirt, leaned back on the grass. She raised her knees, and slowly parted them. He saw the other smile that waited him, and wondered of the two which was the more hideous.

Dimly, he understood. That demons traffic in deceit; that his song had not released her, that nothing would release her. Because she herself had never willed it so. He realised the

215

fiend had played a part; and played it cleverly, to snare him. Now she was his for ever, still in the demon's thrall; he'd forged the bonds himself, bonds no power could break.

He took the knife he carried from his belt, touched the tip to his throat while still she laughed, with lips and loins. He drove deep, one firm and steady thrust; and as the hot gushing began, as his sight began to fade, he realised even death was not an end. She would have followed him through all the world; now she would follow him through every Hell. Because God Himself had permitted him to fall. It was the fruit of arrogance. 'Beloved,' he whispered; then, for a time, the blackness claimed him.

And that is the tale of the Piper, that is the tale of why he waited; and that is the tale of what came.

LISA TUTTLE

The Wound

Once the seasons had been more distinct, but not in living memory. Now, mild winter merged gently into mild summer, and Olin knew it was spring only by the calendar and by his own restlessness.

That morning, Olin's bus took a different route, road repairs forcing a detour through the old city. As he stared out the window at the huge, derelict buildings crumbling into ruin and colonised by weeds, he caught sight of figures through gaps in the walls. No one lived in the old city, but there were always people here. Olin had been one of them once, when he was young, coming here with his lover. He remembered that time as the best of his life.

Recalling the past made him feel sad and prematurely old. His lover had become his wife, and after ten years of marriage they had separated. He had lived alone for the past two years.

Olin reached into his breast pocket for diary and pen, turned to the blank page of that day, and wrote 'phone Dove' in his small, precise hand. About once a month he phoned her, and they would arrange to meet for a meal. Always he went to her in hope, with fond memories and some vague thoughts of reconciliation which would fade over the course of the evening.

As he left the bus two other teachers, senior to Olin, also got off. They did not speak as they crossed the street together and passed through the heavy iron gates onto the school grounds. Olin caught sight of another colleague, a little ahead of them: Seth Tarrant, the new music master. Tarrant was

217

young, handsome, and admired by the students. His cream-coloured coat flared like a cape from his shoulders, and he seemed to be singing as he strode across the bright green lawn. He carried an expensive leather case in one hand, and a bunch of blue and yellow flowers in the other. Olin felt a brief flare of envy, and he touched his breast pocket. He would phone Dove, he thought. She would be glad to hear from him.

During his lunch-break, Olin went into the telephone alcove by the cafeteria, and was startled to see Seth Tarrant there, his long body slumped in an attitude of defeat, his head pressed against one of the telephones. Before Olin, embarrassed, could retreat, the other man looked around.

He straightened up, brushing a strand of fair hair out of his eyes. 'Mr Mercato,' he said.

'Olin,' said Olin, embarrassed still more by the formality. 'Please.'

'Olin. I'm Seth.'

'Yes, I know. An, are you all right?'

'I'm fine. Do you like opera?'

'Opera? Yes. Yes, I do, actually. Not that I know anything about it – maths is my subject, really – but I do like to listen. On the radio, and I have a few recordings . . .'

'You don't think it's tedious, pretentious and antiquated?'

Olin wondered who the music master was quoting. He shook his head.

'You might even think it worth your while to attend a live performance?'

'If it weren't so expensive -'

With a conjuror's flourish, Seth produced two cards from his pocket. 'I happen to have two tickets to tonight's performance of *The Insufficient Answer*, and one is going begging. Would you care to be my guest?'

'I'd love to. But, are you sure?'

'Do I seem uncertain to you?'

Olin shook his head.

'That's settled, then. We'll meet on the steps of the opera

218

house at seven o'clock, which will give us time for a drink in the bar before it begins.'

'Thank you. It's very kind -'

'Not at all. You are the kind one, agreeing at such short notice. Please don't be late. I hate to be kept waiting.'

The opera house was on the river, in an area of the city far older than that part known as the old city. Olin had been there once before, in the early days of his marriage, to attend a performance of *Butterfly*. Dove had been pregnant then, and she had fallen asleep during the second act. It was probably the quarrel they'd had afterwards, and not the price of tickets, which was the real reason Olin had never been to the opera since.

The steps were crowded with people meeting friends, but Seth's tall, elegant figure was immediately noticeable. When he reached his side, Olin began to apologise for his lateness, although it was barely five past the hour. He felt awkward, worried about the evening, certain that Seth had regretted his spur-of-the-moment invitation by now. Seth brushed aside both apologies and thanks with a flick of one long-fingered hand.

'Let's get a drink,' he said.

He seemed distracted and brooding in the bar, but Olin contrived a conversation by asking him questions about opera: after all, music was the man's subject. Olin felt like a student taken on a cultural outing by a master; an odd reversal, since he was at least ten years Seth's senior. It was a relief when the bell rang and they could find their seats and stop talking.

The Insufficient Answer was a love tragedy, a popular story which Olin already knew in outline. He had seen some of the most famous scenes enacted on television, but never with the technical brilliance displayed in this production. By ingenious use of lights and projections, the physical miracle of love appeared to be actually taking place on stage during the opening love-duet. After that breath-taking scene, the familiar tragedy was set in motion as the lovers, Gaijan and

Sunshine, discovered they were not cross-fertile. Because there could be no children, marriage was out of the question. Social as well as biological forces drove Gaijan to take other lovers while Sunshine watched, and wept, and waited. For Gaijan still swore that he loved her the best of all, and he returned to her after every coupling. He told her he considered her his true wife and would never marry. His other lovers, led by the young and beautiful Flower, discovered Sunshine's existence and reproached her in the choral, *We are all his wives*. When Sunshine protested that she could not live without his love, Flower responded with the thrilling *Then you must die*. The duet between Sunshine and Flower which followed echoed the earlier duet between Gaijan and Sunshine only, instead of a transformation, it was concluded by a suicide. In the final act, Gaijan threatened to follow Sunshine into death until Flower wooed him away from the cliff-edge. As Gaijan and Flower exchanged vows of marriage, Flower promised to be to him all that Sunshine had been, and all that Sunshine could not be. The stage had been growing darker all the while, and Olin expected the curtain to fall on the final, throbbing notes of Flower's promise and the lovers' embrace. Instead, Flower turned to face the audience, and opened her robe. Olin caught his breath at the sight of an embryo, seen as if through Flower's flesh, growing within her body. It grew, as he watched, and even without opera glasses Olin could see that the unborn baby wore Sunshine's face.

There was a moment of awed silence as the curtain fell, and then an explosion of applause. Olin clapped, too, full of emotion he was unable to express in any other way. He glanced at Seth and then hastily looked away again at the sight of tears on the younger man's face.

The murmuring, satisfied crowd bore them away, and there was no need, or chance, to speak. On the steps again, Olin began to say his thanks, but was stopped by a gesture.

'Don't rush off,' said Seth. 'I'd really like to discuss what we've just seen. That's why I don't like going to these things alone – it's never complete for me until I've been able to talk

220

about it. Won't you walk with me by the river? I need to stretch my legs, and somehow I think better when I'm moving.'

Olin felt flattered that Seth had not tired of his company after the strained effort of their earlier conversation in the bar, but he glanced at his watch saying, 'I'm afraid the last bus is -'

'Oh, don't worry about that. I have a car; I can run you home.'

'Your own car? On a teacher's salary?'

Seth smiled faintly. 'No. Not on a teacher's salary. Nor this coat, nor a subscription to the opera. It won't last long at the rate I'm going, but I have a little money. From my wife's family.'

Olin remembered the despairing way Seth had leaned against the telephone, and the flowers that morning, and he was surprised. 'You're married?'

'Separated. It lasted less than a year. A youthful mistake.'

The night was dry and not cold, the river path paved and lighted, but they were alone.

'My wife and I separated two years ago,' Olin offered.

'How long were you married?'

'Ten years.'

'Children?'

'Two. At school now.'

'Not a youthful mistake, then,' said Seth. 'Why didn't you stay together? Why – I'm sorry. Please forgive me. It's none of my business, of course.'

It would have been a rude question even from someone less a stranger than Seth, and Olin knew he should have taken offence. But suddenly he wanted to talk about his marriage with someone, anyone, who was not Dove. He had never had the chance before.

'I suppose we separated because we ran out of reasons for staying together. We'd stopped loving each other long since, the children were at school and didn't need us, and there was no reason for two people who didn't like each other very

221

much to go on sharing the same house. We'd never had much in common except the physical.'

'That's supposed to be enough,' said Seth. 'It is in all the operas, in literature, in ballads. The miracle of love is physical love – a biological affinity. Which would be fine, only it never lasts. And nobody will admit that. Everybody expects it to last, and when it doesn't we think there's something wrong with *us*. We're failures. Why can't we be taught to see love in perspective, to see it as a physical pleasure which belongs to one part of life but doesn't ever, can't by its very nature, ever last. We outgrow it, and we're *meant* to outgrow it. So why do we ruin our lives, wasting so much time and energy on love, dreaming about it, waiting for it, hoping for it against all odds?'

Although they were walking side by side, not looking at one another, Olin was vividly aware of Seth's anguish.

'You're too young to be talking like that,' Olin said, trying for a cheerful, bracing tone. 'It's all very well for me to resign myself to a solitary life, but you're still young and you should have hope. You can marry again – you *will* marry again. As you say, the first was a youthful mistake. You'll meet someone else . . .'

'Oh, yes, I'll meet someone else, and start the whole messy process all over again. I won't be able to help myself. But what's the point? To come to this again. Honey's pregnant. Already. I found out today. I suppose I should feel grateful. At least relieved that I didn't ruin her life. It would be so awful for her to find out she couldn't have kids ever, with anyone. It's not so terrible for a man to be infertile, but to be a woman . . .'

'There's no reason to assume you're infertile,' said Olin. 'Lots of people aren't cross-fertile with each other, but that doesn't mean they're infertile. Like in the opera we just saw – it's a question of finding the right partner.'

'So why should it be so complicated? It's just biology. Biological compatability. Why all this stuff about love? It has nothing to do with physical attraction, or being a nice person, or having common interests, or the meeting of souls. It's not

222

spiritual destiny. It's blind chance. It could have been worked out better, don't you think? So that we couldn't fall in love with someone unless we were cross-fertile.'

'But then it wouldn't be love,' Olin said. 'Then it *would* just be biology – we'd just be animals attracted to each other in the mating season.'

'I think we are, and we just don't know it. In our ignorance, we've screwed it up. We try to make it something noble, try to pretend that sex and reproduction are the by-products of love, instead of the other way around. Why should sex get this special treatment? Why can't we see it clearly, as a need like hunger? Why mystify it? Why can't we just admit that we're just animals who need to reproduce, and *do* it?'

Olin was conscious that their argument was operating on two levels. However abstract and intellectual it might become, Seth was speaking out of his own hurt. He was looking for comfort, and Olin responded with the wish to help. But what wisdom could he offer? He was older than Seth, but no wiser. He hadn't found the answer in marriage or out of it. He had told himself that love was for the young, and safely in his own past, but something in him still responded to romance.

After a little silence Olin said, 'We're animals, but not only animals. Yes, we need to reproduce – but we have other needs, too. Emotional, social needs. We have a need for love, however you define it. Maybe it's misguided to connect love with sex, but everyone does, so there must be some sense in it, there must be some hope -' he stopped talking as they both stopped walking, having come to the end of the paved, lighted river-path. The river wound on, out of sight behind the embankment to their left, but ahead of them was a dark, rough wasteland.

Staring into the night Seth said, 'There's a need, but is it natural? Is it something basic in us, or was it constructed? Does it have to be that way, or can we change it? Should we?'

Disturbed, Olin turned away. 'We'd better start back. There's no way through here. It's odd – you'd think the path would go somewhere, wouldn't you? I mean, to pave it, and put up lights – you'd think it would go somewhere. At least to the next bridge, or up to the main road. Just to end like this – Are you coming?'

As they walked back, Olin turned the conversation to architecture, a subject about which he knew little but had many opinions. He soon provoked Seth into disagreement, and by the time they reached the opera house they were arguing as merrily as old friends, all restraint between them gone. Seth's bitter mood had passed, and Olin was glad to agree when he suggested they stop for a snack in a late-night cafe on the way home. Even knowing he would have to get up in the morning to teach, Olin was not ready for the evening to end. He was enjoying himself with Seth, but he didn't trust in their friendship to survive even the shortest separation. In the morning, he thought, they would be strangers again.

But he was wrong. The next day at school, passing each other on the stairs, Seth suggested they meet for a drink after work. He spoke as casually and easily as if they were friends and, suddenly, they were.

Drinks led to dinner and to another walk; to more drinks, dinners and walks. Despite, or perhaps because of, having a car, Seth loved to walk. It was his only exercise – like Olin, he had developed a hatred of sports at school – and after days cooped up indoors, he longed for the chance to move in the open air. He said that it not only relaxed him, but it helped him to think. Olin, always lazy, enjoyed their walks because the talk that always accompanied them allowed him to forget he was exerting himself. Some of their best – and most disturbing – conversations took place while they walked. There were things which could not be said in a restaurant or a bar, looking at each other. But striding along, talking into the open air as if thinking aloud, unable to see each other's expression, anything might be voiced. Anything at all. And one day, Olin thought, Seth would say something . . . Seth would go too far. The thought gave him a strange feeling at the pit of his stomach. It was a pleasurable excitement he remembered from long ago, from the last time he'd had such a close friendship. The feeling was fear, but it was also desire.

Women had friendships among themselves, but women had nothing to lose. Older men sometimes managed it, becoming as if boys again in their age, but for everyone else friendship was a risk. Olin was well aware of this, and thought Seth must be, too. They never spoke of the danger they might be courting, although they came close. For love – or sex, or biology, or marriage – was the topic they continued to be drawn to, again and again, in their night-time, walking conversations. The subject was like a sore Seth could not stop probing, or a cliff-edge he had to lean over. It was during those conversations that Olin became aware of what a dangerous edge it was on which they balanced. If one of them fell
. . .

But if one of them fell, it would be Seth, he was certain. Seth, with his youth, his passion, his sorrow, his 'mistaken' marriage, would fall in love with his older friend, and not the other way around. Olin could imagine Seth in love with him, and the idea of making love to a transformed, newly receptive Seth aroused him. But Olin did not let himself dwell on such thoughts. He didn't really want it to happen. He liked this not-sexual friendship; he wanted to believe that it could last. He wanted to go on balancing. He didn't want Seth to change.

One morning, about six weeks after the performance of *The Insufficient Answer*, Olin's telephone rang before he left for school.

It was Dove. 'I've been trying to phone you for days, and you're never in,' she said.

He remembered his long-ago, never-kept resolution to phone her, and felt guilty. 'I've been busy – I'm sorry I haven't been in touch -'

'It doesn't matter. But I thought you might have forgotten that it's parents' day this weekend. I thought the 8:45 would be the best train to catch. Could you meet me at the station by 8:30 on Saturday morning? Tristan wants a new football, I know – do you think you could manage to buy one? And some books for both of them – you know the sort of thing they'd like better than I would.'

Olin winced and closed his eyes as his wife's voice poured into his ear. He had forgotten. Worse than that, he didn't want to go. There had been a time when he welcomed the ritual visits to his children at their school. Then, his life had been so dull that any events were treasured as a break from routine. But his life was different now. A day spent with Dove and the boys meant a day without Seth. They had made tentative plans for Saturday already: a drive in the country, a visit to some site of historic interest, some place from the old times. Olin knew what he wanted to do, but he also knew his duty. He told Dove that he would meet her at the station.

They embraced as they always did on meeting – former desire transformed to awkward ritual – and then stood back to examine each other for signs of change.

Her hair was too short, Olin thought, the style too severe. It made her look older than she was, harsher and no longer pretty. But she looked fit, and still dressed well.

'You've put on weight,' Dove said.

He was surprised, and a little indignant, for since spending time with Seth he was not only getting more exercise, but also eating less. He tucked a thumb into the waistband of his trousers to show Dove how loose they were.

In answer, she touched his chest. 'Look how tight. That button's ready to pop.'

He flinched away from her hand. 'Maybe the shirt shrunk.'

'Shirts that old don't shrink. I bought you that shirt. You're bigger in the chest, and it isn't muscle. Your face is fuller, too. It doesn't look bad – you look younger, actually. Softer.'

Olin shrugged, annoyed. 'Let's get on the train before it goes without us.' He was dreading the two-hour journey. Usually he told Dove about his life and she listened. But he didn't want to tell her about Seth, and he could think of nothing else that had happened to him in the last two months

226

- nothing that would take more than two or three minutes to tell. He had brought along a book to read, but he was so aware of Dove watching him that he found it difficult to concentrate. The familiar train journey had never seemed longer.

Their children, Tristan and Timon, acted pleased to see them, but they clearly had lives of their own in which parents played no very large role. Olin knew this was normal – he remembered his own school-days. And it was only fair that they be uninterested in him, considering how seldom he thought of them, but, confronted with them in the flesh, with their inescapable separateness, Olin felt his own estrangement the more. Once they had been at the centre of his life, he thought. When he hugged them, and could feel and smell their familiar bodies, he loved them, but when they moved out of reach he was left with only memories. He loved his babies, but his babies had grown into strangers. He wondered if Dove felt the same way. Perhaps it was worse for her. Or perhaps she had come to terms with it long before. It had to be different for a mother, who had brought forth children from her own body. He had *always* been separate from his children. Suddenly, confusingly, Olin wanted to cry. To cover his feelings, he began to rough-house with the boys until he realised he was embarrassing them. He wasn't acting like the other fathers. Desperately, Olin watched the other fathers for clues, and tried to act like them. He tried to remember what he had done six months ago, during his last visit to the school. What had he felt then, who had he been? Surely it hadn't always been this difficult, this painful?

Fortunately the day was structured to make life easy for everyone. Olin and Dove were taken around by their children, reintroduced to their children's friends and teachers, observed various competitions, sporting and dramatic events, and then took Tristan and Timon out for the traditional feast. Presents were given out, and then the farewell kisses and goodbyes.

Back on the train, Olin was too exhausted even to pretend to read his book. He didn't think Dove would have let him,

227

anyway. It was obvious she had something to say, even if she was taking her time about saying it.

'So,' she said at last. 'You going to tell me about him?'

'Who?'

'Your friend.'

'What makes you think I have a friend?'

'You always thought I was stupid,' she said. 'But there are some things you don't get to know out of books. You're different than you were the last time I saw you. You're always out, too busy to call me, instead of lonely and bored like you were before. And instead of telling me in detail about your boring life, you got on the train and stuck your nose in a book. Because your life isn't boring anymore. Because there's somebody in your life. Somebody new. Maybe it's early days yet, maybe you're not really sure, and you don't want to jinx it by saying anything too soon in case it doesn't happen, but – I don't think it's that. I think something's happening that you didn't expect -'

'What are you babbling about?'

'The main thing is, the reason I'm so sure, is that you remind me -' again, she stopped short. It was almost like a dare to him to tell her what she already knew.

He gave in. Maybe, after all, he did want to talk about it; maybe he wanted confirmation from someone else. 'What do I remind you of,' he asked gently. 'Do I remind you of how I used to be, when you and I were first in love? Do I remind you of how I was then?'

She shook her head. 'No. You remind me of how *I* was.'

Dove was right, and he was in hell. He had denied it to her, and had tried to deny it to himself, but Sunday morning Olin woke and saw the blood in his bed and could no longer hide the truth from himself. He had fallen in love with Seth.

It wasn't much blood – a dried brownish spot no larger than his thumbnail. He stripped off the sheet and saw that it had soaked through to the mattress. As he scrubbed at the stain with a wet, soapy towel, Olin blinked back tears and struggled to think logically.

228

He was changing. No doubt about that, but the change was far from complete. Dove had seen the signs, but Dove had been through it herself. It might not be too late to stop what was happening to him. His only hope was to get away from Seth before it was too late. Parents did sometimes save their sons from shame by sending them away when they recognised the threat of a developing romance. Olin couldn't actually go away – he couldn't afford to leave his job – but he might be able to contrive something to keep him safely out of Seth's company.

Olin sat back and surveyed his work. There was a large wet spot on the mattress, but that would soon dry. The blood-stain was gone.

The telephone rang, making Olin jump. He stared at the thing, knowing already who it would be. Maybe he should start now, ignore it. But he couldn't resist the summons.

'Took you long enough,' said Seth's voice in his ear. 'I thought you said you lived in one room?'

'I do. I was in bed – I'm not feeling well.'

'Oh, what's wrong?'

'I'm not sure. I'm probably just tired out from the day with Dove and the boys.'

'Why don't I come over and cheer you up?'

'No!' The leap his heart had given – of pure desire – made him shout.

There was a short silence on the other end. Olin tried not to think about what Seth was thinking, not to worry whether he was hurt or angry.

Seth said, 'What's wrong?'

'I told you. I'm tired. I don't feel well. I'm fed up with people – I just need to be alone.'

'You're the doctor. I'll leave you alone, then. You'd just better be over this by Wednesday.'

'Wednesday?'

'You hadn't forgotten that we've got opera tickets?'

'No, of course not. I'll be better before Wednesday – I have to be well enough to go to school tomorrow. I can't afford to pay a substitute.'

Olin knew Seth's schedule like his own. It was easy enough to avoid him at school, just as, a week earlier, it had been easy to engineer brief, 'accidental' encounters. At the end of the day Olin crept out by a side-entrance and went to a movie and then had dinner in a cafe of the sort Seth would never enter. He felt like a hunted animal, following a similar routine on Tuesday. But on Wednesday one of the boys brought him a note:

Opera steps, 7 sharp, yes? Don't be late! S.

Olin folded the note and tucked it into his pocket, aware that his students were staring at him and giggling.

'Is that a love-note, sir?' asked one of the boys.

Another, in a loud whisper, corrected him, 'Is that a love-note, *miss*!'

The whole class exploded into mocking laughter.

Olin pounded on his desk, painfully aware that he was blushing. He regained control of the class, but he knew how weak was his hold on them. Boys that age were sensitive to hints of sex even where they did not exist, and once they knew the truth about him he would lose their respect forever. He tried to take comfort from the fact that they couldn't really know – and nothing, after all, had happened – and then, with a chill, he wondered if Seth also suspected. If Seth, perhaps, knew.

Against the rules, Olin dismissed his final class ten minutes early. He didn't go to a film or a cafe. He had decided to do something positive, and he caught the bus which would take him to the north-eastern suburb where Dove lived.

She seemed surprised and, he thought, not pleased when she opened the door to him. Entering at her reluctant invitation, he saw that she already had a visitor, a woman dressed, like Dove, in dark-blue overalls. Olin had not seen Dove in her work clothes since the days when they lived together: she always dressed up for him when he came to call. She looked taller and stronger to him now, more of a stranger.

'Is something wrong?' she asked. She did not offer to introduce him to the woman.

'No, no, I just thought I'd like to take you out to dinner.'

230

'Why didn't you phone?'

He shrugged uneasily. 'It was a spur of the moment thing. I thought you'd be pleased.'

There was a silence, and then the other woman set down her tea-cup and rose from her chair. 'I'd better be getting along,' she said to Dove. 'I'll see you tomorrow at work.'

'I'll phone you later,' Dove said.

The two women exchanged a look which made Olin feel even more uncomfortable, and then the other woman smiled, becoming almost beautiful. 'Take care, Leo,' she said.

'Leo?' said Olin when Dove had closed the door behind her departing guest. 'Why did she call you that?'

'It's my name.'

'It *was* Dove –'

'Dove is *your* name for me. I still have my own. I prefer my friends to use it.'

He wondered what she meant by the word 'friend', and what that woman was to her, and he did not want to know. 'I didn't know you didn't like it. I could have chosen another name if you'd ever said –'

'I didn't say I didn't like it. It's all right *you* calling me Dove. Let's not argue. Come in the kitchen and have a cup of tea. Or would you rather have a beer? I've got some.'

'Tea.' He followed her into the kitchen. 'I'm sorry I didn't phone first. I really didn't think about it until I was on the bus coming out here, and then it seemed too late. If you really want me to leave –'

'No, now you're here, stay.'

'I can wait while you change,' he said as she put the kettle on.

She shook her head. 'I don't want to change; I don't feel like going out.' She turned around to face him, leaned against the counter and crossed her arms over her chest. 'Why don't you just say what you have to say?'

He didn't want to talk to her in such a self-possessed, almost aggressive mood. He had hoped to make her pliable with drink and good food, to lead up to it gently, but she

231

wasn't giving him the chance and he couldn't afford to wait for a better time. He drew a deep breath.

'I want to try again,' he said.

'Try what?'

'Us. I'd like us to try again. I'd like to move back in here with you.'

She simply stared. He couldn't tell what she was thinking. The kettle was boiling. She turned away and poured the water into the teapot.

'He's really got you scared,' she said.

'Who?'

'It won't work,' she said. 'You can't get away from him that easily. You can't just pretend you've got a wife -'

'Why should it be a pretence? We loved each other once – why can't we go back to that?'

'Because we've changed.'

'*I* haven't,' he said furiously. 'I haven't changed! It's started, yes, but *he* doesn't know – we haven't done anything – it's not too late – if I stay away from him – I don't have to be his woman -'

'And I don't have to be yours.'

Olin stared at her. 'But you can't – you can't change back. You can't ever be a man again. Becoming a woman – that change is forever. I changed you.'

She smiled. 'What makes you think I *want* to be a man again? There are other kinds of change. There's such a thing as growing.'

'Have you met someone else? Who is he? Do you want to marry someone else?'

'No.'

But there was something . . . Olin felt sick. 'Not her – that woman who was here? Is *she* your lover? Do women do that?'

He saw her tense, and it occurred to him that she wanted to hit him. But she was very controlled as she said, 'We're friends. We'll probably make love some day. But not in the way *you* mean. It's not that kind of thing. There aren't any men and women among us.'

'I wouldn't try to stop you,' Olin said. 'If that was what

you wanted, if you wanted her as well . . . You could do as
you liked. Let me move back in here.'

'No.'

'Why won't you help me? Do you hate me that much, for
what I did to you?'

She sighed. 'Olin . . . I don't hate you at all. If I can help
you, I will. But I'm not going to live a lie for you.'

'Why should it be a lie? We were happy together once,
weren't we?'

'We were, but that's over. Olin, you know it is. You spend
an evening with me, and by the end of it you can't wait to get
away. The Dove you've got in your mind isn't me. You'd
know that if you weren't so afraid right now. Why are you so
afraid? It's natural; it happens to people all the time. Why
can't you just accept what's happening to you?'

'I'm too old,' he said, anguished.

She almost laughed. 'The fact that it's happening means
you're not too old. All right, maybe too old for babies, but
that can be a blessing. Since you've done your bit for the
species already, with Timon and Tristan, you don't even
have to feel guilty. Let yourself enjoy it. There *is* pleasure in
it, you know. Pain, too, but you might find that the pleasure
makes up for it. I remember the pleasure, Olin. You don't
have to feel guilty about what you did to me. Oh, I know you
feel guilty. Otherwise you wouldn't be so afraid of it happening to you. Don't be. It isn't *so* terrible to be a woman.'

Of course it was terrible to be a woman. Olin had feared it all
his life. Everyone feared becoming a woman. Parents feared
it for their sons. And friends, in their intimacy, battled
grimly not to lose. To lose was to become a woman. Olin had
been through that in his youth, and he had won. He thought
he could relax, then, he thought he was safe. He had not
realised, until it was too late, that the battle to retain man-
hood never ended. He had not truly understood that one
victory was not the end. He had not realised until now that he
might yet lose.

After leaving Dove, Olin rode around the city on buses,

unable to think what to do next, unable even to decide upon a restaurant. But eventually he became restless and decided that, like Seth, he would be able to think better if he could walk. He left the bus at a stop near the old city, so that was where he went to walk.

Darkness had fallen, and the broken pavement was treacherous underfoot. Here and there among the looming vastness of ancient buildings tiny lights glowed and flickered: candles lit by lovers in the abandoned rooms which were their trysting places. They were all around him – he heard the indistinct murmur of their voices and, occasionally, a cry of pain.

He broke out in a sweat. Once these surroundings would have induced nostalgic memories of his time with Dove. Now they brought only fear. Why had he come here? Why had he chosen these streets, of all there were in the city to walk? He had to get away.

Olin turned around and there, in the darkness, unmistakable, was Seth.

'I knew you'd come here,' said Seth. 'I knew I only had to wait.'

'It was a mistake,' said Olin. 'I'm leaving.'

'You'll come with me first.'

'No.'

As he tried to go past, Seth caught him by the arm. It was the first time he had ever touched Olin, and now Olin knew that it really was too late. They could fight: although Seth was taller, Olin was heavier and better co-ordinated and under other circumstances he could have taken Seth. But as he stood very still, feeling Seth's fingers like a chain around his arm, feeling the unwanted, unmistakable trickle of wetness between his legs as his wound began to bleed, Olin knew that Seth had already won this fight. He shuddered, as his fear was transformed into desire.

'Where will we go?' he asked.

'I know a room. Come on.' Now Seth, seeming kind, released his bruising hold and laid his arm gently across Olin's shoulders. 'Don't be frightened,' he said, leading Olin away. 'I'll be very gentle; it won't hurt so much.'

It was only the first of his lies.

Contributors

TANITH LEE was born in London and began writing at the age of 9. She has worked as a library assistant, waitress, shop assistant, clerk, and spent a year at art college before becoming a full-time writer after the publication of *The Birthgrave* in 1975. Since then she has published over thirty-five books and has also written radio plays and scripts for *Blake's Seven*.

CHRISTOPHER EVANS was born in South Wales and now lives in South London. A full-time writer since 1979, he is the author of three novels, the most recent of which is *In Limbo*.

M. JOHN HARRISON's early novels include *The Pastel City*, *A Storm of Wings* and *In Viriconium* (runner-up for *The Guardian* Fiction Prize), which introduced the mutable city of Viriconium, the setting for numerous short stories. Now resident in London, he is currently completing *Climbers*, a novel arising from his passion for rock-climbing; and at the same time is working on *The Course of the Heart*, a metaphysical thriller.

IAN WATSON's first novel was *The Embedding*, and since its publication he has been a prolific and inventive producer of science fiction. His other novels include *The Martian Inca*, *Alien Embassy* *The Book of the River* and *Queenmagic*, *Kingmagic*, while his short stories are collected in *The Very Slow Time Machine* and *Sunstroke*. He was born on Tyneside, studied at Balliol College, Oxford, and now lives in a Northamptonshire village.

BRIAN ALDISS's recent books include the *Helliconia* trilogy and a revised version of his landmark history of science fiction, *Trillion Year Spree*. He was born in East Anglia but now lives in Oxford. His other books include *Non-Stop*, *Hothouse*, *Report on Probability A*, *The Malacia Tapestry* and *Life in the West*.

GRAHAM CHARNOCK published his first short story in the 'New Writers' issue 184 of *New Worlds* (along with M. John Harrison and Robert Holdstock). His fiction has also appeared in *Orbit* and *New Writings in SF*. He works as a bookseller in London and has recently completed a novel, *Vanishing Acts*.

ROBERT HOLDSTOCK has been a full-time writer since 1975. He has published science fiction (including *Where Time Winds Blow*), horror (including *Necromancer*) and a mythological fantasy, *Mythago Wood*, which won the World Fantasy Award.

MICHAEL MOORCOCK's many novels include *Stormbringer*, *Behold the Man*, *The Final Programme* and *Gloriana*. Former editor of *New Worlds*, his most recent books are *The Laughter of Carthage* and *Letters from Hollywood*, which tells of his encounters with the film world and the West Coast way of life.

GARRY KILWORTH was born in York but is widely travelled and has spent much of his life overseas. He began writing for publication in the early 1970s, and has six novels and forty short stories behind him. His latest novel is *Witchwater Country*, to be followed by *Spiral Winds*. He lives and works in Essex, close to the site of Edmund Ironside's defeat by King Cnut.

R.M. LAMMING was born on the Isle of Man and now lives in North London. Educated in Wales and at Oxford, she is the author of two novels: *The Notebook of Gismondo Cavaletti*, which is set in sixteenth-century Florence, and won the David Higham Prize for Fiction in 1983, and *In the Dark*, a contemporary mainstream novel. She formerly published science fiction stories under the pseudonym Robin Douglas.

DAVID S. GARNETT lives in a rambling old grange in the village of Ferring, near Brighton. He has published several novels, including *Mirror in the Sky*, *The Starseekers* and *Time in Eclipse*, and recent short stories have appeared in *Interzone* and *The Magazine of Fantasy and Science Fiction*. It was he who originally suggested the idea for this anthology.

DAVID LANGFORD is the author of the novels *The Space Eater* and *The Leaky Establishment*, and non-fiction books such as *War in*

2080 and (with Brian Stableford) *The Third Millenium: A History of the World: AD 2000 – 3000*. A lapsed nuclear physicist resident in Reading, he also edits the scurrilous and indispensable sf news magazine, *Ansible*.

KEITH ROBERTS currently lives and works in Amesbury. He trained in the visual arts and produced covers and interior illustrations for *Impulse* and *New Worlds* in the 1960s and 70s. His books include the now-classic *Pavane*, *The Chalk Giants*, *Molly Zero*, and, more recently, *Kiteworld*, *Kaeti & Company* and the forthcoming *Grainne*.

LISA TUTTLE was born in Texas but has lived in Britain since 1980. Her novels are *Windhaven* (co-written with George R.R. Martin), *Familiar Spirit* and *Gabriel*, while her short stories are published widely and have been collected in *A Nest of Nightmares*. She has also written the *Encyclopedia of Feminism*.

Also in Unwin Paperbacks

DAYBREAK ON A DIFFERENT MOUNTAIN
Colin Greenland

Walled off from a world it no longer remembers, the city of Thryn decays in arrogant isolation. Its ancient scriptures tell of the god, Gomath, who will one day return to perfect his city. But his return has been long awaited.

'The writing is good, the observations intelligent and the tone and imagination individual. I think it's an excellent book.'

Michael Moorcock

DRAGONSBANE
Barbara Hambly

A thrilling new fantasy by the author of THE DARWATH TRILOGY.

It was said to be impossible to slay a dragon. But Lord John Aversin had earned himself the name of Dragonsbane once in his life and had become the subject of ballad and legend. Fired by the romance of his tale, young Gareth travelled far and wide across the Winterlands from the King's court to persuade the hero to rid the Deep of Ylferdun of the Great Black Dragon, Morkeleb.

With them on their quest went Jenny Waynest, half-taught mage and mother of Aversin's sons.

Morkeleb was the oldest and mightiest of the dragon race — the most fearsome opponent that the Dragonsbane had ever had to face. But Morkeleb was not the greatest danger that awaited John Aversin and his witch-woman. The once-ordered court had fallen into decadence and dissolution, and the beautiful sorceress Zyerne held the King in her sway. Just as Morkeleb posed the hardest test of skill and courage for the Dragonsbane, so Jenny Waynest would find her powers pitted against an adversary as deadly as the Black Dragon, and infinitely more evil.

'This is literary alchemy of a high order, and it confirms Hambly's place as one of the best new fantasists.'

Locus

VIRICONIUM NIGHTS
M. John Harrison

'Harrison is the most elegant stylist writing fantasy, or indeed most forms of fiction, in the country . . . With each book I have wondered how much better M. John Harrison can possibly get; and the question has yet to be answered. There seems no limit to his talent, and after reading this stunning, captivating work of staggering imaginative power, one is wondering: what next?'

Vector

'Harrison writes beautifully, weighing and shaping words with the practised precision of a man building a dry-stone wall, wanders his latterday Byzantium of the imagination with a confident curiosity that at times . . . becomes bewildered wonderment. Altogether, a strange sea in which to swim: an evening's read and at least a fortnight's dreams.'

Time Out

THE SUMMER TREE
Guy Gavriel Kay

Guy Gavriel Kay's *The Summer Tree* is a book of exhilarating scope and intensity. The novel is the first book of a fantasy trilogy on the grand scale, a work within the rich tradition of books like *The Lord of the Rings*.

The Summer Tree focuses on five young people who are dramatically precipitated out of their lives in this world into the midst of a terrifying war in Fionavar, first of all the worlds.

'one of the very best of the fantasies which have appeared since Tolkien ... The cliff-hanging ending leaves me eager for the next volume. An outstanding work all the way round.'
Andre Norton

'A strong individual book by a splendid new writer . . . *The Summer Tree* merits the highest recommendation.'
Locus

THE LADIES OF MANDRIGYN
Barbara Hambly

From the best-selling author of *The Darwath Trilogy* and *Dragonsbane* comes a stunning new fantasy – *The Ladies of Mandrigyn*.

When the evil Wizard King Altiokis sacked the city of Mandrigyn and sent its menfolk to labour to their deaths in his foul mines, he had reckoned without the ladies of Mandrigyn.

Determined to win back their men and destroy the wizard, they set out to hire the services of the mercenary leader Sun Wolf. They offered him a fortune in gold. But Sun Wolf was not fool enough to match his sword against sorcery . . .

Sun Wolf awoke, some hours later, on a ship bound for far-flung Mandrigyn, lethal anzid coursing through his veins. The ladies held the only antidote, and Sun Wolf found himself an unwilling participant in a very dangerous game . . .

THE INITIATE
Book One of the Time Master Trilogy
Louise Cooper

The Seven Gods of Order had ruled unchallenged for an aeon, served by the Adepts of the Circle in their bleak Northern stronghold. But for Tarod — the most enigmatic and formidable sorcerer in the Circle's ranks — a darker affinity had begun to call. Threatening his beliefs, even his sanity, it rose unbidden from beyond Time; an ancient and deadly adversary that could plunge the world into madness and chaos – and whose power rivalled that even of the Gods themselves.

And though Tarod's mind and heart were pledged to Order, his soul was another matter. . .

THE OUTCAST
Book Two of the Time Master Trilogy

Tarod alone knew the nature of the supernatural force locked within his soul – and he knew that it must be thwarted, no matter what the sacrifice. Denounced by his fellow Adepts as a demon, betrayed even by those he loved, he had unleashed a power that twisted the fabric of time, to put himself beyond the reach of that monstrous force and avert the pandemonium that threatened the world.

He thought that nothing could break through the barrier he had created.

He was wrong . . .

Also available in Unwin Paperbacks

All these books are available at your local bookshop or newsagent, or can be ordered direct by post. Just tick the titles you want and fill in the form below.

Name ....

Address ....

....

....

Write to Unwin Cash Sales, PO Box 11, Falmouth, Cornwall TR10 9EN.

Please enclose remittance to the value of the cover price plus:

UK: 60p for the first book plus 25p for the second book, thereafter 15p for each additional book ordered to a maximum charge of £1.90.

BFPO and EIRE: 60p for the first book plus 25p for the second book and 15p for the next 7 books and thereafter 9p per book.

OVERSEAS INCLUDING EIRE: £1.25 for the first book plus 75p for the second book and 28p for each additional book.

Unwin Paperbacks reserve the right to show new retail prices on covers, which may differ from those previously advertised in the text or elsewhere. Postage rates are also subject to revision.